His Sweetest Song

A NOVEL

VICTORIA H SMITH

HIS SWEETEST SONG: A Novel

Copyright © 2018 by Victoria H. Smith

All rights reserved. No part of this book may be reproduced or transmitted in any form, including electronic or mechanical, without written permission from the publisher, except in the case of brief quotations embodied in critical articles or reviews.

This book is a work of fiction and any resemblance to any person, living or dead, any place, events or occurrences, is purely coincidental and not intended by the author.

One

ALICIA

I slid my hat off as I crossed the threshold of the large home, the sun terribly high today on my way from the train station. The trip had been long and my feet felt it, my heels clicking atop hardwood floors. The floorboards creaked like an old oak tree's branches, the smell of the room reminiscent of that same great oak. I imagined the smell on the train ride over here. I imagined many things. A soft huff came from behind me and I turned, the real estate agent finally joining me. She hadn't been as fast despite my heels.

"It's truly something, isn't it?" she asked, a layer of sweat beaded on her upper lip. She had a bleached mustache there, a nice woman, but didn't overly care about her outward appearance. There was nothing wrong with that, but quite different from what I was used to. The people of Chicagoland put value in different things.

My own done-up tresses pinned behind my head, I smiled at her, removing the wide-rimmed, black hat that sat pertly on top of my head. I often had my hair pulled back for a day at the office and that remained consistent today. The style was clean and flawless despite the heat here in Kansas and my makeup, I was sure, not far from pristine. I took a lot of care in that, again working in an office mostly dominated by men. They always looked for a chink in one's armor in my day to day but I never gave it to them, especially being a woman of color on top of that. My skin was the most pigmented in the office with its bronze glow and that went for both male and female.

Saddling up beside me, the woman who accompanied me on my journey today breathed hard. Dragging my single bag behind her, she stopped it in the center of the living room where I stood. The stout woman, known as Marilyn Williams, insisted on helping me with my bag today. Though, I told her I could manage. I only had the one, but I guess being my real estate agent, she felt the need to assist me in whatever way she could and had been since she picked me up in her Ford Escort at the train station.

Smiling at me, Marilyn smoothed out her pleated skirt pulled up well above her waist.

"We've kept up the place real nice for you," she said, gazing up at the framed photos and decorated touches of an elder. The home had a feel I remembered vividly, despite not visiting in years.

If I was being specific it'd been around seventeen years since I'd been in my aunt's home and because it had been so long I didn't recall much of the faded wallpaper and unfinished runners directly above. The carpet too, felt foreign under my feet as well as the woman who smiled amongst many faces on the decorated walls. I knew this woman to be my aunt, her silvery locks framing around a face only slightly deeper than mine.

Reaching out, I touched the frame of the photo behind an upholstered couch, the woman beautiful and classic just as my mother had been. They had the same eyes, brown and hypnotic like from a sweet dream. Naturally pink lips and high cheekbones, they could play the sisters on an aged sitcom, both women just as cheery and pleasant to be around. I remembered my aunt's spirit because it'd been just as similar to my mom's before I lost her. God, that had been so long ago.

Leaning back to my heels, I released the memory on the wall, seeing my aunt Josephine like a jolt to my childhood brain. I only spent a few summers here and so young, the memories hadn't been much for lasting. I'd only been eleven the last time I came here, twenty-eight now.

Maneuvering around, I took in the rest of the room, the walls the most decorated out of everything with its polished sconces and floral elements. The house really was in good condition. If not very similar to the last time I'd witnessed it.

I ran my fingers over the upholstered sofa, the bump and groove of the fibers rough against my skin.

"Lovely, right?" My real estate agent said, watching me study the sofa.

"Devine," came from my lips, as my fingers returned to my black hat. It coordinated with my high-waisted shorts and five-inch heels. I may have overdressed for today, but I wasn't sure in fact how exactly I *should* dress for something like this.

I mean, how was one supposed to dress to accept an inheritance?

When I'd gotten the call last week about my aunt's home, I'd been more than shocked. I hadn't seen my aunt or her home in so long, and in the end, I guess she'd left it all to me.

I sat on the arm of the sofa, still in shock by it all. The place really was managed well. No dust donned the coffee table and the piano in the corner, from what I could see, layered nothing but age across its black and white keys. My aunt Jo's little world had been locked in time, a sea of old rugs and vintage lamps of a distant memory.

Marilyn took her seat as well, more formally on the recliner in the corner.

"You must be tired," she asked, lacing her fingers across her wide bosom. "How far is it from Chicago to here again?"

"Just long enough to annoy," I joked, the travel from Northern Illinois to the remote city of Mayfield, Kansas, took over seven hours. My body ached and fatigued from the trip, I pulled off both heels and set them in front of the sofa, my feet singing at the feel of carpet underneath them.

I'd only taken the train because I didn't own a car. I both worked and lived in downtown Chicago. As a corporate lawyer, I didn't see the point in investing in a vehicle. When I needed to get somewhere beyond the use of the metro I simply used one of the practice's cars, my comings and goings usually work-related anyway.

Marilyn's laughter at my joke had been overly inflated, a bit *too much*, but remained consistent with how she and her husband had been since she first made contact with me. I guess it'd been quite a feat for them to find me. My aunt had lived here by herself for many years and didn't keep up much with anyone outside of the small town she lived in. I guess that had something to do with my mom. She was my aunt's only sister, the two each other's only family. I'd heard stories of my grandparents, how they hailed from the South. They passed when my aunt and mom were very young and their travels headed them upstate. I guess they'd been free spirits from what my mom told me.

Mom...

My only link to this place and how I missed her. She died after my last summer here, sickle cell disease.

I assumed that's why it had been my last summer.

Mom had literally been my only tie to this place and, well, I supposed after she'd gone my father saw no purpose in bringing me back. My dad was a business man from the Chicago world as well.

I laughed a little with Marilyn, but there'd been no reason

to draw it out. Like so many people I found myself around in my job, she was basically being pleasant for a purpose. She had intentions as my real estate agent and was humoring me.

She stood up signaling the end of her laughter. "Well, I'll leave you to it then to look around. I don't want to hover. You can do what you wish now that you're here. This is your home now."

My home... so weird since I'd spent so little of my life here. I appreciated what she said, though. I preferred her not to linger as well. I may have been able to deal with false niceties in my day to day, but I tried to avoid it if it could be helped.

Standing to the rug, I shook her hand.

"Do you know the name of a nice hotel in town?" I questioned before she left, pulling out my phone. "I was going to call a cab after I was done and—"

"Oh, you won't be staying here?" she asked, frowning. My words seemed to surprise her.

I held my hat in front of me. "I wasn't planning on it."

Actually, I wasn't planning on staying here or *in this town* very long at all. I had a job to go back to, a life, and after I got everything with the house and my aunt's property squared away, I was going to go back to it.

Without answering me, Marilyn waggled her little hips. I followed her into the home's kitchen, which could only be described as quaint with a touch of country. My aunt even had an old cuckoo clock, the tic and tock running above a big kitchen sink. Marilyn went over to it and turned a knob. The pipes hummed around us for a second, but then a rush of water fell into the wide basin.

She smiled. "You have running water and everything here, a market up the street if you're hungry to fill the fridge. The power is on in the whole house."

With a squeak she turned off the faucet.

"Fresh linens, too," she continued. "But if you'd really like to stay somewhere else there's a nice bed and breakfast in town, hot food in the morning and—"

"Internet?" I really wanted to get some work in while I was here, my laptop in my bag.

Marilyn laughed. "There should be some there yes. I'll write the address down, as well as the local cab company. But really, you shouldn't need to use that. Everything is pretty much within walking distance here."

That usually came with a town so small the property line from its welcome sign to its end didn't stretch much farther than that of the home I grew up in, in upstate Illinois. My father's house resided in the country on acres and I recalled the sign into *this* town stating the population wasn't more than a few hundred people.

I took Marilyn's information for both the BNB and the cab without question. With the shoes I wore and the ones in my bag, anything longer than a few dozen steps would need assistance. Especially considering the entire property was surrounded in gravel, not pavement. Even the roads had been rocks on the way up here.

After thanking Marilyn for the information, she bid me farewell with promises that her husband would be in contact with more information surrounding my aunt's estate. He was apparently my aunt's estate planner and wanted to meet with me personally to go over the details regarding the extent of my aunt's property.

There doesn't seem like much to go over, though, I thought, my steps taking me inward. My aunt had been a very modest woman and my strides around the home only reiterated that.

She had no clutter, the walls simply decorated and the floors only that of a rug here and there. This was the exact *opposite* of how my grandmother had been, my dad's mother. She kept every little thing myself and my half siblings had given to her. My dad remarried a few years after my mom died, so I wasn't without family, *noise*. There had always been people and there had always been *things* in my life, my dad and my stepmom, Sandra, very generous people.

But I guess when there was no one to give to, receive from, one didn't have much, did they?

My aunt didn't have many pictures, mostly vintage paintings like one might pick up from a secondhand store. They each displayed personal taste but lacked something. The place felt more like a display at a home furnishings store than a home and I wondered if Marilyn and her "upkeep" had something to do with that. She said they'd cleaned for my aunt, dusted and everything.

It all made me quite sad really. I hoped by looking at my aunt's things I might connect with her a little more. I couldn't really feel anything in this place. I couldn't feel her or who she was really at all.

I wandered the home looking for anything of her and I found myself looking through a window in the kitchen. She had a shed out back so I decided to explore a little. Marilyn welcomed me to.

Grabbing my heels, I slipped them on before heading outside. I left my hat inside so the sun hit my sew-in like a sauna, my brown locks pinned to my head absorbing heat.

Guess I won't be out here long...

But I did want to go look. If anything, I intended for my trip here to result in some kind of keepsake I could take back to the city with me. I wanted *something* of the woman who allowed me to stay here a few summers as a child. Everything else would obviously be auctioned of course, and the house going on the market. I had no use for or the means to care for something of this caliber. Especially considering how far away I lived. I could manage a thing here or there, though, and I went in search of it, my steps taking me down a back porch.

The entire house was surrounded in gravel, but beyond

that were trees of oak and green. She had a canopy of wilderness over her property and I ventured out into it, my heels bracing the rocks. My steps careful, I made it to the shed all right, but the sight of a lock had me cursing internally.

It hit with a thud against the shed when I let go of it and I put my hands on my hips, disappointed by what really *wasn't* out here. My aunt really had very little, just some furnishings and a large house, a quiet house.

Lowering my head, I decided to go back inside. It was hot. I was *tired* and really just wanted to put my feet up at the BNB. I had my phone in my hand to call a cab when my sight latched onto something back by the house.

The hard crunches of gravel hitting the underside of my Louboutin heels sounded in the air with each step I made and I dipped, finding something spherical and pink behind some prairie grass under the porch. Moving the blades of grass around, I picked up a rubber ball, a child's toy with pink and white stripes.

This is unusual.

The ball looked abandoned. Like it hadn't been handled in a while, but it wasn't old, the colors not faded.

The shelter of the porch must have protected it.

I brought it inside, but only because it happened to be in my hand.

After quickly observing the toy and now *myself* after handling it, I put the ball down on a table in the hall, then went in search of a bathroom to wash my hands. I wanted to see the rest of the home anyway, so my search provided the completion of two goals today.

Hitting the stairwell, I discovered what I sought rather quickly when I made it up to the top, but not because I happened to have good navigator skills.

The man on his knees in the bathroom... *my aunt's* bathroom, couldn't have been here when Marilyn and I arrived.

I feel like I would have noticed.

A lift of his arm and a sharp and *unpleasant* sound reverberated across the bathroom, a tool in his hand hitting a pipe under the bathroom sink. The *noise* had been the very sound that summoned me to him in the first place, the man following up with several small hits. He went to *whack* the pipe again, but my very audible and very necessary, "Hey!" caused whatever tool he had in his hand to dance in the air with hesitation.

Strands of ruffled deep-brown hair cut the air when he turned his head, and when he pushed out from under the sink, I saw his face.

A jawline scruff with dark hair matched that atop his head, the few gray stands sprinkled throughout telling of age I supposed, but I found that hard to believe. He didn't look that much older than me, maybe a few years or so.

He grew to full size when he got up from his knees and the fact that a man was in here... that I was *by myself* with him settled on me.

A set of broad shoulders took up much of the tiny bathroom and his wide chest rose and fell from behind a dirty white t-shirt. He had that same dirt on his hands, his fingers wrapped around what I now saw to be a wrench.

"You must be the niece," he said, pulling a rag from the back pocket of well-worn jeans. He rubbed his dirty hands with it and I only shook my head. I was glad he knew who *I* was.

Because I had no idea about him.

I put my hands on my hips, shocked that this man was casually wiping his hands down in front of me when he was clearly trespassing.

"And you are?"

Like he only realized himself that he'd left *that* part out, he pocketed the rag, then put his hand out. His palm was still dirty of course. I mean, how clean could one get their hands with that of a simple rag? The thing had been dirty to begin with.

"Sorry," he said, then took the proper action by washing his hands in the sink, a bar of soap there. After using the air to quick dry, he returned his hand to me, but by then the whole "introductions thing" seemed pointless. He'd made me wait and, well, had been kinda rude from the jump.

He closed his hand, taking a step back.

"I'm Gray," he said. "Short for Grayden. I, uh was working on your aunt's sink."

That I could see, eyeing around him, but what I didn't know was why and he didn't tell, watching me.

His hands came together. "I didn't mean to barge in, but I wasn't sure what day you'd be here so um..."

He paused for a second, ruffling around those dark locks on his head. Like I said, he couldn't have been much older than me. Possibly a half a decade at best, but he did have that gray, not unlike his name. He had age around his eyes as well and I noticed when he narrowed them the irises were a soft blue.

"You just get here um...?"

"Alicia," I said, since it seemed that's what he'd been looking for. I gazed around and he watched me while I toured the little space of the bathroom he didn't take up. He had tools everywhere, a mess everywhere and none of it made sense. If Marilyn was having a handyman come over today she should have told me so I wouldn't be surprised at his presence.

He took a step behind me as I'd turned my back.

"Sorry about the mess—"

"I'm sorry," I started, turning around. "But did Marilyn send you? She never mentioned someone coming by today to fix things in the house."

"And Marilyn would be?"

"My realtor?" I told him, looking up at the mass of him. He was quite tall.

I stood my ground. "She brought me here today and didn't mention a handyman. She actually said the house was well cared for."

Gray nodded with the words and when he came toward me I stiffened. He just said he had no idea who Marilyn was, which meant he was an intruder.

I blinked, as he gained. "What are you—"

The flush of a toilet sounded when he pulled the handle, his wide frame reaching around me.

"Well your realtor's idea of well cared for is your toilet slow flushing," he said, standing upright. A *whoosh* of oak scent thickened in the air around me, the smell combined with the faint smell of cotton, his t-shirt.

Soft blue eyes flicked right and I followed the direction.

Dipping my head, I noted the toilet had flushed just fine.

He navigated around me, causing me to do a small dance in the bathroom when he took my place and turned on the faucet of the sink he'd just been under.

"And your water coming out brown," he said, the droplets slow at first, but then full stream. Clear water came in a steady current and I watched until he moved. "That was until I fixed it," he finished. After splashing his hands under the stream and turning the water off, he rubbed his hands on his rag again.

"Neither was working properly until I did."

An air of smugness I gathered from his tone, but I didn't comment on it. If he did what he said, I supposed that was good.

And he was staring at me again, a long and well-observant peer like he was taking me in...

As well as sizing me up a little.

I squared my shoulders. "I suppose you want something for it? Your trouble?"

Dark eyebrows shot up. He pushed the rag behind himself, back into his pocket, and when he leaned back on the sink, he crossed an ankle over the other.

"What I did with the toilet was a temporary fix," he said, moving on the conversation like I'd said nothing about money, nothing at all.

Bending down, he picked up the back of the toilet and repositioned it.

"The toilet will back up," he said. "It will fail, so you're going to have to get someone out here to take care of it soon, as well as look at the motor on your fridge. It's crap and will eventually be the reason your food spoils if you let it. I told your aunt about this and a few other problems many times but—"

"My aunt?" That'd been the first and only thing really to get my attention.

He knew my aunt? He... knew her? What did he know?

There went that gaze again, sharp and intense in his stare and when he kicked a leg off the other, he stood to full height.

"Yes," he said, then dipped, picking up his tools. I could only watch, stare as the man went about his actions and gathered his things like it was nothing. Like this was routine for him and he'd done this before.

Maybe he had.

His final item of retrieval had been a pencil, which he pushed behind his ear.

His toolbox hit his hip when he lowered his shoulders.

"You'll take care of all this, right?" he asked, his eyes narrowing. "Get someone in here soon? I'd hate to see this place fall apart."

I could only nod, on autopilot by what he said and the tone in which he'd stated it.

He'd sounded so serious.

After he got that from me, that single solitary movement of acknowledgement, his gaze parted from mine. He looked away and then up like he was taking it all in, absorbing it. Without a goodbye or I guess even a hello, he left my side. He asked for nothing from me when he went down the hall, not for the sink, toilet, the advice, or anything. He simply walked away, the top of his head disappearing down the stairwell.

The front door clicked shut not long after.

Two

ALICIA

THE CAB DIDN'T COME after I called and I waited for almost two hours before I began walking.

She said everything is within walking distance.

Banking on that, I closed the door behind me, then locked the entryway to my aunt's house. I'd been waiting the better part of the evening for my ride and dusk had started to settle in —hence the lights. I had no idea how far or how *long* I'd be traveling, so I decided taking only the necessities from my overnight bag seemed like the most reasonable action for travel. I got my toothbrush and a pair of panties, which I stuffed into my oversized purse. The final element had been a pair of more sensible shoes. I had a pair of flats in my luggage and decided those were my best bet for tonight's journey.

I headed onward after that, using my cellphone light after a while, as I ventured into the wildness known as my aunt's small town. The area was completely surrounded in trees and landscape despite the single gravel road leading out from the country home and I wished I would have paid more attention on the drive up here with Marilyn.

Or taken her advice to just stay at the house.

The concept just felt inappropriate. This really wasn't my house and to stay there like I lived there didn't feel right.

Then there had been that guy...

Maybe it was just normal that country people walked into one's home, fixed things because they felt like it and didn't take or ask anything for it. Maybe this was all normal, but for me none of it made sense and the need for refuge and comfort was something that I needed right now.

That and cell service.

I hadn't been able to make any calls besides the one to the cab company. Not that anyone in a hundred-mile radius could help me anyway. I was on my own here, out of my element and ideally wished I would have taken my dad's advice to handle all this—the inheritance—himself. He'd offered graciously, but I wanted to do this. My aunt was my only link to that side of my family and I was grown. I had this.

My cellphone died.

I don't have this.

My feet in an aimless sprint, I shuffled in the only direction I knew of. The rocky road underneath my feet wasn't easily made out, but it could be seen and I stayed on it, suddenly wishing for the obnoxious noises of city life to guide me to some sort of civilization. The only thing out here were owl calls and cricket chirps.

The lights of a small city took my vision about halfway between me being kinda freaked and completely losing it, a cluster of tiny buildings ahead in the night. As I moved forward, they got bigger and I realized immediately this was it. This was the town, downtown.

All the buildings faced each other like in a square and as I had no idea what building was which, I headed in the direction of the closest. It happened to be a bar judging by the flashing neon lights of *Budweiser* and *Guinness* and I gave a silent prayer of relief at the sight of something familiar.

Shrugging my bag up my shoulder, I cracked the door and entered a room so lively I questioned if I'd been in the middle of nothing only moments ago.

I guess this is where everyone is, travelled my thoughts, as well as my sight. I normally felt at home in environments such as this, partying and bars nothing new to me. Stuffy, suited businessmen and women partied hard if not harder than the rest of them and I'd always been along for the ride.

But that was in Chicago.

People, faces—*white male faces*—ventured in my direction. Heads cocked, I got more than a few stares my way and the fact that I was in a small town came to fruition in my thoughts.

Brushing next to burley men at high-top tables eating wings and guzzling beer, I lowered my head, looking for a kind eye to latch upon. I needed someone to tell me where the BNB was and at the sight of the bar, came my saving grace.

What happened to be the sole woman in this place resided there.

And we just happened to share the same skin.

The woman looked a bit hipster, slender in frame with a beanie cap on her head. She'd actually pass for a boy had I not looked twice, but she was clearly female, her tight-fitting jeans and slight bump of bosom beneath a plaid shirt evident.

I hustled my way toward her, not stopping for anything.

I dropped my heavy bag of currency and personal items on the counter, sighing relief as I slid onto a bar stool. The bartender didn't see me right away and I waved my hand, attempting to get her attention. When I didn't get that I waited patiently. She passed shots and mugs to customers a mile a minute so I figured I'd wait my turn. A soft "Can I help you?" eventually came my way from her direction, muffled behind that of the bar's music, but as the woman was still turning out drinks, she didn't look at me when she asked the question.

I placed my hand on the counter, wanting to ask her about the BNB, but figured I should at least order a drink first.

I got out my wallet. "A vodka tonic, please, more vodka than tonic."

My order got a few eyes, but only a slight smile from the bartender. She looked up finally, looked at me, and at the sight of me, she did a double take. She did like a legitimate double take, stepping back.

She blinked at me. "What?"

I guess a place such as this might not have what I ordered, small town, small bar.

I smiled. "If you don't have that I'll take whatever is on tap?"

This seemed the safer option, but the woman's eyes didn't do anything to lessen in size. Eventually, she stepped forward.

"Um, yes, yeah, um?" she pulled her hat off, revealing the tight, short coils of natural hair, big and bushy in nature despite how the hat had concealed them.

Forcing the hat under the bar, she exchanged it out for a mug.

"*Budweiser* okay?" she asked, looking up twice.

Then a third.

My eyes shifted. Looking down, I thought I might have had something on my white blouse or something. When glances came up unscathed, I set an arm on the counter.

"Yeah, that's fine."

A curt nod and she filled the empty mug, the glass pumped full with frothy booze. She slid it over to me and I thanked her, placing her a tip in the amount of the drink. I was sure she worked hard here, bartenders tended to do so.

Lifting the extra bills, she muttered thanks before pocketing them. I thought she'd move on to someone else, but she chose to let the other guy behind the counter handle the others, choosing instead to wipe down the bar in front of me.

I sipped the alcohol, not exactly what I was used to, but not bad. I grew up with three half brothers and saying they liked to *drink* in their youth was an understatement. I got about a quarter of it down before I noticed the bartender girl was still there.

And was still very much looking at me.

What was with people in this town...

"You're not Alicia are you?"

I blinked now.

How did she know my name?

She must have realized how unusual what she just said came across to me because she stopped wiping the counter, chewing her lip a little.

"Small town," she said, bunching up the rag. "I think everyone here knows who you are. We all knew Josephine, and well, there's not very many of *us* here."

She gestured her rag back and forth between us, laughing a little, and gazing around, people did glance at me from time to time. But if they did, they just went back to their conversations. I even got a couple smiles when I locked gazes with a few people.

Relieved by that, the friendliness, I nodded.

"Uh, yeah," I said, breathing. Quite a day so far. I put my hand on the bar. "I just got in earlier today. I'm in town to settle my aunt's estate."

At the words, the girl's lips went tight, a slight sadness with her nod. She said she knew my aunt, that everyone did, so I bet this all affected her quite a bit, the loss.

"I'm sorry for your loss," she said, leaning on the bar. "We loved Jo."

And so it was confirmed. What I remember of my aunt

had been positive memories and I wished I could have had more of them, had something like they all seemed to.

"So you just uh, came into town for a drink or..."

"No, actually." I was glad she brought it up. I'd nearly forgotten after sitting down, my senses on overloaded. "My realtor told me about a bed and breakfast. I'm trying to find it for the night but wasn't sure what building it was. I walked from my aunt's house."

"You're not staying there?" she asked, sliding a brew over to a patron. What she said had been similar to the realtor.

"I plan on working and I need the Internet for that. It'll only be for a few nights while I'm here."

I'd blocked off the whole week for the finalization of the details surrounding the estate, but didn't plan on using the time if I didn't have to. I had a very fast-paced job and didn't want to get behind.

The girl's expression cringed after she brought her attention back to me.

"It's actually undergoing repairs," she said, resting her arms on the bar. "There was a fire earlier this summer. Some stupid kids. It hasn't been in commission for a bit now."

Something my realtor failed to mention. She didn't live in town, though. She and her husband had been someone my aunt apparently hired from a nearby town, which was more heavily populated, no estate planners in the area I guessed.

I'm not surprised.

There really wasn't anything out here let alone the tools needed to settle an estate. I was just wrapping my head around the fact that I'd have to travel in the dark all the way back to my aunt's when the woman behind the bar got my attention again.

"You don't remember me, do you?" she asked, smiling a little. "I guess it has been a long time and I do look different. I used to come over a lot to your aunt's when I was a kid. I wore glasses at the time, big round ones."

My memory pulled for those elements, a little girl with big glasses lost in the sea of twenty-eight-year-old memories. That in itself made the feat damn near impossible, but as I worked through the muck for anything of who she could be, my thoughts did pull something.

I remembered a girl coming over sometimes. We'd played with my aunt's doll collection and Aunt Jo had been so annoyed when we did. The dolls had been precious, had glass faces or something, but the girl and I played anyway. Ava had been her name.

I said the name with the thought and when the woman said the same name, my eyes widened.

"Oh my... God. You look so different."

And she did. I recalled her being a chubby little thing, round cheeks and all.

Ava's head bounced back and forth in the air.

"Thinned out a little I guess," she said, laughing. "You look different, too. So smart and fashionable."

I sat back with my crisp shorts and flat-ironed hair I styled up today. I used to not care so much before, getting just as dirty as any kid my age. Things changed, though. We grew up.

"I guess we both did a little changing," I said, gripping my mug. "And you're still here. Didn't leave or anything?"

"I left for a little while. College. I didn't do so well, so I came back."

My mouth made an "o" and she waved me off.

"It's fine," she said. "This is home. It always seems to pull you back and I did come back in the end. Most do."

I respected that, smiling at her. She excused herself for a moment, obviously needing to help others, and by the time she came back, I finished my beer.

"You headed out?" she asked, flipping her tiny spirals in my direction. She was filling up a mug for someone.

I slid off my chair. "Yeah, I should head back to the house. Though, I'm not exactly sure what direction to head in."

I had no cellphone for light this time and almost got lost the first time—going in a straight line.

Ava frowned. "You walking there?"

"I think so," I said, patting my purse. "I tried to call a cab earlier but—"

"Oh, if you wait a second I can take you home. I get off in about," she paused to check the clock on the wall behind the bar. "Thirty minutes? Or is that too long for you?"

It was like she asked if I minded chocolate. This girl was turning out to be my saving grace.

After thanking her profusely, I slid my way back onto the barstool, making light conversation with Ava in the minutes she wasn't serving.

"You don't happen to know anything about a guy named Gray, do you?" I asked, catching her during a moment of rest. I shrugged. "A little scruffy? Tall."

Huge, actually and would be a little intimating for a girl not able to hold her own. I'd been around people like him for most of my adult life. From gaining my MBA and law degree to my position now, senior associate at one of the most successful law firms in the country. Powerful people with an often brooding force came a dime a dozen in my life and didn't easily throw me.

Ava flipped her head of bouncy curls in my direction, her hands steadily filling a cup with brew.

"I don't know him per se," she said, topping off the glass. "But I know of him, yeah. He's actually like you. New to town, fairly anyway."

"Really?" I found this surprising considering he knew my aunt. At least, he said he had.

Her fluffy curls bopped with her nod. "Yeah, moved around here less than a year ago, which is uncommon for people living here. Like me, I've lived here my whole life. He's pretty quiet for the most part, keeps to himself."

I moved in. "But you said you don't know anything about him?"

"Not really. He lives on the outskirts of town," she said. After slinging the beer mug she filled down the line, she placed her hands on the bar. "Like I said he keeps to himself."

"Do you know where exactly he lives on the outskirts?"

I didn't really know *why* I asked, but I was curious about him. Besides the brief, unusual interaction I had with him I found what she'd said about him being a loner completely contradictory. *Loner people* didn't tend to make sudden appearances in peoples' homes and honestly show genuine concern for the state of the homes' well-being. He did, though.

He definitely did.

Ava dipped below the counter.

"I don't," she said. Popping up, she retrieved a glass. "But he's sitting just over there if you want to ask him."

Her chin jutted in the direction of her right and, sure enough, *down the bar*—I mean, the exact very bar I sat at—the man I'd been questioning her about resided. He had a glass of something clear in his hands, his tall body arched over the busy bar with steady traffic in and out from the counter.

I froze, the man literally four barstools away from me. I had no idea when he came in or even if he had been in here the whole time I'd been, which reminded me of our initial encounter earlier today, the surprise of it all.

Hugging my bag, I snuck a casual glance in his direction. He was sitting by himself, a loner like Ava said. He tipped his glass of whatever back and forth on the bar and the other bartender came over, speaking to him briefly.

Gray simply lifted his glass in response, then went back to nursing it. He smoothed his hand over the short layer of scruff on his jaw and in the movement, he turned.

Our gazes collided immediately.

Gray's body lifted, his eyes narrowing and the fact he knew exactly who I was and where I sat in position to him was evident.

Turning on his stool, he faced me in much of the same way he'd done before, full on and unrelenting. I thought maybe he'd turn away or... something, but he didn't. He simply picked up his glass, then came right to me.

My purse's strap slid under my slick hands. I had no idea why this man was making me nervous. Perhaps, it was how in my face he was. He talked right at me before, and was coming over here now.

His glass clinked the bar when he set it down, only a barstool between us.

"Can I get you anything?"

The flare of blue that was his eyes only severed their gaze from me when Ava asked the question.

He smiled at her, tight, but genuine.

His dark hair tousled more when he shook his head, some of that brown curling over his eyes with the movement.

Dismissed, she nodded, then tipped her chin at me. "I'll be ready in five to take you home."

I thanked her with a wave, truly appreciating her generosity. Especially considering Gray was here now.

"Can I uh," he started, pushing a hand behind his neck. His eyes creased hard in the corners. "Can I take a seat here or are you meeting someone?"

Like I knew anyone here. In fact, other than Ava, he was the only other person I'd associated with.

I waved to the barstool next to me, but not before I stood. Ava said we'd be leaving soon.

He watched me as I gathered my things.

"Allie, right?"

I closed my eyes slowly.

"Actually, Alicia," I said, facing him. "*Grayden*, right?"

"Gray."

Well, now that we were acquainted again.

Ava, where are you...

"I see you're leaving, but I wanted to catch you."

"Really?" I asked, more than sarcasm dripping from my voice when I tossed my gaze in his direction. I put an arm on the bar. "What exactly for?"

"To apologize I guess," he said, opening his hands. "If I scared you by being in the house—"

"You didn't." And I did *partially* mean that. I wasn't scared after a minute or so. He didn't scare me or intimidate me.

His lips went firm with his nod. "Not even a little? I was in your house, your aunt's house."

"And what was that about anyway? Are you just a creepy lurker or—"

"No," he said seriously. He shook his head. "I was trying to help. I probably didn't go about it the best way, but honestly didn't expect you to be home."

"And that makes it right? You breaking in—"

A key stamped down on the bar, his fingers slipping away from it when he pulled his hand back. The overall design and grooves looked eerily familiar to me.

Because it looked exactly like the one my realtor gave to me.

"Where did you get that?" I asked, glancing his way. "Is that a key to my house?"

Broad shoulders lifted and dropped, but I doubted it was because he didn't know the answer to my question. He put his hand back on the bar and his finger danced over the key.

"I knew your aunt well," he said, flashing dark lashes at me. "I did work for her before. Lots of work when she needed it. I checked up on her too sometimes, made sure she was okay and…"

His words drifted off when I retook my seat. Silent, I didn't exactly know what to say to that, to what he'd said. He helped my aunt. He checked up on her, which was more than her own family had ever done, *me* despite the fact of not knowing that I could. I'd been so young when I had last been here, the memories of the past and my times here faint.

Those were crystal clear for Gray, this guy who'd only been in this town not even a year. He took a swig from his glass he'd been nursing.

"You got something hard in there?" I gestured to his glass and he shook his messy locks again.

His smile after he swallowed took me by surprise, the hike in his strong jaw playing out all over his face. He didn't look so aged when he smiled.

Sitting back, he put his arm on the bar. "Not tonight. I actually don't drink a lot. It's just seltzer water."

"Seltzer water? In a bar?"

His head dipped once.

Now, I'd seen it all.

From over his shoulder, my ride came down the lane, Ava sliding on a jacket.

I got off my stool again. "Apology accepted, Gray. But only if you don't break into my aunt's house again."

His lips lifted in the corner, his hand rising from the bar. "Is it considered breaking in when you use a key?"

And since I didn't have the answer to that, I didn't respond. Instead, I got my bag and moved past him to meet Ava.

"Wait, Allie— Alicia. You forgot your key. Your aunt's—"

"Are you as good at fixing things as you are at diagnosing them?" I asked facing him. He'd stood up, the key in his hand.

He pushed the barstool behind himself with his leg. "Yes?"

I nodded. "Good. Then you'll need to keep that key for when you come back. I'll need you to fix all the things you mentioned. You got time in the next few days? I'm here for less than a week."

Three

GRAY

My boots crunched gravel when I left my pickup and I shut my door behind me to approach a house with deep-blue shutters, the property lights on and the house bright inside. The entire property was surrounded with a white picket fence, the temperate air of a summer evening breezing about the leaves of the two large oak trees planted in the front yard. White-walled with the brown porch wrapped around created a vision of security, a stable home and a steady life that no doubt went with it.

My feet moving, I cracked the harmony of that home when I creaked the white gate open, closing it softly behind me. I looked up to find my presence already known despite how quiet I tried to be. I didn't want to disrupt the flow of the environment more than I already had been doing as of late.

Ms. Jolene Berry came with her smile, always with her smile no matter how early in the evening I tended to be. I really tried today, took my time by going to the bar and everything.

"Gray," she said, waving, her pants cuffed at the ankles. She had her powder-blue blouse tied at the waist over her cotton t-shirt, the young school teacher casual in the final days of summer. Stepping from her doorframe, she met me midway onto her lit porch.

"We actually just got done," she said, not acknowledging the fact that I'd come early once again today. I could thank her for that.

In the past I had.

My smile small but always genuine, I nodded at her, then panned to her left a little. She was shy one person today, my little person.

Laura could be quiet, but I never lost her. I always found her. Always.

A head with a crooked ponytail bobbed and tilted not far behind Jolene, strands of deep, dark silk hiked high atop her head. I'd been getting better at doing her hair, but we'd been running late today. I had a repair job in the town over at an office building and could be mismanaged in regards to time sometimes. I always made sure we got where we needed to be in the end, though. That was my job.

That was my honor.

On her belly, Laura colored in Jolene's living room with a colored pencil, her location within clear view of the school teacher's foyer. She and Jolene must have gotten done early like the teacher said. She'd never let Laura color unless she was done with her schooling.

My smile widening, I made moves forward, toward her, but stopped when Jolene flagged me down.

"I wanted to speak with you about something quickly if we could," she said, cutting my view off from Laura a little when she shut the door a bit. She didn't do it much and I assumed so sound couldn't travel.

I guess that explained why they finished up early. She wanted to talk to me.

"About?" I asked finding her eyes when I removed my gaze from Laura. "Everything all right? Did she—"

"She was an angel as she always is," she told me and I believed her. She'd only spoken highly of my daughter, *honest* about my daughter.

Sometimes to the point of overstepping her boundaries.

I felt she was on the cusp of that now, a change in the summer air I spoke about before.

Her vision panned to Laura through the glass window on her door.

"I'd like to see Laura join regular classes in the fall," Jolene said, confirming my earlier thoughts. She faced me. "She'd do well in a traditional school environment. She's smart. You've seen her work."

My daughter was smart. She was.

But that wasn't the problem.

Moving my jaw, I faced that same girl through the window Jolene stared upon. She'd continue to color, keeping to herself as she always did. My daughter never bothered anyone. She'd never been trouble for me.

Squeezing my fist, I stared at Jolene. "We've had this talk before."

In fact, too many times to count. The discussions had only gotten more frequent as the summer months dwindled down. I took Jolene on to teach my daughter all she could before the regular school year required more of her time. The tutoring would allow my daughter the best education possible as I took on repair and maintenance jobs.

This had been a big step for me.

I didn't trust easy, but I gave this woman before me a chance. She came with questions and answers I never had, but she took on the job. She seemed happy to, especially after meeting Laura. Like I said, my girl didn't get in trouble.

I breathed. "My daughter won't be starting school and I

can go back to homeschooling her in the fall if you don't have time—"

"That's *not* what this is about, Gray," she said, her expression serious. "You know I enjoy teaching Laura. I just want her to have the best learning experience possible."

"Which is?" I asked, my face doing nothing to cool in the soft heat of the night.

She shook her head. "Interaction. She needs friends, Gray. She needs something I can't give her and people her own age."

"And you'd know exactly what she needs wouldn't you, Jolene?" I told her, raising my head. "Because you're a parent? You know how to parent my child?"

Because she didn't and last time I checked, she didn't have children. She was a teacher, an educator and a damn good one judging by the work my daughter brought home.

But that didn't give her any right to parent.

Having enough of this, I went to move around her. She did move out of my way. I gave her that, but that didn't stop her words.

"She's getting... worse, Gray."

I closed my eyes, my hand sliding from her door.

Worse...

"Her withdrawal..."

The woman's eyes were cringing when I turned around, her face sad as strands of her red hair swept her face in the wind on her porch.

She pulled it away, shrugging a little. "It's like some days I don't even know if she's there. If she hears me at all when I'm teaching her."

My eyes cringing now, I faced my daughter, barely an expression on her face while she colored in her coloring book. I got so used to that, so much so that some days...

My fists tightened at my sides, my head shaking when I faced Laura's teacher again.

Jolene came forward and the genuine concern on her face was evident. She'd had it that first day she met my daughter, but it got better. It got better.

"She needs interaction with others, Gray."

"She has me," I said, lifting my head.

Jolene nodded. "She does and she's blessed to have that."

Was she, though? Sometimes I did wonder.

I wondered if I brought more hell than happiness into Laura's life, but worse, I worried if I was the cause for her *lack* of happiness. She didn't have fun like most children her age, didn't laugh and barely played. Jolene was right. My child was withdrawn.

And only one had been able to get through to her.

I squeezed my eyes, hearing Jolene's steps creak closer. Those slats on her wraparound porch were giving way under subtle movement.

"Consider school," she said, then made it worse when she said, "I think Jo would want that for her."

I watched my daughter in the dim evening of our drive home, her head leaning against the half-open window of my old truck. She had her fingers curled tight over the top of the glass, wisps of her chocolate-toned hair touching her cheek in the open wind. Flush and round, her cheek peeked beneath the strands, her dark-brown lashes framing eyes I knew to be just as brown. She looked like me in so many ways, but more so resembled her mom. Her skin toasted and tan, Laura held strongly to the Puerto Rican roots of her mother and I was proud of that. I was glad she *had* that, something if anything positive from her mom.

She'd never have much, a reality I knew more than she might ever even as she grew into adulthood. I worried for those times, the days and years that passed for her.

I worried who she'd end up becoming.

Swallowing, I forced my eyes on the road, my thoughts

taking me away as they always did. I was always thinking, my mind a web of anxiety and unease.

"Ms. Berry said you did well today," I told her, referring to what little good did come out of my conversation with her teacher.

There hadn't been much.

I breathed, facing Laura. She reacted in no way to my words, her hand playing at the window. Some guys couldn't get their kid to *stop* talking.

I unfortunately never had that problem.

Trying to get her out of herself, trying *anything* I moved her leg, forcing a smile at my little human.

"How about we make your favorite tonight?" I asked her returning my hand to the wheel. "We got a bunch of mac and cheese last grocery trip."

I knew she liked it because she ate a lot of it, always going back for more and being assertive about it.

I didn't know what I hoped for by telling her I'd make her favorite dish, but in the end, I didn't get much. I just got Laura, Laura ignoring me and maybe listening. She only did when I was forceful about it, obedient when she needed to be and nothing more.

We listened to the road a long time before I spoke again, and by then, I found myself grasping at straws. I told her about my day and all the work I'd done. I took on about three repair jobs today before settling in at that bar this evening and I told her details about every one of them.

Which may have been the problem.

I noticed her head lift when I mentioned Jo's place, her fingers stopping entirely when I moved on to details about my time at the house.

"It's looking good," I said to her, smiling when her hand returned to her lap. She rose up. She was listening.

My smile widened. "It's been cleaned up real nice and I got

a job fixing the place up. I'll get some of those things done that fell by the wayside a little."

The older woman had been maddeningly stubborn in her days. I couldn't work on anything without her getting on me about it. She literally wouldn't ask for help until things broke down.

That's how wonderful she'd been.

She'd been so kind to Laura and me, and in the back of my mind, I knew that's why my daughter was paying attention. She was listening about the woman and home she cared about and because she was, I kept on. I kept talking, kept pushing, and mentioning everything, which occurred today at the house outside of Josephine's niece. I would have gotten to that. That came next.

Until Laura.

My daughter rarely looked at me when I spoke. Like I said, only when she knew she needed to. She did so in instances of urgency and because those occasions were so rare it was hard to know if she was paying attention like Jolene said.

I damn sure knew when something was wrong, though.

My daughter didn't scream. She didn't shout. She didn't yell and sometimes... well, sometimes I wished she would. It'd let me know she was in there.

It'd let me know my daughter existed.

The smack of her hand on my truck's dashboard rang in my ears, then reverberated in both the cabin *and* my head when she hit against the truck's window. Laura wasn't much for strength. Eight-year-olds really weren't, but I heard those hits, those *pounds* against the glass and the door. Her other hand joined in, fists slamming and hands slapping and the violent sounds surged bile to chase up my throat.

"Laura," I urged, trying to make her stop while I kept my eyes on the road. I grabbed her arm. "Laura, stop."

But my kid wouldn't stop. Her hits, her thrashes only hit

harder, and when her little hands tugged at the door handle, I had to pull over. We'd made it close to the house but still had a couple of miles.

That didn't seem to stop my daughter.

Going for the lock, she tugged it open, and before I knew it, I caught nothing but her back. She was out of my truck then and on her feet, running out into the world.

What the hell...

"Laura!"

I called through the open door first before unbuckling my belt and getting on my feet. Free, I sprinted into the prairie grass after her.

Until I realized I didn't need to.

My steps slowing, I knew exactly where she was headed and I found her there. I found her past the seemingly miles of land.

And gravestones covering them.

A tiny girl out of breath lay against one of them, holding herself while she stared off into the distance. Despite where she was, *what she was doing*, she looked at peace. In fact, I knew she was.

A short time ago, she always looked that way when she watched Jo's hands, her head against the back of the piano while the older woman played it. She'd sit for literally hours if Josephine's hands held up and some days they did.

My breath all but lost, I stepped up to the gravestone that was engraved with the woman known as Josephine Bradley, a woman who'd done more for me, hell more for my daughter, than I'd been able to do in the last three years of her life. Since I'd gotten Laura I hadn't known what to do with her, for her, but this woman had. She'd gotten my daughter to open up and if she'd lived longer...

I might have been able to hear my daughter's voice again.

Four

ALICIA

Bastian picked up on the third ring and I breathed easy, settling back into my bed. It was lonely out here in Kansas, dark, and I needed to hear a familiar voice.

"Off the train maybe twelve hours and you need me already?"

His warm chuckle drummed into the phone and I grinned at the fact he poked fun at me.

I pulled up one of my aunt's old quilts around me, staying in the guest room of her wide home. I still felt like a guest here and that seemed appropriate. I turned on my side, making sure not to unplug my phone that had only been charging in the few minutes since I got in.

"Shut your filthy mouth," I said, being mean too, and he only laughed again. He had a voice like smooth velvet and a laugh just as rich.

"Filthy, huh?" he asked, showcasing that depth. He barked another chuckle before continuing. "I can show you filthy."

And I knew he could. I *wished* he could. It was so lonely here, the only sounds deep in the dark of the woods around me.

My thigh warmed the other, my legs curled under the sheets. I pressed my hand between my legs and hummed at the feel of the touch to my thighs.

"You know, you could come out here," I said. "Join me?"

I spread my legs open and purred into the phone. "I promise I'll make it worth your while."

And even more tonight if he was game. About to suggest that, I gripped the sides of my panties to pull them down.

"You know I can't do that, Alicia."

I removed my fingers from my panties, sighing when I fell to my back.

"It wouldn't be for long," I explained. "You could come down for a few hours while I'm here, take the jet one day."

He had many. His status as CEO of a Fortune 500 company allowed him perks beyond that of many. That's how I met him, the firm I worked for represented him.

"Work doesn't stop for play," was all he said and I knew he wouldn't be coming.

I didn't even know why I asked.

A pregnant silence filled the seconds of our connection and if not for his soft breathing, I'd think we lost our call.

"Besides, you'll be home soon," he said. He let out a sound like he turned over and I assumed he was in bed just as I was. I didn't call that late, only choosing to go to bed because I had nothing else to do without Internet. Bastian, though, always chose to go to bed early, rising with the day.

"You will," he went on, "and then...."

And... then. What would happen next? I didn't know but had high hopes. Feeling light, I wanted to discuss what that "then" might be, but some chatter in the background took my attention.

The sound of small voices overtook the air and a softened, "Dammit," drummed into the receiver from Bastian's own lips. He didn't speak to me next and I knew right away.

The hurried dips and peaks of an Asian dialect moved into the line, Bastian's native language. He was second-generation Japanese and Brazilian, hailing for Brazil before coming to America and self-making his billions.

The softened chatter continued on, not much of which I could understand. I picked up a few things here and there since knowing him, but was still a novice until I had time to take in a few classes, which I definitely planned to. Especially, if we intended to have some kind of a future together.

"Erik wet the bed," was what finally came my way into the line, Bastian's deep groan following. Moving sounded in the background before he spoke again.

"I'm sorry, Alicia, but I have to go handle that."

He sounded incredibly frustrated, but I on the other hand found it adorably sexy. A man taking responsibility for his children and whatever problems turned up showed off his responsibility.

I smiled, rolling on my back. "Okay, no problem. You go take care of everything. Can you call me when you're done? Only if you remember of course."

"Probably not the best idea," he said. "Long day tomorrow."

I tried to hide the disappointment I felt within myself, but the ball in my chest couldn't be unknotted. Instead, I tried to respect the fact that he valued his work and the company he ran. I supposed that had to be enough for me.

I told him I understood and then goodnight.

"I miss you," I said on the tail end of it all. I wanted him to know that all jokes aside he was right. I did miss him. I did want him no matter how far away.

He didn't respond to what I admitted immediately and a few seconds ticked by before he actually spoke again.

"Alicia, we are taking things casually, right?" he questioned, breathing a long breath into the phone. "The divorce... It did just finalize."

My throat tightened, silence between us both in the air. It was true that he just finalized a divorce. In fact, he'd been married for over fifteen years and the settling of the union had been messy. But not once did he talk to me about slowing down during the period of separation when we originally got together.

If anything he only begged for me to go faster, harder while he fucked me for nine months.

I said nothing at first, really not knowing what to say, but I guess I knew the answer to my earlier question now. I knew where we stood officially.

I knew now what came after the "then."

Five

GRAY

"Grayden...?"

She'd answered the door in a negligee, pink silk hugging pert breasts the tone of caramelized honey. Robe open, the extended length and overall thickness of sugar-brown thighs were on full display as well as how subtle silk could play along the curves of a clearly unsuspecting woman. She hadn't expected me today.

But she'd invited me.

Alicia had given me back the key Josephine gave to me for emergencies, but I obviously wasn't going to use it if her niece was still inside the property. I thought I was doing the civil thing by knocking.

I severed my gaze from the view of her thighs and back up.

I barely hit breasts before she closed her robe.

Alicia apparently hadn't realized she answered the door this way, and under my gaze, she suddenly shied, wrapping herself like a mummy in her silk and pushing strands of hair the color of various golds and browns from behind her back and over her shoulders. Maybe she believed this concealed her better despite the length. Her hair only came to her shoulders.

Full lips pressed together.

"What are you, um," Alicia started, pushing her hair around again. "What are you doing here?"

I picked up my toolbox from the porch.

"At the bar you mentioned more work done on the house," I said. "I'm here to get going with that."

Her lack of argument told me she at least knew the conversation I was referring to, but her squinting into the low light of the day behind me clued me in that something still felt off to her.

"It's like six o'clock."

"Five actually," I corrected, rocking back a little in my work boots. "I'd like to get started as early as possible."

If I got done even a fraction of what I wanted to accomplish to Josephine's home and property overall, I'd consider today a job well done. There were things lingering around her home that had been niggling at me for a while. Like I told Alicia at the bar, the elderly woman had been a little stubborn when it came to things that needed to be fixed at her house.

I shrugged. "That is if you don't mind," I said, seeing as how I did kind of barge my way in here today. Alicia had never really given me a set time to roll through at that bar.

Perhaps, that explained the deep lines of unsettlement on her face.

I'd seen the expression before, unease... discomfort. She'd seemed displaced in the bar, which was why I had been so shocked to see her in such a place. She'd walked in wearing fancy shoes and a white blouse, a towny only a beer slip away from drenching that silky top of hers.

Alicia's hands did something similar to a grip action on her robe, again like I hadn't seen what had been behind it. Her nightgown hadn't been see-through or anything, but I'd seen people wear more on the beach.

"I suppose that's fine," she said, pushing her hand into the crown of her hair. She dropped her fingers. "But I don't know where anything is so I can't help you in that department. And if you need anything extra—"

"Not a problem," I told her, pushing my way into her home. She reluctantly followed her way behind me, closing the door.

I turned to her. "I have all I need right here and if I need anything else I'll retrieve the resources myself. I'm assuming I have a budget."

Some of these repairs wouldn't be free considering the parts and supplies and I had no plans to lie to her about that. My labor I'd do on the house, though. It'd be my gift.

It'd be an honor to a woman who'd been so kind to me.

Knowing that kindness, I passed a look through Josephine's sheer curtains, my pickup out there.

And my kid in the front seat.

I didn't take Laura with me on jobs if I could help it, but today had unfortunately not been my choice. She didn't have school today with Jolene and the other potential set of eyes to watch her...

I gripped my hand on my toolbox. Alicia had wandered off somewhere and I called to her.

"Do you um," I started, hoping she'd find my voice wherever she was at. "Do you mind if I brought my daughter in? She's in the truck. She's eight and won't be any fuss to you. She'll probably sleep the whole time I'm here."

Which was part of the reason I came here so early today. I wanted to outwork my daughter's sleep schedule. I usually got her up around nine and that gave me a few hours to work.

I was well aware my child should get up earlier than that, but the fact of the matter was getting her up even *that early* was easier said than done. She slept a lot, my kid. She slept more than I liked.

Alicia's silence wherever she was had the hairs on my arms

standing on high end. It took a lot for me to ask her such a request and she could easily say no.

"What was that?"

Her voice came somewhere in the general direction of the kitchen.

I stepped into the living room, which was closer. I pushed my thumb behind myself. "My kid. She's in the car. Can I bring her inside? She's sleeping. I'll put her in the spare bedroom—"

"Yeah, sure, fine," she said, voice clearly distracted by something.

But since she said what I needed to hear...

Placing my toolbox down, I sprinted out to my car, a quickness on my heels as I kicked up the rocks and gravel lining Jo's driveway. Laura was on the passenger side and I gingerly cracked the door.

She fell into my arms with the gentle weight of a child, her smell of sunshine and things like honey bees and summer emanating off her. I'd bottle that scent if I could. I hiked her up, pushing her arms around my neck and letting her rest her chin on my shoulder. Holding her head, I pushed the door of my truck closed with my hip, giving it an extra kick with my boot to secure it closed. Sometimes it needed the extra muscle to close, as I didn't always keep up with such things.

Holding underneath my daughter's legs, I took her inside, keeping a look out for Alicia when I crossed the threshold of the house. She may have given me permission to bring Laura in, but I wasn't going to take my chance by letting Laura actually see Alicia. Her sudden appearance might startle Laura.

And my girl could be easily startled.

I took Laura up to the spare bedroom like I told Alicia, figuring it'd be the perfect place as Alicia was probably staying in her aunt's room. Upon going in, the sheets were tossed, but that didn't mean anything. I'd never seen this bed made once when I came over here. I put Laura on top of it, then took off her shoes. I knew where a quilt was in the closet and I grabbed it to cover her. After giving her a kiss on the forehead, I left the room, making sure to close the door quietly. I'd let my kid sleep all she wanted if that made her feel any ounce better. I had no idea what she was feeling half the time.

But I had a notion her incident at the cemetery was an indicator.

Dipping my head, I attempted to block that out as I went down the stairs. My daughter was clearly taking Josephine's passing hard.

She wasn't the only one.

Making my way into the kitchen, I found a surprise in a woman wearing lingerie. I wasn't surprised she wore such things to bed considering her dress at the bar, but I was surprised she was actually *still* awake and humoring me. She was clearly trying to get her day somewhat started, rooting through pans and other things under the counter.

"You're not going back to bed?" I asked, allowing her to know I was there by the appearance of my voice. Instinctually, a tiny hand went to a pink silk robe, and I smiled as I came up behind her.

Again, it wasn't anything I hadn't seen.

Almost dismissively Alicia passed a look over her shoulder.

"I figured why not," she said, putting her attention back on the pots and pans. She rooted through them. "I'm up. Might as well start my day."

I could respect that, and though I didn't regret my plans to come over, a little guilt settled that I ripped her out of her bad. For that, I figured she was at least owed a cup of coffee from me so I got the pot from under the coffeemaker then went over to the sink to fill it with water.

My hand hesitated at the many bottles in the sink.

Empty, Alicia had cleared out some of her aunt's best wine

in little more than forty-eight hours. I knew because I'd just seen her at the bar and had been well-aware of her arrival only earlier that day.

Not knowing what to make of that, I ignored the bottles and pushed the coffeepot over them, filling it with enough liquid for one.

"Let me get some coffee started for you," I said, turning off the faucet before pouring the water into the machine.

Dark eyes flashed up at me from the floor.

She sighed. "You're a godsend."

I had to admit that'd been the first time I'd been called that. I considered myself personally less of a god and more of something a bit darker most days.

My hands moving, I made the motions to get that coffee for a woman I barged in on this morning. When she got up from the floor and made her way to the kitchen table, clearly waiting, I figured I relieved her of a task she'd been trying to embark on by herself.

Silent, I kept my back to Alicia while the pot brewed, the notes of fresh roasted coffee beans spinning themselves through the air. I'd picked the beans up for Josephine not long ago, thinking she'd like them when I went into the next town over for a job. I had been so quick to buy them and even quicker to get them back to her, my foot heavy on the gas. Little did I know she'd never get to taste them. She'd passed in her sleep that very morning, due to her age I was later told.

It'd been the first time I ever had to use my key to get in.

My lids covering my eyes, I finished the coffee on autopilot, trying not to shake when I opened and poured the single cup for Alicia. She was still sitting at the table when I turned around, and right away, the fact I had an audience settled itself upon me, her gaze drifting up from the broad shape of my back and to my eyes. Perhaps noticing that, she flitted them away, again appearing dismissive about the action before accepting her coffee.

A soft and cool, "Thanks" on her breath, Alicia accepted the cup and I nodded in response, grabbing the fridge handle.

"Cream?" I asked her, knowing there was some in there. I'd been popping back in to do little fixes here and there and kept the fridge stocked with at least that for myself.

"Please."

Again, I nodded to her, getting the cream and the sugar for her. After placing it down, I started cleaning out the coffeemaker. It was just something I did while I was here. I assumed Alicia watched me again while I did so, the soft heat of lingering eyes I felt in my direction.

She spoke after a while, saying my name.

"So you're a handyman?" she asked, her voice followed by a slurp of coffee behind me. "Does that take a lot of schooling or...?"

I had never been one for small talk and the condescension of a typical occupational question did nothing to turn me over to that particular type of conversation. I assumed she didn't really want to know anything about what I did. Asking me about such things was simply easy and made things less awkward for her about me being here in her home.

I figured I'd save her from that.

I'd brought my toolbox into the kitchen and after I put the clean coffee pot back underneath the maker, I retrieved it.

"Not much schooling," I told her, humoring her as I stood to my feet with the toolbox. "And I'm going to go ahead and get started."

My job actually didn't take any schooling at all, something I picked up in a pinch. It was the closest thing I could do for money to what I used to do in my more than nine-to-five. Truth be told I could work up to eighty-hour weeks in my old life.

I now gratefully knew it'd been a half life.

Alicia's foot touched the floor in my thoughts. She'd had one on the legs of the chair next to hers. Closing her robe though the garment fully covered her, she stood.

"All right. Well, don't worry about anything. If you need supplies just let me know. I'll give you whatever you need and as far as payment that's fine too—"

"No payment required," I said, dark eyebrows jumping in my direction with the words. "It's my pleasure. Jo was a friend."

The fact I'd severely minimized the role the elderly woman had in my life and the life of my kid quite frankly turned my stomach a little. A friend didn't just sit back and allow you to come into their lives day after day and be at peace with all you could give them—which wasn't much. I couldn't give Josephine much, but that didn't matter. She never asked, not once about why my daughter was so withdrawn and why I never talked about the road that brought us to this small town in Kansas. She just let me come in, day after day and help her with small tasks she couldn't do herself, the woman playing the piano in her living room while I did.

She sat and played for my mute daughter.

She played without question or reprieve, Laura's eyes opened while she watched her play on the piano bench beside her. It brought my daughter peace, which was why Jo played. She'd play for hours.

A friend wouldn't do that. A friend would try but they'd always wonder. They'd always question. The fact of the matter was Josephine Bradley wasn't just a friend.

She was the epitome of family.

Moving my jaw, I nodded at Alicia before leaving the kitchen. She could keep her money, buy herself a purse or something.

My work took me outside for the better half of the

morning, not surprising considering all the work that needed to be done out there. In reality, the entire property needed an overhaul, siding falling off and the roof of the house basically shot. Alicia had a few months at best with that. Whoever the realtors brought in to care for the general landscaping of the house should be fired. They mowed enough to create a partially symmetrical square around the house and didn't even touch the current state of the trees or overgrown shrubs. It looked like no one had been out here in months.

Standing with my back to the house, I gazed out into the horizon. Josephine's property line stretched far. I knew because she took Laura and me to walk out there many times.

A smile tugging at my lips, I recalled it had actually been my daughter to take Jo and me out, leading the charge with her run of the temperate land. There was actually a lake out there, an abyss beyond the canopied woods.

I saw my daughter come to life out there, smiling as she actually used to... play.

The pressure behind my eyes I squeezed away, pushing those visions that weren't my current reality from view. I never once heard my daughter's voice during those times, but that had been okay. She'd been getting there however slow.

I'd never been affected much by death before Laura came into my life. I lost both my parents at a young age and after their tragic car accident, I motivated myself. I'd be successful, take care of myself, and I had done just that. Then came Laura, her appearance not changing my life like it should have. I had been selfish when I found out I had a kid. Despite the knowledge, I still took care of number one. It wasn't until I truly feared for her well-being that this fact changed, however late. I changed and because I had, I'd been utterly gutted by Josephine's death. The difference between Laura and me was my status as an adult changed the ways in which I could mourn. I *couldn't* mourn with Laura around for fear it might break her more than she already was.

I checked on her several times that morning, several unnecessary times but several nonetheless. She was still asleep, fine...

I drove a nail into Jo's shed, securing the wall that no longer hung. If I had it my way, the means, people would be out here getting this whole place turned right side up.

I guess that was the perfectionist in me.

Driving one more nail for good measure, I stood back, the dark hair on my forearm catching sweat when I used it to wipe my brow. Taking a rag out of my back pocket, I used that instead, catching a vision when I returned the rag to my back pocket. Brown eyes widened in my direction, and slowly, Alicia lifted a hand from the kitchen window. She no longer had her coffee in hand, but she was still half dressed from what I could see, the summer breeze blowing about pink material against the swell of her full hips. She had her other hand on the half-open window and I assumed she'd just opened it.

Her fingers moving, she waved at me, her smile stiff before opening the window the rest of the way and escaping my gaze.

Bending back down, I ran my hand down the siding I just secured, the wall of stable wood running smooth under my palm. I knew this, construction and architecture. I knew the science behind it and what a man or woman's hands needed to do to create art.

I moved away from the structure, not everything that had come into my life I understood so simply. I got this, though. I *understood* this.

I stared at the house, the breeze pulling sheer white curtains in and out of the window. Smells of femininity, faint and soft like roses in the wind lingered in the air around me and I found my time outside may have been too long.

Must be my mind playing tricks on me.

The temperature rose high even with the early hour already. I was in for a sweltering heat if I didn't wrap up what I was trying to do soon. I'd stay all day normally.

I looked at the window again, my eyes flashing at a sudden sound. Closing my eyes, my chest felt on the brink of caving and I grabbed onto the shed I'd just finished working on. I needed to hold on for stability.

The heat really was being an angry bitch today. It had to be because no way was I hearing what I thought I heard, the sounds of a piano...

Josephine?

Gripping my head, I was soon squatting, trying to wake myself up or something. She couldn't be playing, Josephine.

She couldn't be still alive.

But I felt... her, the essence of her while the notes played in the air. She lingered in the wind as notes soft and incredibly dulcet sounded into the morning. The elderly woman could play like an angel to their harp, easy and natural.

And beautiful.

I hadn't known so much beauty until she came into our life. I had been surrounded by anger and greed much of my adult life, most of which stemmed from myself. I had no reason to be angry. I had everything back then.

I pressed my hands on the shed, the notes still playing from the house, and suddenly, I found myself lost, the sounds of the piano inside moving through me. So deep, I held my heart. I could feel them there, alive within me.

Something told me I should go find out what all this was about, who was playing the piano inside and why, but I couldn't make my boots move. I just stayed there, listening and pretending my reality was that of only weeks ago when Josephine had been alive and my life was finally, *finally* starting to right.

The sudden notes ripped themselves out of me with the

abrupt way in which they stopped. They ended too soon and I faced the direction in which I'd heard them, that kitchen window with the white, breezing curtains. I stepped in that direction.

I ran at the sound of a scream.

Six

ALICIA

There was a little girl under my aunt's sofa...

And I think I scared her more than she scared me.

I screamed in the end because I could only determine I'd been shocked. I heard something coming up behind me while I'd been playing my aunt's vintage piano and that terrified me. I had never been much of a jumpy woman, on my toes constantly in the often male-dominated environment I worked in. Because I worked with men, strong and powerful leaders in both business and law, I had acquired somewhat of an iron stomach. I didn't *do* flustered. But this girl, well, she unsettled me.

Especially, with what she'd done after the scream.

I barely caught a glance of deep-colored hair with tones reminiscent of a foul's shiny coat before she'd fled, scurried really. With quick feet, she'd dropped to the floor and pushed herself underneath my aunt's couch. She had been so quick I might have missed her had my senses not been so vigilant. I'd heard someone behind me, felt the ray of an intense gaze on my back.

I guess I had been correct.

She had been staring at me at least for a little while. I knew by how deep she'd gotten into the room. I heard her literally *right* behind me. Maybe only three feet away.

I had never seen anything like it, the way she'd reacted to me and her behavior. Yes, I had screamed, but the highest capability of that reaction to a stranger was a jump at best. This little girl hadn't jumped. She'd *cowered*, shrinking to the floor before tucking herself away under the sofa. One might have seen that reaction from an animal, a terrified being in attempts to flee a predator.

Not another human being such as myself.

My fingers to my robe, I wrapped the material tight around myself, my body at odds with standing versus trying to say something to her. Finding an option in the middle, I bent at the knees. My intention had been to speak to her, do *something* in this situation.

But I paused right away by what I saw.

A tiny human lay formed up in a tight ball, her arms and legs secured as well as they could be in her tight position beneath the couch. She faced away, her shoulders and back donned in a red-and-white-striped t-shirt, which currently all shook like a leaf. Her knees also knocked against each other in the same way while covered in a set of blue jean coveralls. I knew because the material crisscrossed at her back, a real, live kid under there.

Pushing my hand into my hair, I fell back a little, the reality in front of me I literally couldn't believe.

I went back for another look at what'd happened, *what was happening* as plain as the oak floor underneath my feet. There was a little girl under my aunt's couch.

And she truly was terrified.

I swallowed, not knowing what to do. Should I call the authorities? I didn't know the answer. She could be a runaway or something and found her way into a house that was usually vacant.

I looked again, her body still racked with tremors. Reaching, I figured I should do something. I couldn't leave her there.

She looked so scared.

My hand got within inches of shiny locks of a deep brown before the resonating sound of thick boots filled the room. Steps followed in from behind me and I turned to find Gray in my aunt's hallway, the door open and the sheer size of him nearly filling the archway leading into the living room.

"Alicia?" he questioned, eyes wild, *everything* wild. His dark hair and brow shined with perspiration, his white t-shirt dirtied and sticking damp to the outlines of his defined chest.

He crossed the room over to me in two strides.

"You all right?" he stumbled, his words stumbling. His hair cut the air when he shook his head. "What...? You screamed, right?"

I had screamed. I had been scared.

But not nearly as much as her.

In all my own flustering by what happened I couldn't voice any of that though. I could only point down to... her.

He followed my hand with his gaze, confusion and all-out wonder on his face.

"I didn't know she was there," I started, mouth opening and closing. "She was just there and—"

"What are you talking about?"

I pointed with vigor to the floor. "The girl. I don't know who she is. She scared me and I screamed."

I didn't think anything of what I said made any sense. My words were jumbled up, my body wracked and thrown, but somehow through my rambles something got through to him.

And whatever did put nothing but pure terror on his face.

His features visibly transformed from worry about me to dread about something else and whatever that was had him on the floor in not a breath, not even a whisper of it he'd been so quick.

A soft and raspy, "Laura?" hummed from the depths below me, within *him*, and I stepped back, my hands to my mouth. Gray had himself close to the floor on his side with his scruffy cheek pressed to the dark wooden slats on the floor.

He spoke to someone, tones of cool and soft vibrato in his normally gruff and sometimes terse voice. There had always been somewhat of an edge to his voice when we exchanged words. I figured that was just how he communicated.

I couldn't have been more wrong.

My steps continued to the outskirts of the living room, then later the hall. He spoke as if he definitely knew her and the feeling in there, the love in his words...

He talked her down. There was lots of "stay with me" and also "just look right at me."

My hands warmed my lips, my breaths on my palm. Like so many things today, I didn't know what to make of this. That girl was *scared* and there was no way she'd come out willingly.

A tan and muscular hand lined with dark hair across the knuckles disappeared underneath the couch and when it came out, it wasn't alone.

Tiny fingers with little nails on top of them wrapped around a hand that could literally devour it whole, Gray's hand so vast. Hell, his hand could do that to mine and I was a grown woman, but his hold was so gentle with hers. He tugged slightly and soon the small hand turned into an arm, a shoulder covered in red and white t-shirt stripes.

And then a face, a baby doll face. Round cheeks and big, dark eyes I'd only seen on the likes of puppies. Her skin dark, so much darker than Gray's, the girl looked to be of an ethnic origin, possibly Hispanic.

She pressed her forehead to the other side of Gray's neck,

which I couldn't see. He let her stay there, using both her limbs to wrap around his neck. He picked her up in the next moment, using only his legs to get himself off the floor before pushing his hands under her tiny legs and holding her. I think his next move would have been the door, his long strides taking him right out of the living room and quickly into the hallway.

Gray turned just before he would have, his hand on this little girl's head. He wouldn't let her see me, her head cradled as if to protect her. She wouldn't even know I was standing not three feet away from her if she wanted to. He made sure of that.

The largeness of his chest rose and fell.

"My daughter," he said, something I suspected had I not known by the care he displayed on that hardwood floor.

His lips moved. "You told me she could rest in your spare bedroom."

Spare bedroom... my aunt's spare room and the one I'd been sleeping in? She'd been in there? I hadn't recalled giving such permission.

But then again, I'd had so much wine yesterday.

The sudden feeling of that wracked my brain, no more adrenaline or coffee to see me through. The liquor's after affects ran rampant within me, my way of not dealing with my emotions when it came to everything that went down last night on the phone with Bastian.

I pushed my hands into my hair. I probably hadn't heard Gray. He no doubt had asked, but I wouldn't have heard anything this morning. Especially considering how early he came over today.

The man in front of me breathed deep.

"She must have just heard your playing," he started, his voice cracking a little. He pressed a hand to her back. "Your aunt... She used to play. She—"

A shake of his messy hair must have shaken him out of the rest of what he'd been about to say.

Standing back, he held the girl closer than he had just a moment before, backing toward the door.

"I'm sorry," he said, large boots retreating. One hand reached for the door. "I'm just so sorry, Alicia."

He turned and I managed to get one look at that little face, her eyes on me and absolutely haunting in their beauty. She was like a tiny angel, a lost child in Neverland, but that's all I got before Gray cut us off with the close of the door.

He left me wondering, long after he departed, what he was actually sorry for.

Seven

ALICIA

"Alicia... did you hear me? *Us*, my dear?"

The words parted my view of passersby, the people on the street walking their dogs and sipping coffee in a natural bliss. I'd been watching their goings-on for a while, lost by the many words exchanged in this downtown office.

As well as so many other things.

I was still in a state of confusion and overall wonder by what happened at my aunt's home the other day, by what happened with Gray's child and her unsettling reaction to me. I carried the heavy weight of that before I set heels into the office of my aunt's estate planner today.

And then the estate planner dropped the bomb on me.

"She owns all this?" I questioned, coming back to him. The map had been placed in front of me, wide and seemingly went on forever on the conference room table. The dimensions of the modest-sized home sat on the outskirts of a property line.

But that had only been its start.

Breathing, truly coming back, I pushed my hand over my mouth, the estate planner known as Mr. Williams, nodded his head of salt-and-pepper hair. Burly, he matched that of the general look and stature of his wife who sat beside him, the kind woman very much along for the entire conversation. Mrs. Williams, Marilyn, had picked me up from the train station a few days ago, got me settled, and in no way during our pleasant back and forth did the woman touch upon what would happen in her husband's office today. She'd left all this, *what my aunt had*, out.

And it was a lot.

The property line literally went from the house and onward, the home itself the starting point of an actual estate, which wandered way past what I'd been ready for when I came down to accept an inheritance. I thought I was receiving a home to fix up and later sell.

Not half of an entire town.

She owned the land in which many of the properties of downtown Mayfield sat on, which included both businesses and even homes once hashed out. Most of what was in my aunt's name was undeveloped land and truly beautiful by the pictures in the book the Williams' sat in front of me. They had a whole collage of expanded woods and scenery. There was even a lake back there, a gorgeous one with glistening waters when the sun above shined through the clear sky that day.

I ran my fingers over that sun.

"Its estimated value I'm sure exceeds what you believed."

Mr. Williams had shared that with me too before his last words. What my aunt had acquired came in somewhere around six-point-five million dollars and that was just estimated, no offer for purchase. The real estate had a potential for development well past that.

I knew because I worked in business law, knowing a bit about commercial real estate as well in my day to day.

The tourism industry could come in and clean up here,

build extensive campgrounds with the lake as its focal point. It could be something, truly something.

"We'll help you through the whole process, my dear," said Mrs. Williams, smiling ever so wide at me and I was sure she and her husband would. It wasn't lost on me she'd never mentioned any of this on the phone or when she met me for the first time the other day. She'd kept this information all to herself and later she and her husband tag-teamed me with it.

No, it wasn't lost on me.

Moments later with more than enough decisions on my hands, I found myself outside, my red-bottom heels scraping the sidewalk of a neighboring town. The Williams didn't have their office in Mayfield, the town perhaps a little small for them. Mayfield was perhaps too small, quaint, and maybe not appreciated by all.

Pushing the small chain of my purse up my arm, I sought out my ride who lowered her Converse sneakers from the dashboard when she saw me.

Ava beamed at me from behind big Aviator shades, the dark, ebony skin of her arms resting on the open window of a Honda I might see in a high-schooler's driveway. The vehicle was young, *rough* with patchy spots and nearly bald tires, but the ride suited her. She was young at heart where many of us, i.e. myself, sometimes took themselves way too seriously. She waved viciously out the window and I couldn't help the smile tugging at my lips. I waved back, happy for a familiar face after all that happened inside.

I had a lot of decisions to make in the next few days, what would ultimately be done with my aunt's property and later the logistics. It'd take a lot to prepare such a wealth of land for sale, and though my aunt and I didn't have a close relationship, I wanted to do right by her. I felt something in her place, her home, something familiar that I knew went beyond me. People lived here and the situation needed to be treated fairly.

One of those locals stared at me now, her head of curly, bouncy natural spirals tilting at me.

"That was quick," she said, getting her car started with a roughened hum after I got in. She apologized for that with a small smile and I laughed, happy she spotted me running earlier that morning and offered to take me into town today. She'd been receiving an alcohol order at the bar when I sprinted past in my athletic shorts. We got to talking and since she only had to work evenings, she said taking me into the next town for a few minutes wouldn't be a big deal.

It'd been nice to see someone who always radiated friendly. I made a note to read people in my day to day and had been doing so since I arrived in Mayfield, Kansas. I knew when people were being nice just to be nice to me, and with Ava, I never felt like I had to wonder whether or not she was being genuine in regards to her kindness toward me. Pretty much an open book, I felt like I got her.

It'd been Gray who'd been all over the place for me.

Not dwelling on the fact and *still* in wonder by that, I was handling one thing at a time today. My aunt's property and my decisions about that became priority.

"They were very organized," I told Ava in response to what she'd said before. She pulled out into traffic at this point and I put my arm over the open window. "I have a lot to think about."

The statement in itself seemed like the understatement of the year. I had no idea how an older woman from Mayfield, Kansas, had come to acquire such wealth, but according to her estate planner she very much knew what she had, hence investing in his services. My aunt had apparently made some very savvy business decisions over the years, not acquiring the land in one lump sum but over time, the bulk of which had come from someone she'd been close with in town. Well, when that friend passed and the woman proved to have no living heirs all that abundance went to my aunt. Through that, she'd been able to acquire much more.

And now it all came back to me.

I didn't necessarily feel worthy of such of gift, feeling really I was gaining it all by default. I just happened to be related to her, the only one who also happened to already come from an affluent family. Outside of that of my parents, I had my own money, my own job and my own mark I'd made in the business world. I never wanted to be dependent on the acquired wealth of my attorney father or doctor stepmom. I wanted my own and had gained it just like myself and my three brothers. We'd all gone to prestigious black and high-ranking colleges outside of my eldest brother, Peter, but he went Ivy League just the same, MIT. Between the four of us we had a young CEO, two attorneys, and one doctor. We were doing all right.

Why me? Why would she give it all to me?

I knew why, convenience and only that.

Smiling at Ava, I tilted my head at her. She didn't say anything after what I said, but I did notice that constant smile of hers did waver a little for some reason. She opened her mouth as if to say something but I supposed thought better of it. We drove for a while, getting back on the highway before she turned to me and I noticed her smile had suddenly returned.

"You should hang out with my friends and me tonight," she said, turning down the stereo a little. She'd turned it on when we got on the highway. "After my shift at the bar, we're all meeting up for a bonfire. Actually right off the lake behind your aunt's house."

Her gaze trained on me after she spoke and I felt kind of bad for what I had to say to her. Hanging out with her friends might not be so bad considering the downside of being outside and in the elements. I hadn't really packed for anything like that.

I sighed. "I would but I'm probably going to work tonight. I'm an attorney in the real world."

"An attorney? Wow," she proclaimed, bouncing her shoulders before facing me. "That's why you're always so smartly dressed."

One could be called worse things than fashionable. Grinning, I shrugged my shoulders a little.

"Anyway, yeah. I'll be working. The Internet guy is supposed to come by today and get me all hooked up with service so I can get some work done."

I called just this morning and after the day's events so far, I was glad to have been vigilant enough to make that call. Dealing with my aunt's inheritance would take some time.

And definitely more than a week.

Ava and I chatted a little bit on our way back into town and I found myself happy for it. She pointed out all the basic highlights like the courthouse and large library, but also more individualized establishments too. I got to see the places the town's youth liked to visit after a long day at school and where adults liked to hang their hats after getting off from work.

"We line dance there," she said after pointing out a restaurant known by three words: Brown & Hobs. My brow hiking, Ava lifted her eyes in response.

"Don't knock it until you try it," she told me and I laughed.

I couldn't see myself at all *ever* line dancing. I may have hailed from the Midwest such as herself but the concrete jungle of Chicagoland was very different from that of Kansas.

Humoring her, I sat back and let her go on about all the fun things they liked to do in town, even events like a pumpkin festival the locals put on every year. She truly did enjoy living here and she had to, considering she came back after going to college.

That made the decision on who I chose to sell my aunt's

property to that much more important. I wanted the right people to have it, the money in all this secondary.

I didn't speak a lot with Ava talking and she must have noticed. Stopping abruptly in her speech, she suddenly shied.

"Did you ever think we'd be here again?" she questioned, turning my way once she pulled up in front of my aunt's home. The drive hadn't been far, a nice one. She rested her chin on her palm, her arm lounging on the window. "In the same town, like when we were kids?"

I definitely gave her that one, herself and this town far from my mind before the call I got about my aunt. I hadn't forgotten about her or my time here on purpose. I had just been so young last time I'd visited.

"It doesn't seem to have changed a lot," I told her, smiling a little. "But you sure have."

She'd been quite different, both physically and personality wise. She'd been way shier before from what I remembered and, yes, rounder as well.

Giggling, Ava let her curls fly in the wind when she shook her head.

"Not really," she said. "But I guess it can seem that way since it's been so long since you've seen me."

Knowing the truth in the statement, I nodded.

She pushed her hand over the wheel. "If you can make it tonight, to the bonfire, you'd have a good time. We'd all love to have you and show you some more of Mayfield. It's a beautiful place."

I'd never question her about that even with the little bit I did see.

"Also hit me up if you ever need anything while you're here," she went on, that smile of hers still full. "I'm just a walk or a cellphone ring or text away. I don't live far from here, up the street and a few blocks."

Thinking I might take her up on that offer in the future I went to thank her, but paused when I realized something.

"Do you happen to know where that guy from the bar Gray lives?" I asked, belting my seatbelt again. "If so I'd... well, I'd love a ride there if you have the time."

Eight

GRAY

THE EVIDENCE SOBERED ME, my reality in the form of the financial spreadsheets I kept displayed in a weathered-down notebook on my kitchen table. The notebook had seen a few replacements in its day, but the general information inside remained the same. I wasn't organized in many things, but when it came to Laura and me and our livelihood, I didn't cut corners with that. I wanted to know what we had at all times, and right now, it wasn't much.

Another move would literally cripple us financially, not to mention what relocating would once again do to the currently fragile emotional state of my daughter. Laura had always been fragile and might always be, but she did tend to do better with routine. Places like Mayfield were small, intimate and that allowed for less emotional stimuli for my kid who never had a great time dealing with pretty much anything new or unexplored. She didn't do well with change, but I wasn't sure I had a choice.

Josephine was no longer here, both Laura's and my mental rock, and with Jolene Berry, Laura's teacher, getting on me about putting Laura in school in several weeks...

Then there was that thing with Alicia.

Caging my face with my hand, the incident itself had caused me to open up the books and see if moving was an option in the first place. I had given up. I literally saw nothing for us here anymore with Jo gone. I couldn't possibly go back to Alicia and do any more work on the house with her in town, she might not let what happened at her aunt's house go. She might question.

They always do...

My hand fell from my face and hit the table, a noise from an adjoining room getting my attention. Laura always watched afternoon cartoons around this time, Bugs Bunny messing with Daffy Duck on the screen in her bedroom. I went ahead and set her up with her own small television set, the box sitting on her dresser while she watched cross-legged on her bed.

Head tilted, the braid I did for her this morning draped across her back. The entire image of a young child watching afternoon cartoons completely normal.

She was normal. In there, inside her, was a kid just wanting to be a kid. I think she was just trapped and didn't know how to express herself.

I wish she'd just talk to me...

I stopped wishing that long ago. I guess I got tired of disappointing myself in dreaming and wishing.

My arms crossed over my notebook and my gaze severed from my daughter at a rumble clunking down the road. I didn't hear many, Laura's and my trailer on the outskirts of town.

My hand hit my knee and I rose as the sound suddenly stopped. It hadn't passed by or moved on.

That sent me on red alert.

Standing tall, I peered across the room as well as I could through my trailer's sheer curtains. A car had stopped in front of my house. Tilting my head, movement from inside the car could be witnessed, clear and distinct, as well as the sound of distant voices. The door of the car slammed suddenly and the hairs stood up on the back of my neck.

What the...

Not thinking, not doing anything but acting, I got a visual on my daughter still at her position on the bed. She hadn't heard the activity outside and if I had my way, she never would.

Quickly, I moved around my chair in the open kitchen, which joined with the living room. Our trailer basically only had four rooms, the living room/kitchen area, my daughter's bedroom, my own, and then the bathroom. I knew the schematics of this place like the back of my hand, our bags —*our lives* tucked away in the closet could be moved with a single grab. We could literally pack up and leave at a moment's notice if need be.

And sometimes there was a need.

I slid my notebook off the table, traveling across the room with gentle steps. Whoever was moving outside the house was getting closer, too close.

A glance in Laura's direction told she hadn't budged or made any type of movement at all and I crossed in front of her open door, pulling it closed a little. Letting go, I grabbed the handle of the closet door next to her room.

I'd cracked it open just a little, my attempt to get our single bag in there and grab my kid next when I caught a glimpse of someone.

A woman who seemed vaguely familiar.

My palm sliding off the closet door, I lowered, inching closer to get to the living room window. Getting there, I pushed the curtains open, which had been the very moment the visitor had closed our chain-link fence behind herself.

Alicia...

Feeling as if I was seeing things, I pushed the curtains fully open, an unease prevalent and deep within me as I watched stiletto heels stamp and sink in the earth outside my house. They actually slowed her a bit and she had to stop for a second.

What is she...?

But she was coming *here* for some reason in her short skirt and top, which flowed gently in the wind. Every soft stride exposed a sliver of the creamy brown skin at her waist and I immediately let go of the curtains. She couldn't knock.

I couldn't risk the repercussions of the sound.

The presence of sudden visitors generally lacked at my home. People didn't come here. People didn't see either of us and that'd been a general understanding by both my daughter and me. People weren't usually seen unless planned. That's how I preferred it.

My palm covered the trailer's living room doorknob and I pulled it open to a pair of wide eyes and red painted lips. Alicia's hand had been poised to inflict that very knock I sought to prevent. I moved between her and the door, pulling it with me a little. Even in her heels, Alicia barely reached that of my chin.

"Hi," she exclaimed, a shot of breath escaping her lips when she took a step back. I'd clearly surprised her, which hadn't been my intent. I just didn't want anything unnecessary happening today if I could prevent it.

I told her hello, gazing above the top of her head at the car she'd arrived in. Powder blue, the Honda could beat my truck with its condition, but that spoke of nothing of the way it drove. My truck was very sturdy considering the road and miles it had experienced.

Upon squinting the driver appeared familiar and when she bounced her head of full spiral curls once at me in acknowledgement, I remembered the owner worked at the bar in town. She'd always been nice, causal and didn't linger to talk when I took my business there.

I nodded back to her, my hand still firmly on the doorknob. Closing the door wasn't an option and neither was keeping it open, the door lingering somewhere in the middle between open and closed.

Noticing my hand, Alicia ventured a little more away from my personal space though she'd already taken a healthy step back.

"I, um," she started, not ever seeming like someone to lack words. She'd been quite confident around me in the past.

Your daughter hadn't freaked her out before.

My palm warmed the door handle. "What can I do for you?"

My voice sudden, her lashes lifted up and she took another step back.

"Nothing urgent. I just..." Pausing, she played with the ends of her skirt. "I wondered if you had a moment. I'd uh... I guess I'd like to talk if possible."

Talk...

Talk.

Nothing sounded worse considering the other day and I think she had an indicator of that, how I felt about a talk, when her gaze escaped mine.

It drifted in the direction of the door I had partially closed and bracing the knob, I made sure her sight didn't have the opportunity to go any farther.

I moved my lips.

"I'm not—"

"We can talk outside," she said, blinking. She messed with the chain of her purse on her arm. "And it won't take long. I don't want to bother you. I really just came to ask you something. A... quick something."

The fact she'd taken one more step back wasn't lost on me. We could have easily stretched two or three people between us and still would have had room with the space she'd created between us.

Rocking on her heels, she awaited my answer, her travel companion behind her and trying not to watch. The bartender's thumbs played at the wheel, her gaze facing forward.

Breathing, I stretched my arm up, scratching the back of my head. The odds of Alicia coming down here to confront me about what happened at her aunt's home I found highly unlikely. The situation had been uncomfortable for all three of us.

I moved my jaw, lifting a finger to indicate one moment to her before going back inside the house. Not quit closing the door, I stepped back from it and then found my daughter where I left her.

Completely unaware to the presence of our visitor, Laura continued to watch television, the tube playing old episodes of SpongeBob SquarePants.

"Laura?" I questioned, hoping I didn't have to do more than that to know she was listening to me. But like many things, they couldn't be easy when they came to my daughter.

I pushed my hair forward, messing with it again. "Sweetheart, we talked about this. What do we do when people speak to you directly?"

She knew the answer. One *faced* people when they were acknowledged and my kid knew that.

Using her knuckles, she turned softly from her position on her bed until she was doing just what I asked, facing me. Sitting cross-legged on the bed, she placed her hands in her lap, expressionless with neither anger nor annoyance by me telling her to do something, or anything else. She just sat, not so much in contentment but something else.

I supposed I'd take that. At least she listened to me when I forcefully told her to. Some parents might not find value in that but when one had an essentially mute child the situation changed.

Breathing, I scratched into my hair, not knowing for how long I actually did have her attention.

"Dad's got a visitor," I said to her, not expecting much from that statement, which was what I got. I dropped my hand. "She's going to come inside for a little bit, the living room, but she won't be any bother to you. You don't have to do anything."

Again, no reaction. My kid had the endurance to be silent and still as an oak tree's trunk.

I breathed again.

"You just stay in here," I went on. "I'll leave your door cracked if you... well, if you need me."

She never did, and sometimes I really wondered how much my kid actually did need anything outside of the obvious of food and shelter over her head. She trusted me, that was a given, listened to me when I needed her to, but she was absolutely absent from anything else. I had a blood-related child, but I didn't feel like her father sometimes, my kid passing through life like a zombie.

The hole in my chest just expanded that much more before I inched the door closed, Laura's eyes still on me until they couldn't be. I closed it silently and, standing for a second, I heard shifting, what I assumed to be her moving on the bed and watching television again.

Shaking it off, I returned to the door that hadn't been tampered with since I left it. I opened it so quietly this time Alicia's gaze didn't sever from the ground, her fingers wrapped around the chain of her purse at her hip.

"You can come in... if you want."

Dark eyes the color of midnight found mine, the delicate skin of her neck moving a little with her swallow shortly after.

Blinking, Alicia faced the woman from the bar who still sat in her car. She waved the woman off, and shifting, her ride buckled herself in and then started the Honda. The beater chugged down the street and Alicia smiled at me.

"She's going to tour around the block a little before coming back for me. I didn't want her to wait or anything."

I could drive her home if she wanted. Though, that probably wasn't a good idea considering Laura.

Choosing not to suggest the option, I pushed a hand behind my neck, guiding Alicia inside with the wave of a hand. Gingerly, she parted from the grass and stepped from in front of me into the house and I had a little smile at that before I closed the door behind her. She was literally trying not to disturb the peace of the environment or possibly even rock the situation with me.

I'd given her a reason for that I supposed and the expression eased away from my lips. Especially, as I watched Alicia circulate the room with her gaze. She took in that of a beat-up couch and dated carpet that came with the trailer. I was happy to find a place outside of town. I didn't always get that when I moved, the privacy.

"You said something about talking?" I questioned and stopping at her side, I lost her, attention on a particular part of the room.

The part in question happened to be the very room my daughter sat in, the sounds of SpongeBob SquarePants traveling from underneath the door.

"Uh, yeah," she said, turning away from the direction of the sound. Crossing in front of her, I directed her toward the kitchen, moving a chair out for her.

She took the seat and I moved my notebook over to the side and away when I took mine. I placed my hands on the table, Alicia doing the same.

She looked up at me. "I guess I thought it was important I come out here."

I sat back, not understanding why.

"For what reason exactly?" I asked shaking my head.

Hadn't the other day been enough for her, the awkwardness of it?

It'd been enough for me and there'd been no intention on my part to ever go back to her and her aunt's place. No matter how much it hurt to know I would never be able to finish fixing up Josephine's house.

Perhaps Alicia felt differently than I had.

She faced that room again, the one containing my daughter, and I started to question whether or not letting Alicia inside, so close to my skittish kid, had been a good idea. I didn't think she'd come all the way here only to bring up events of the other day but maybe I had been wrong.

"You seem to care a lot," she said, returning to me. "About my aunt's house. I remembered what you said about working for free. That's a big deal."

"Not really," I told her, tapping my finger against the triangles that made up the table's design. "Your aunt was good to me, my daughter and me. Laura, she doesn't—"

"Laura?" Alicia questioned, soft. "That's her name?"

I swallowed.

"Yes. She doesn't get along with a lot of people, but your aunt was one of her favorites. And I did ask you if she could come inside. You said yes at the time."

Though, she had been distracted.

It had been something I took advantage of.

I had a task to do that day and my daughter unfortunately had to be there with me. I knew full well Alicia had sounded preoccupied, but I didn't care. I guess in the end I paid the price for that.

I swallowed before I found dark eyes on me.

Pushing her fingers together, Alicia leaned forward, that flowy blouse of hers brushing the table. "I don't remember that, but I'm sure you're right. I was just a little out of it that morning and the night before."

My memories of the wine bottles in the sink stapled themselves at the forefront of my mind. Had she drunk *all* that over the course of one night? She didn't seem like an alcoholic, but then again, no one ever did.

"The situation had nothing to do with you of course," Alicia continued, shaking her head, "but I brought all of that with me that morning. I was already flustered, so I ended up screaming—surprised at any little thing."

The "any little thing" happened to be my kid that day.

Alicia ran her teeth across matte lipstick that didn't wear away with the motion.

"I apologize," she told me finding my eyes. She blinked once. "I didn't mean to scare her and if you could please pass that apology on for me? I really didn't mean to scare her. I feel so bad about that."

She was apologizing... to me?

My mind pushed in wonder of that. She'd definitely done nothing wrong. It had been myself who brought an already timid little girl into her house with barely any permission at all to do so. I probably should be apologizing to her.

I stared at her, that remorse on her face, as she played with her fingers.

"Anyway," she said, looking up. "I'd like to ask you a favor. You don't have to do it of course. Especially with..." Her gaze traveled in the direction of Laura again before returning. "Basically, you can tell me to leave right now if you want. I just don't know who else to go to."

I watched her shrink in her chair and gripped my arms before I leaned forward.

"What is it? I mean." I paused, moving my jaw. "What do you need exactly?"

I was still in awe that this woman was even here and apologizing let alone asking me for something, and yet, here she was.

Alicia chewed the inside of her cheek. "I just came from my aunt's estate planner's office. I was there for only an hour, but what they loaded on me in that time I wasn't expecting. My aunt has more than just the house, quite a bit more, and I've got a lot of thinking to do in regards to how the property should be handled."

Because she wasn't staying in it or on it. She wasn't keeping the property.

She was leaving.

She didn't have to tell me any of that in the end, though. I just assumed.

I knew nothing about this woman before me besides the generalizations I'd already made. She had obvious quirks about her personality that could be easily discerned. She walked and talked in a certain way that spoke of the city and a possible higher upbringing. Between that and the general state of her dress, well, I figured she wouldn't be staying in Mayfield, Kansas, long. She didn't particularly *fit* this place and I believed I could be correct in assuming that.

But she was suddenly surprising me, her appearance here today to apologize amongst other things.

Clearing her throat, Alicia reached a finger over to play with, *what I assumed to be*, a diamond tennis bracelet on her wrist.

"Regardless of what ends up happening to the property I want my aunt's home to be preserved. I spent a handful of summers there as a child and I guess I have a place in my heart for it. I also want something of my aunt's to remain in the state in which she left it. I'll be making calls to the city to see if I can get the home recognized as maybe a local landmark.

From what the estate planner told me, it's got quite a long history."

I took her at face value with her comments, not knowing the history of the house or the property itself other than the clear understanding I had with my own history. That place was special to my family and me, just as her aunt was.

I opened my hands. "That sounds nice, wonderful actually, but I don't know what that has to do with me."

I wasn't trying to be smart with her, but genuinely wanted to know my role in all this. She said she had a question for me and sought me out for it.

Something of a soft light touched her eyes after my words, bringing out the various tones of brown in them and I recalled such a detail in someone else I used to know, the eyes more aged around the corners and the face fuller. She looked so much like her aunt. Like sneaking a beautiful glance into the past of one who'd been so special.

My gaze severed from those haunting eyes when Alicia moved her chair over and spread out what looked like a map on my kitchen table. Her smell wafted with the maneuver and I watched the top of her head while she adjusted the map. Light and airy, the woman had a subtle aroma reminiscent of roses in the wind and I realized I hadn't smelled anything like that in many years.

"This is everything the property entails," she said to me, looking, and I realized she needed my attention. I'd seen diagrams like this before, again many years ago, but yes, I understood them.

I leaned forward, my eyes wide.

Josephine owned... all this? I mean, I had a bit of an indictor of the property's width with the lake and all that, but still this was quite a surprise.

I blinked up. "What will be done with it?"

Shrugging, Alicia leaned back. "I have some ideas, but my

priority is the house and the surrounding land. I want it as beautiful as can be and that's where you come in."

I shook my head, not understanding.

Alicia's eyes crinkled in the corners. "You have a care for this place that no one I could hire would have. I'd like you to lead a complete restoration. You don't have to do anything technical if you're not comfortable with that. I know you're a handyman so I wouldn't put that type of pressure on you, but I want you there to consult with the team that's brought in. You'll be paid of course. Anything you want. The value of my aunt's land is quite high, but even if it wasn't I have the means to make this happen. I want this place to look the best it could be and I feel I need your help to do that. You knew my aunt. I just feel in my heart you'd know what she'd want done."

Everything she'd laid out before me had my mind lost in a sea of possibility, generosity, as well as her own care and graciousness she had to have to take on such a task. She could easily sell this place to the highest bidder and be done with it.

But she wasn't.

My hand moved across the map.

"What you're asking could take months," I told her, spelling out her reality. "You have to know this won't be easy."

Alicia's eyes worried a little after my words and I immediately regretted saying them. I didn't want to make her feel bad, but this would be a challenge. Not just for me, but especially her. She'd be in charge of all this. Essentially, the boss of the entire project.

She blinked at me.

"Are you not up to it?" she asked, chewing her lip a little. She moved her hair around. "I mean, if you don't want to commit to this I understand. I could find someone else. I just feel like... I don't know..."

She trusted me, and more than that, she trusted that I knew what Josephine would want. She was right about all that she assumed. No one else would care about this house like I would. I'd put everything I had into it and I owed that to a wonderful woman. I had something invested in Josephine's house and land that no one else she hired would, as well as an expertise that went far beyond what Alicia could ever imagine. I acquired it in a life I had before, and though happily left behind, I'd never forgotten.

I couldn't even if I wanted to.

"I'd like to hire my own team," I told her, pushing my hand over the property map. I looked up at her. "And we need to talk about my daughter."

Nine

ALICIA

"Dearest, you have to know this will take months. You can't possibly undertake such a project on your own."

This was the second man to have said such a thing to me in a twenty-hour period and I wondered if I had something stamped on my head that said I couldn't do things for myself.

I understood where Gray had been coming from yesterday. He didn't know me and hence wasn't aware of my capabilities.

But my father knew better.

My lip stiff, I tossed down a blouse I had gotten from my bag and switched it out for a floral dress. I was in the process of unpacking all my stuff and putting it in the closets, but was still currently living out of a bag. Going over to the mirror, I put the gown in front of myself, tugging out the fabric to see where it'd sit at my hips. I didn't have a lot of options since I'd only packed long enough for a week's stay, but I would have to make do until the rest of my stuff came in. I had a service pack up some of my things from home and ship it down to Kansas just this morning. Gray and my father were right. This project would take months.

Sitting on the soft seat of the armoire my aunt had in her guest room, I adjusted the phone I had lodged between my ear and shoulder.

"I get that, Daddy," I told him. "But I need your support. I didn't call to ask for permission. I just wanted to let you know what I was doing and where I'll be for a little while."

I had to do this. I *had* to be here for a woman who *did* have family. I was Josephine Bradley's family and I was going to take care of her and her legacy.

"But this isn't your crusade, honey," Daddy said, sighing into the phone. I caught him in the middle of a meeting in which he stepped out of to take my call. He always did though I told him not to. My dad was a good man and I came from a good family. He and my stepmom took care of all of us. My brothers and I went to the best schools and had the best lives because of it.

In my silence, I played with the hem of the floral dress that currently sat in my lap.

"At least let me use my resources," my father went on. "I'll send people down there and you won't have to do a thing. You come back home and can be involved in the decisions via email and video chat."

"You know good and well if I go home I'll bury myself so much in my life and work that I won't have time for anything down here."

Daddy laughed a little. "I do know that, which was why I suggested it," he said, laughing more. "I was counting on you and your work ethic."

He wasn't sly at all and I would roll my eyes at him if he were here to see it.

"You get it from me," he chimed.

"And my stubbornness?" I questioned.

He laughed again.

"That you actually get from your mother," he said, serious

now and I went quiet. He didn't say my mama. *Mama* was my stepmom, the woman who had been my mom over half my life.

Mother was my birth mom, a woman I wished I had the pleasure of knowing longer than I had. She passed when I'd been so young. I only recalled glimpses of her now, the same ones that connected me to this place.

Looking around, the room bare with nothing but the essentials, I stood. My bag was on the bed so I started putting everything in it but the dress I planned to wear today, chatting with my dad more as I filled my bag back up, then wheeled it down the hall. I had decided to move rooms, going to my aunt's room.

"I suppose I'll let everyone know your status then," Daddy said, finally understanding that yes I would be doing this and yes I would be staying here. "You'll call us if you need anything, though?"

"I promise," I told him, opening the door. Inside, a room very similar to the one I'd been staying in resided.

I stepped into the wonderland, a wide window leading out to an exquisite veranda. Filled with light, the room glowed like an iridescent heaven with the way the sun played through the sheer curtains on the windows and the white bedding.

I stood there, ready for this.

"You better," my dad went on. "And when you come back we'll meet that boyfriend of yours."

I told Daddy what he wanted to hear in regards to that last bit. He knew full well about Bastian, my entire family did, the young CEO who'd made his way into my life. What they hadn't gotten to hear about was how he'd been married—albeit separated—for the majority of our relationship.

As well as how he'd broken my heart and I boozed myself to sleep recently because of it.

Sitting on my aunt's queen bed, I pushed my hand into

my hair. I had no idea what would happen between Bastian and me. I did know I had been trying.

But that took two people in the end, didn't it?

I took the time to dress a couple hours later, my Internet provider had come and gone. He'd finished up the job he started yesterday after Ava dropped me off at home. The serviceman arrived severely late and had also come with the bonus of being underprepared on top of that.

"I'll be back tomorrow with the cables," he'd said yesterday, literally leaving one of the most important things back at his company's base a few towns over. Mayfield didn't have an

Internet provider so I had to outsource. The man was back as promised today, but needless to say, I hadn't gotten much done in regards to work prior to that.

Not that they needed me there anyway.

I called in earlier that morning informing them of my leave of absence. I was basically being dubbed the task of organizing my cases enough to pass on to the other attorneys as well as being on call for my particularly special and more affluent clients. The latter in itself would always keep me busy. I took the time to make sure my clients were always cared for and their needs met.

Pushing my hands down my dress, I made my way through the house, foolish I knew, to make sure things were tidy and clean before Gray came over. I mean, he'd been here just a few days prior.

I tended to clean when I was nervous.

And the situation, what was about to happen, was definitely making me nervous. Last time Gray's little girl had seen me she ran and she'd be here with him today. He apparently didn't have a sitter for her, as she didn't take to many people. He explained to me she'd be with him on the majority of the days he'd be here.

He also explained a few other things.

He'd emphasized her shyness and had been adamant that she should do the approaching if she did any and that I shouldn't expect her to say anything to me.

He literally said she wouldn't say anything to me. I had no idea if that meant she wouldn't be talking to *me* in particular or didn't talk at all. Either way, I figured she had special needs, autism or maybe something else.

I supposed in the end it wasn't my business.

I employed her father and that's the only exchange that really mattered. I understood the need for child care and I, of course, was okay with it though I had no children myself. I guess lately I figured I'd be inheriting Bastian's, their own mother nonexistent in her globetrotting and international excursions. She was apparently an international buyer and businesswoman.

My lip pushed across the other, all other thoughts lifted from my mind at the sound of a pickup truck pulling into my aunt's driveway.

Exhaling breath, I messed with my hem again. I wore nothing flashy. Autistic kids could be easily over-stimulated I'd read on the net that morning.

Angling my head to gaze through the curtains downstairs, I made no sudden movements, letting the pair come to me. The slam of a truck door sounded and I moved away from the curtains, standing into the middle of the hallway until that telltale door knock entered the hall.

It hadn't been loud, not surprising.

Braving up, I knew it was just a little girl behind that door, and her father.

Eyes of a crashing blue displayed before me, a child underneath Gray's palm as his hand was on her tiny shoulder.

His daughter truly was angelic. Her face China-like and round, she had a haunting glow about her, her hair dark and messy like her father's. It pooled down past her shoulders today, her dress that of a t-shirt with a printed cartoon on it and shorts that matched the same blue of her worn tennis shoes. Her hand gripped Gray's pocket beside her. Her skepticism was abundant in her gaze. She slid an arm up to Gray's waist and he pushed his across her shoulders.

She really was a skittish little thing.

I stood stationary, waiting to be presented and Gray didn't disappoint. Looking down, he spoke to her, saying, "This is Alicia.

"We talked about how this is her house now," he went on, his voice kind of rough in its usual tone but incredibly soft despite. I heard him sound that way before when he'd helped guide her from under the couch. He faced me. "Alicia, this is my daughter, Laura."

She did look like him from those high and slightly hallowed cheekbones to that messy, dark hair on their heads. She was quite darker than him though and I wouldn't be surprised if she did have that Latina in her as I assumed before.

Then there'd been her big brown eyes.

Someone else was there inside her, Gray only half the piece of the puzzle. He himself was a maze of mystery but I didn't hire him to know his life story in the end.

"Nice to meet you, Laura," I said subtly squeezing my hands together. I smiled. "I'm Josephine's niece."

Laura gave no reaction to that, at least not with her expression. She simply let go of her dad.

Then she walked past me.

Giving herself a wide berth, she made soft steps into the house and I turned, watching her disappear into the living room. Like she knew what to do, she lifted an ottoman, taking out what looked to be a book and some colored pencils.

Venturing inside a little, I watched her open up a coloring book, while getting on her belly and using those pencils I saw her retrieve.

"Please don't be offended."

Gray had apparently flanked me in my strides to see what his daughter had been up to.

Closing his eyes to her, he opened them to me. "She's used to milling about this place. She knows the house well."

The obviousness of that statement rang true.

The little girl flipped to her page of choice, doing her thing by doodling in the book.

His bearded jaw moving, Gray breathed deep. "She'll no doubt do that most of the day. When she's not doing that she'll probably nap."

"Will she need food?" I asked, closing the door behind us. "I can go to the store."

"You really won't have to worry about her. I'll take care of everything in regards to her care. You're doing me a huge favor by letting her be here."

I nodded, pushing my hands over my arms. "Well, I'm out of the guest room. She can sleep in there if she needs to."

"Thank you. I appreciate that."

As if on autopilot his daughter took our attention, the soft etches of color wearing down on paper before us. After a while of staring at her, Gray pulled down the pencil he had secured behind his ear.

He pulled out a notepad from his back jean pocket. He had arms the size of most men's thighs, generally built all over.

"I figured I'd use today to make notes. I've already got a crew in line and they'll be coming in the next few days. I'll alert you when people start coming through here, no surprises."

Appreciating that, I smiled. "Well, you'll have whatever you need from me. Just let me know."

"Thank you."

Rocking on my heels, I moved my lips. "I guess I'll leave you to it then."

He watched me venture to the staircase, my hand on the railing.

"And do you personally need anything?" I asked, shrugging a little. "If so..."

All he had to do was ask.

His bottom lip lowered from the other and the smallest crease in the corners of his eyes could be made out in the hall of my aunt's house.

"I'll let you know," he said. "But really both of us should be fine."

I supposed I had to take his word for that and guessed this could be considered day one.

Ten

ALICIA

I HAD to give Gray's kid one thing, her continued quiet only aided in my ability to get work done. I basically had one foot in Mayfield, Kansas, and one back home in Chicago. My days consisted of conference calls and telecasts, my headset on as I spoke with clients. My aunt had an office and that worked out well for my situation. I stayed in there pretty much all day, taking my breaks to ask Gray if he needed anything—which he never did—or take care of the essentials like eating or sleeping. A week went by easily this way, then a few more days after which I lost count. When it came to work I could easily get lost in it.

I had to admit the first couple days had been... intense. I wasn't sure how all this would work, a child in my aunt's house. I mean, children played and generally made noise.

But not Gray's daughter.

When she wasn't in the living room or at the kitchen table coloring, she was—I assumed—taking a nap. I figured this because when I didn't find her in all the usual places the door would be closed to the guest room. Gray did say if she weren't coloring she'd be napping, so yeah. I decided that was my best bet on her location. She actually slept quite a bit, more than I thought children usually did. But then again, I didn't know much about kids. Kids did nap, though. So yes, I figured this was all normal. Besides the fact that she was eerily quiet in demeanor and play, she was normal.

But then there was the piano... thing she did.

I couldn't remember what day it'd been when I found her a certain way at the piano in particular, but after I continued to spot her sitting on the piano bench by herself I lost count how many times I did after. She didn't do this often, but when she did, she sat for what seemed like hours.

Back facing the room, she'd have her palms in her lap. I knew because I wandered a little bit into the living room. I never came directly in, not wanting to bother or scare her. But once I was in, what she was doing could be easily seen. She sat there, quiet of course and she'd have her little forehead rested on the upper panel of the piano. Eyes open, she'd watch the keys, sometimes her little fingers in her lap moving. It was as if she was imitating playing, hearing it in her mind.

One day, I wondered if she did play or if her fascination with the piano had to do with something else. Gray did say my aunt used to play for her.

Maybe that's it.

I got lost watching her one day, truly fascinated. My headset still on after a call, I turned it off, my head tilted at the little girl. Her wild locks pooled on the piano keys, her fingers moving.

"She's not bothering you, is she?"

Despite his size and overall stature, Gray could be as quiet as a weeping willow's branches in the wind.

I turned to find him behind me, his hands together and lips pressed firmly in concern. His intense blue eyes creased hard in the corners and I realized he had a constant worry there even when he seemed at ease, the day we met coming back to me. He looked the same way then and as I'd seen him nearly every day for a little bit now. I noticed he always seemed to look as if he had the weight of the world on his shoulders.

I think the little girl currently resting on my aunt's piano gave me a clue as to why.

I pulled my headset off, fixing and fluffing my hair, a stubborn habit with me I supposed.

"Of course not," I told him, slipping the mobile device into my pocket. "It's like she's too well behaved sometimes."

In fact, it was exactly that. His daughter didn't play at all besides with her coloring book, which, if not for her extreme quiet, I would find surprising. I figured after she got herself settled in she'd at least go outside and play while she watched her dad work. Gray spent the majority of his time out there, though, he had brought in a handful of guys over the past few days. They'd completely torn down the shed and a garage that hadn't looked usable. They'd been restructuring that, as well as making repairs to the roof and his title as a "handyman" didn't seem much to suit him now. He obviously knew much more than he let on about his trade.

What else is new?

The man had been a complete mystery to me since he came into my life, so why not add another thing?

With the tension that left the crease of Gray's brow after my words, one would think I had given the man the greatest gift. Maybe in a way, I had. He had a tool in his hand, a large mallet of some sort and he stamped it restlessly on his palm.

"Well, good," he said, hurried like this conversation was taking everything for him to keep going. His throat hiking, he started to walk away.

"It's going well outside?" I asked, choosing to make small talk today. I didn't often. He made it hard.

His large boots stopped in the hall.

"We're making progress," he told me, nodding. "We'll

probably be *in* the house after while. I'll let you know when that happens."

"Okay, thank you."

He bounced his head of dusky locks once in acknowledgement. Passing a look back to the living room, he gripped the top of his mallet. His daughter still had her head rested against the back of the piano, little shoulders moving up and down with her breaths.

"Does she know how to play?" I asked him. He looked back at me and I shrugged. "She just sits there a lot."

That worry touched his lips this time at the question and he turned his broad body to me, shaking his head.

"Jo just used to play for her like I told you," he said. "She probably just misses that."

But there was no probably in his statement. She did miss someone and that was easily discerned.

He left me in the hallway after that and I had no choice but to move on to my next conference call.

A few days later, I was surprised by a soft knock to my door. The surprise came from the fact that workers were warned—mostly by Gray—that knocking was strictly prohibited. He'd even put a note on the door that said to come to the backyard and bypass the house entirely. Under that, another note said there was a child in the home that needed quiet so if one had to knock, to do so softly.

Which was why I only heard Ava's knock because I happened to be walking past the door. She'd caught me on my way from the stairwell and into the living room, my intent to get a cold drink on this terribly hot day. My summer clothes had come in from my downtown apartment, but still, it seemed the heat down here in Kansas was tenfold over that in Chicago and I'd experienced some hella hot Midwestern climate changes.

I knew it was Ava by the way her curls bounced through

the glass design on the door, my eyes traveling that way and smiling a little.

Rerouting, I stopped on another pair of eyes, though.

Laura sat in her usual position in the middle of my aunt's living room, color pencil stopped in her hands as she looked up. She wasn't always in the house on days Gray worked, but most. Sometimes she had summer school with a local school teacher in town.

I wonder how well she does with her?

I had to say I wasn't really getting anywhere with the quiet little girl, not that I'd been trying. I pretty much kept my steps swift when passing in front of the living room, already feeling awkward since I generally didn't know what to do around children. Laura seemed to be getting used to me being around. Normally, she didn't even look at me when I passed by.

But today she did, those little eyes dark and wide in their doe-eyed demeanor. Her expression somewhere between content and disinterest, she watched me and I did something incredibly random.

I waved at her.

I literally lifted my hand, moving my fingers just as randomly and awkwardly as I did the first day I caught Gray working and sweating his backside off on that shed. His t-shirt had been stuck to his back, his sizable arms engorged. He could be a very attractive man on a good day.

Had he not seemed so tortured.

Like that day, my wave went without a return, not surprising. Like father like daughter. Laura barely looked at me when I did it let alone wave back. Her gaze leaving mine, it returned to the coloring book, her hand moving underneath her.

I let out a breath, Ava waiting at the door for me. Moving, my gaze slid back to Laura absentmindedly.

And imagine my surprise when I managed to gain her attention again.

I didn't stop this time, moving toward the door, but she was definitely looking at me and for the first time, I felt I could make out a little bit of expression on her face. She wasn't smiling or anything.

But she didn't look expressionless anymore.

My notice of the acknowledgement could have been wishful thinking on my part to get something out of her, and in the end, I did take it for that when I opened the door. Ava had actually started to leave, I took so long, and she had a case of beer in her hands.

Turning in her combat boots, she bounced her curls, the nicest grin on her face.

"Wasn't sure if you heard me so I was going to go to the back like the note said," she exclaimed, swiveling around. She lifted the beer. "You didn't go to the bonfire before so I was going to bring the party to you."

That was very sweet of her. I was coming to associate her in that way regularly.

"And what *is* with the sign?" she questioned, angling her head a little toward it. "I mean, did I do it right? The knock and—"

I waved her off, not even having the energy to explain it to her. Stepping inside, I grabbed my tennis shoes from inside the door.

"You said something about a party right?" I asked, tipping my chin toward the beer. "Because if so, let's go. I'd love a break."

Ava took me deep into the woods later that day, behind my aunt's property and away from the working men and women who operated on my aunt's house. Case of beer in hand, Ava asked about that during our strides to which I could only say, "progress." We'd been getting there and I wanted to surprise both her and the rest of the town with what I had planned.

Among working over the passing weeks, I'd been speaking to some developers and potential buyers of my aunt's property. If it went to the right person, some serious money could be flowing in and right into the pockets of the people who lived here. If my aunt's land ended up being transformed into a potential attraction for tourists that could only be good for Mayfield and its small businesses.

And would they have a site to see.

My sneakers scraping the sand, I took it all in, a scenic landscape of a crystal-clear lake and the expansive display of trees surrounding it. Winding, the lake weaved along the bank and behind the trees, its soft run rushing over smooth rock and algae.

"Beautiful," I said, my hands bracing my hips. I wasn't much of a nature girl, but this, yes, this was amazing.

Flanking me, Ava came up on my side in her shorts and tank. Setting the beer down, she popped a squat and began taking off her boots.

I joined her, wanting to feel the sand under my feet as well.

"It's your aunt's you know," she said to me, stacking her boots beside her. She opened up a beer with a device on her keychain, then handed it to me before opening one for herself.

Sipping the cold brew, I was well aware this was all Josephine's. I just hadn't experienced it.

Ava smiled, taking another swig. "Do you remember all this?" she asked, tilting her head. "She took us here before as kids and didn't mind us coming out here before she passed. Like I said, we have our bonfires out here all the time."

Waving her off, I told her of course I didn't mind too, but I wished I could tell her what she wanted to hear about the former.

I dragged my finger across the sand, trying to feel something.

"I don't," I told her, looking up. "I don't remember. I want to remember."

The brain was selective. While I had faint memories of her and of course some of my aunt, this place seemed to have been a casualty of my mind.

Ava's smile wavered a little by what I said. Nursing her beer in her hand, she shook it toward the lake.

"Well, that's okay," she said. "It's been a long time."

It didn't seem like it was okay, but I guess I had to take her word for it.

I took another drink, not a beer drinker, but seeming always to find one in my hand around her. I guess I just found comfort in her. We had a history. She was really my only link here besides my aunt's actual house.

"So how long will you be here?" she asked after a while.

I shrugged.

"A little bit," I said, then bumped her arm. "So you're going to have to show me more of this place."

Laughing, her curls rocked back.

"I think you saw about all of it when I showed you before, but I'm happy to show you whatever you want to see."

I appreciated that, clinking my bottle against hers. We watched the babble of the lake for a little while before I heard her voice again.

"You got something for Gray?" she asked, then hit her default shyness when she lowered her head. She bit her lip. "I mean, with me taking you over to his place and all."

She was referring to my visit with him obviously, something she didn't ask me about after I returned to her car. Then, with my questions about him in the bar, the man seemed to have always been on my lips. I wasn't surprised by her assumption.

"Oh, no," I told her, emphasizing the fact. "Anyway, I have a boyfriend."

Kinda... well. I still wasn't sure and when I went silent Ava definitely noticed. Choosing not to say anything, she looked ahead.

I sloshed the beer in the bottle. "He's just helping me with a project. He knows my aunt's house pretty well and he's fixing it up for me."

She lifted and lowered her head.

"That one's definitely different," she said. "And his daughter..."

"What about her?" I asked, my attention definitely hers. I didn't ask Gray about Laura, not my place.

But if she knew something...

Shrugging, Ava leaned back, elbows in the sand.

"Nothing really," she said. "Like I said, I don't really know anything about him or her, but this is a small town and people talk, is all. I don't make it my business but yeah people talk when you choose not to associate with anyone. I guess people assume he thinks he's better. He's only ever spent extended time at Jo's house and no one knows anything about his little girl."

That's because she didn't talk, not to her daddy, me, or even herself as kids sometimes do. She spoke to no one and I definitely noticed.

Deciding to join Ava in the sand, I put my bottle down and leaned back.

"Did Jo ever say anything about either of them?" I asked. "You said he spent a lot of time over there."

The smile went full over Ava's lips with her laugh.

"Don't get me wrong, Josephine Bradley could *gossip* just like the rest of them and was particularly bad at church on Sundays. But the thing is, despite all that she'd never talk about Gray and his kid. Very tight-lipped and I know she was asked. Like I said, I try to stay out of all that, but yeah. She'd never talked about Gray. Almost as if he and his were out of bounds. Eventually, people stopped asking and then with her passing..."

I'd heard she'd died in her sleep, old age.

I watched Ava, the beam on her face leaving.

"Anyway, I sound like my mama and I'm not trying to be a gossip hen with the rest of them."

We laughed together at that and I was happy to see her smile returning. Drinking our beers, we lay back, watching as the sun lowered below the trees. I guessed I wouldn't get anything out of her. When it came to Gray and his secrets, I supposed my aunt decided to take all that with her in the end.

Eleven

GRAY

THE SUN WAS high when Alicia made her way outside. She hadn't come out often over the past month or so we'd been working on her property, but when she did, she garnered a lot of attention.

I thought her chosen attire had something to do with that.

As per usual, she sported the highest shorts imaginable, her navel showing with the sway and swish of a canary-yellow top that left her shoulders exposed due to the tiny straps. Hair bundled behind her head, she brought a tray of lemonade and cookies I knew she spent the morning making. The smell had wafted into the backyard through the kitchen window and caused my mouth to water most of the morning.

Taking a definitely unscheduled break, both the men and women left their stations and sprinted up to Alicia with her baked goods and cool beverages. They devoured the tray, bantering with her and making her laugh, and I could only shake my head as I rammed a nail into the roof from my position on the garage.

Pulling another from my teeth, I slammed the nail into a shingle, the sweat beading down my arms and to my knuckles.

Alicia's... generosity was very nice. I didn't particularly believe she enjoyed being outside, but she did come out to make sure the workers were cared for. Though nice, it was very much a distraction and messed with everyone's pacing.

Especially mine.

I had to make sure everyone got back to work when all they wanted to do was laugh and talk after their work pace had been messed up.

I passed a glance in that direction, Alicia's tray more than empty but my workers still talking to her. Some had gotten back to work, but a few remained. Eventually, our distracting guest went inside, but that didn't keep a couple of the guys from lingering on—talking—and I was well aware what their gazes did after Alicia left from the backyard and back inside.

Borderline leering, their more than observant gazes travelled up the full extent of Alicia's shapely bronzed legs and it took a couple howls of "back to work" before I could even get them to go back to their stations.

We can't be doing this.

Not if she wanted us to finish that was, not if *I* wanted to finish.

Knowing it wasn't possible for my kid to be here any more extended time than we were, I got down from the roof.

Many workers watched my back as I strode from the garage to the house. I didn't say a word, but a look told them to mind their own business. They went back to their task and I pushed the screen door open, going inside. Alicia was at the kitchen sink, washing the empty tray of cookies she brought out and a few cups my people had siphoned down in front of her.

I cut the air into her space, her rose scent travelling around me within seconds of setting foot into the kitchen. She could fill the room with whatever perfume she wore. She often did with the soft scent. Sometimes I'd catch it outside, always on the wind.

"Hey," she said to me, watching as I made my way over to her. She smiled. "Sorry I didn't make it over to you. Everyone cleaned me out before I could get to the garage."

I had no idea what she was talking about at first.

Right, her cookies.

Precisely the reason I came into the kitchen, to tell her about that and the distraction of them.

"It's all right," I said to her, not wanting to come off as an asshole, but we really needed to get our work done out there. I bunched my hair in my hand. "Can I talk to you about that? The cookies?"

"Did you want me to make more? I can."

God, no.

I raised a hand. "Actually, I'd like it if the cookies, at least their frequency, stop for a while. It's getting distracting and it's hard to get everyone back to work after you leave."

There, I said it. I put it out there and it all sounded reasonable enough.

So why did her expression sock me like a mallet to the chest?

It was like I told her Santa wasn't real or something with the way her expression fell and I nearly wanted to take back what I said.

Her gaze severed from me.

"I wasn't aware of that," she said, plucking a cup out of the sink before washing and rinsing it. "I'm sorry. I won't do that so much."

I should be grateful for what she said.

So why did I suddenly feel like an asshole?

She made me feel that way a lot when I was around her, but of no fault of hers. I just didn't know how to talk to her, *act* around her. She threw me off when we were in the same room and my reaction was always clipped and abrasive because of it.

Silently, I stood there while she rinsed the rest of her dishes. I thought I should probably apologize for the way I came off, but I noticed her attention passed both me and the situation.

Drying, she stood in the middle of the kitchen with a glass and rag in her hand. From her position, she could see right into the living room.

We both could see my daughter.

Laura had taken to the piano again, her hands hovering over the keys this time, but not in front of herself. She stretched them to where Jo usually played.

"Gray?"

I barely heard Alicia's voice I was so focused on my kid, and had I not been, I might have been able to anticipate what she asked me next.

One of my worst nightmares.

"Where is her mom?" she asked.

Where. Is. Her. *Mom*.

"Laura's," she pushed when I didn't answer her quick enough I imagined. She lowered her drying towel and her dish, her finger playing along the top of the glass.

"She's irrelevant," I stated, the best I could do by a first response. She'd caught me off guard.

Alicia, though in our short weeks of knowing each other, had never once asked anything personal about myself or my kid. She had many opportunities to, but she never did.

Really, she should have let it all go after that, the topic of Laura's mom. The information wasn't her business and I didn't feel comfortable discussing the matter with her—essentially a stranger.

But then I guess that would have made it all easier, wouldn't it?

Grabbing the glass, she looked at me before placing it into the cabinet above the counter.

"Irrelevant," she stated, as if testing the word. She grabbed another dish, drying before looking up at me. "Irrelevant?"

I wished to escape those eyes at the moment. She shouldn't mess with this, especially with my daughter right in the next room.

We didn't talk about her mom, Laura and me. We didn't need to and that was understood, but Alicia didn't know this, the can of worms she was attempting to open here.

Moving away from her, toward the door, I opened it to the backyard.

"The topic of Laura's mom is a moot point because the woman is irrelevant," I told her, the snip in my voice readily known to me. I moved my jaw. "She's not in our lives and hasn't been for a long time—"

"Does that mean she's alive or..." Alicia's voice came down as she made the journey to me by the screen door. "I don't mean to butt in or step where I shouldn't here."

But she was. She *was* and quite frankly, the place in which she was speaking out of turn did nothing but unsettle me—as well as piss me off.

The words flew form my lips before I could stop them and because they had I couldn't take them back.

"She was abandoned," I said, nostrils flaring. "If you must know, the mother of my kid didn't want her child. She left her, tossed her away like she was trash."

I spoke too much, but I couldn't quit.

Why couldn't I stop?

"That's what makes her irrelevant," I went on, more emotion in my voice than I liked. I pushed my hand across my lips. "And I need to go back to work."

I pushed the door open so quickly Alicia's hair breezed back. I'd never forget the expression on her face when I left her standing there by the screen door. The shock was evident.

But the sadness trumped it ten times over.

I had no idea if it had been sadness for Laura, me, or just the situation we were both currently in. In a different reality, I might have accepted that sadness for me. I might have had our situation not been my fault, which it was. Laura's mom had definitely abandoned us both.

But it had only been to take a shot at me.

My thoughts, wild and angry at no one but myself, I tossed around tools and hammered at the structure too long before I finally came out of it, *finally understood* what I said and who I said it to. Alicia had only asked questions, honest ones because she was human. I never spoke about anything in regards to my family and she was naturally curious.

And she definitely didn't deserve what she'd gotten.

Shaking my mallet, I took an unsteady breath. I'd gone off on her/reprimanded her literally twice today, each of which had been uncalled for. Knowing that, I got off the roof of the garage again, hoping to find her in the kitchen though not surprised when I didn't find her there. Too much time had passed.

A glance into the living room, I spotted Laura still steadfast in her position at the piano. I left her there, then backpedaled through the kitchen and into the hallway, my intent to take the stairs and find Alicia on the second level. I planned to apologize to her amongst other things.

I didn't make it past the first step.

Something about that hallway, a change in the air or something made me look. I *needed to* look in the direction of my kid, feeling the necessity of that.

Letting go of the banister, I found something I'd never seen, not just my daughter in there but Alicia too.

She wasn't two feet away from my kid.

Laura's head angled in Alicia's direction, she watched the woman, Laura's hand sliding away from Jo's area of the piano and I left the staircase, not knowing what Alicia was trying to do but definitely feeling the need to put a stop to it. She knew the situation at hand. She *knew* she couldn't approach Laura or talk to her but something about the moment had the woman ignoring the warning. She stepped lightly toward Laura, softly, then suddenly her hand was on the piano.

She was *playing* the piano beside her.

My breath, all wind seemly knocked out of me, left me dry, a sucker punch to the gut literally leaving me with more air. I knew I needed to move, but I couldn't.

I watched, watched my little girl's shoulders tense as someone was clearly getting in her personal space. Shifting, Laura looked as if she suddenly might flee.

But then she didn't. She stopped. She *listened* like I was currently doing.

I couldn't help it, the notes, the playing, so beautiful. It'd been like that day I first heard the notes after Josephine had passed. I thought I'd been losing my mind and it'd been Jo playing, my head tossing tricks at me.

It hadn't been Jo. It'd been this woman, her niece playing an older woman's piano like an angel.

Struck silent by it all, I watched, my daughter in awe as I was. Her shoulder's relaxing, she moved not an inch as Alicia got closer to her, her gaze on the keys and not Alicia. She let Alicia come near her, her notes sounding through the room like a gift from the heavens. That's when I realized they *were* a gift.

∽

Alicia

I didn't know how long I played that afternoon, how long it took for my hands to finally perspire and my brow shortly before. I was unaware of a cramp in my hands until it was there, nor the stiffness that rode in an achy wave across the length of my back. These things just all of a sudden seemed to appear, the music the same. I knew I was producing it. I *knew* that much but after a while I disconnected from my hands and their role in the creation of the music. Oddly enough, once upon a time, my parents believed I might do something with all the years of piano lessons behind me. I'd gotten quite good and probably could have gone to a prestigious school such as Juilliard or somewhere else quite equally proficient. That hadn't been the life I chose and the playing ended up falling to the wayside. I enjoyed tinkering with it all once in a while and did have a keyboard at home for such days, but usually for the most part, I didn't play. That had been another life.

No, I didn't remember how long I played that day in the old house of a woman who'd since passed, but I did remember that moment I finally sat down. When I sat next to a child who had been motherless for who knew how long for. Gray had been elusive about those details about Laura, not surprising as that's just how he was. He didn't let on about himself on a personal level or even a cosmetic level. He didn't let on at all, himself and his daughter a world of privacy I never thought to understand before. It hadn't been my place, and though it still wasn't now, I couldn't ignore what he did allow me to hear. He and his daughter were alone in this world in the sense they were shy a third party I had twice in my life.

His little girl didn't have a mom.

That had been enough for me I guessed. It'd been enough to impulse me to do something I never usually do. I played piano again and I played for a little girl who seemed to not only love it, but also *breathe* because of it. She didn't shy away from me when I had sat on the piano bench beside her. If anything, she welcomed me to it, a place beside her needing to be filled. I knew it to have once been by my aunt.

"She doesn't get along with a lot of people..."

She probably wouldn't, would she? A quiet little thing that most people wouldn't or didn't bother to understand. My aunt must have taken that time in the passing moments underneath this roof. She must have been there and let the earth move around them.

Laura had to be just as stiff as I was, her head angled and her long and flowing locks breezing across the piano keys on her side. If she was uncomfortable, she didn't voice the fact. She probably wouldn't in the end.

I continued to play, never looking too long at her before staring off above the piano. I watched the sun travel down over the trees, the air change and turn to a soft breeze instead of thick with heat. I listened to the sounds of the workers outside dim down until there was no trace of them at all. I listened until it was just me, playing tunes through both muscle memory and the titles filtering in my brain. I had dozens upon dozens in there locked away, ready to pluck for the most opportune moment.

That moment must have been now, the perfect time to play and feel. I only stopped playing when a little hand moved into my designated zone, the sound from the key I last stroked fading off into the dimly lit room. I never turned on the lamps in the house after it'd gotten dark, but in the end, someone must have.

Laura's hand stroked above the keys I last played and when she looked up at me, I saw something in her both large and vibrant brown eyes I hadn't before. I saw something of a change, a life there I realized in that moment I had never seen. It was like not noticing something was there until one saw it. I saw it now.

I saw *her* now.

Something strummed heavy in my heart upon catching it and that something made me want to play for forever and an hour. I wanted to play so the life in this little girl's eyes would never leave.

The room lay silent after my last stroke. I allowed the tunes to fade out in the wide living room, Laura and I both sitting there on the piano bench. I think we might have sat there forever if not for a voice, Gray.

He'd called his daughter from somewhere in the house and when she heard her name called her feet touched the floor.

Turning, I realized someone had indeed turned on the lights in my aunt's living room, a single lamp lighting our way into the evening. We really had played for a while, no sounds in the room and dusk settling outside.

I could see it from beyond the piano, the workers gone for the day and myself all alone. A creak in the floor had me turn around and I rose to the sight of Gray, Gray and Laura.

His hand holding hers, he must have found her, but he wasn't looking at her. He was looking at me.

I stood from the piano bench, his gaze moving with me. He said nothing and made no moves toward me, his deep-blue eyes focused, yet soft in my direction. Squeezing Laura's hand, he guided her out the front door before I could get to the pair. I might have followed them out had I not seen the note by the door.

I assumed it was from him, reading it as I heard his truck pull away outside. It didn't say much, cementing how a man of few words he really was, but that didn't take away any of the meaning from them.

Nor how they made me feel.

"Thank you."

Twelve

GRAY

IN THE DAYS AHEAD, I heard Alicia's music without it even needing to be played. My ears always seemed to be reaching for it. It was as if my eardrums were always trying to be in a position in which to touch the music. Like I said, she didn't even need to really be playing for me to hear it. The sound had become an instinctual part of my memory like breathing was to air or sight to a vivid image. My ears *needed* to hear it and the effects I heavily valued.

I heard her playing even through this evening's storm, my trailer's windows a wash of raindrops and restless branches that scurried against it from the oak tree outside. It'd been storming all day, the sound a constant drum in my head, but despite the endless turbulence I still heard the music. I heard *Alicia* feeling her way into my soul.

She'd played for my kid for countless days, not just the first time I caught her at the piano. After the first instance, I didn't believe I would hear it again. I mean, I *hoped* I would but my note to her hadn't been a requirement of it. I just wanted to thank her for what she'd done and acknowledge her in some way. She'd allowed Laura into her life for a brief time and that meant something to me. It meant something real, something special she didn't have to do. It was something Jo would have done for my daughter.

It was something she would have done for me. Something she did do.

Moving on to the days that followed that first time, I'd been surprised to hear the music again, but not just that.

She'd played every day, every damn day like she'd been formally asked or even paid, neither of which she received from my end. Despite no presence of monetary value, she continued to play.

Sometimes before Laura and I even arrived.

Most days, the notes would already be sounding in, a soft pull as if from the sweetest piper. The house simply hummed with sound, *feeling,* and since it's occurrence, getting Laura up and moving in the morning had ceased. I never even had to nudge her awake anymore, my daughter sitting on her bed and sometimes dressed before I even went to check in on her. She'd always be ready to go after breakfast and actually beat me to the door to leave some days.

She'd always wait patiently, never opening the door herself, but once the knob clicked, she'd be outside and in my truck in the next second. The drive over to Alicia's was seamless, and once I opened my door, she followed suit, into Alicia's living room before I knew it. Some days she'd sit on the floor, coloring while Alicia played.

And others...

Those were the sweetest days, the ones I lived and breathed for. She'd sit right at the piano, never asking and Alicia pretending she was never disturbed. Perhaps, because she wasn't. Her playing always went uninterrupted, her hands moving and playing melodies. About midway through, Laura would place her little head on the piano, listening and feeling the music from the back of the instrument.

I never disturbed them, always going about my business, but even I couldn't pretend how her playing for Laura made me feel.

I stopped to talk to her more when I passed by her, the smile on my lips hard not to have each time. She was just like another piece of my life, like Jo had been once upon a time.

Jo...

The evidence of her was in the room, as if she was channeling herself through her niece. The walls of my trailer were covered now, in coloring book pages, pages Laura colored but didn't rip out and give to me until after Alicia made her way into our lives. In all her coloring, Laura hadn't once given me any pictures she'd completed.

Yet, she was now.

I put my hand on my favorite on the cabinet above the kitchen sink, wild roses brightly colored in the wind. I didn't know why it was my favorite, but then again, maybe I did.

The evening storm settling in, it shot the walls of my trailer with its heavy downpour. It'd been raining for two days solid and not looking ready to let up. I never found I much minded rain before. It hadn't bothered me until, well, it had.

My gaze lifting, I turned toward the living room, my kid sitting on the recliner. She'd been doing that for the last two days as well.

I guess not much else to do since I hadn't been working.

These days Alicia and her project had taken the majority of my attention. I declined my usual work for that, and because I had, nothing could be done on days, which consisted of crappy weather. My men and I were mostly working outside for the present, which made working on rainy days like today more than a challenge. We couldn't work through storms and because we couldn't...

Laura had turned the chair completely toward the window, her cheek pressed to the back of the chair. She looked so much like she did when Alicia played for her and I turned from the image, knowing exactly what she wanted. My kid had grown used to Alicia's playing, hearing it all the time now.

Hell, I'd gotten used to it too.

Dampening my lips, I reached into the cabinet, taking out a couple cans of tuna and some canned peas. I'd been in the middle of making dinner, another one of Laura's favorites, tuna casserole. I figured it'd cheer her up if not a little.

I breathed, turning my head in her direction.

"Hey," I said, smiling at her, though she wasn't looking at me. "Want to help me with dinner? I could use a hand."

She normally never did, but then again, I hadn't asked. I just cooked, not expecting much from her end.

Not surprised, my kid hadn't budged by the sound of my voice or even my request to ask for help. She simply lay there, gaze through the open window. It was almost like she was willing the storm to stop despite it being too late in the day to work.

I don't know how many more of these days we can take.

I personally couldn't take them, wanting the storm to lift myself. I'd been watching the forecast constantly on the television, Kansas' biggest drought in history apparently being corrected for the next few days. The meteorologist expected flooding, which meant nothing good for my daughter and me, we the casualties.

Letting my hope for a response go, I grabbed the electric can opener, opening the first can of green peas. After draining, I dumped the peas into the glass dish I had waiting, tossing the can into the trashcan. I went to start opening the can of tuna before I thought of something.

It's worth a shot.

"Laura?" I questioned behind me, loud so I knew she'd hear. I put the can under the opener.

"I bet Alicia might like some dinner," I said. "Do you think we should take some casserole to her?"

I waited with bated breath. I waited for something to happen, what, I didn't know, but I needed something.

I needed anything.

Nothing sounded behind me and I started the can opener, opening the tuna. I drained it before putting the tuna into the glass dish, reaching to toss the can in the trash beside me.

But when I turned around I wasn't alone.

Laura was making her way to me, my gaze following as she travelled across the room. She stood beside me, watching me while I tossed the can into the trash.

My heart moved.

"Want to help?" I asked her, my throat jumping a little. "Like I said, I bet she'd like it if we took some to her."

I held the next can of tuna to be opened out to her on will and was finally able to breathe when she took it from me. She held it while I got the opener ready, the two of us opening it together.

I made sure her fingers cleared before I pulled the handle and she held the can, guiding it through with my other hand above hers. I lifted the lever and she didn't even wait on what we had to do next. She traveled to the sink, draining the tuna. She'd seen me do this a million times.

Swallowing, I told her good before asking if she could get the pasta I had already drained in the sink. After giving it a little shake like I asked her, she brought it over, the pair of us tipping the noodles into the dish.

She assisted me with every request and sometimes did steps before I even asked them, but I think it really hit me that this was really happening, when she lifted her chin after sliding the baking dish into the oven on her own. She had something in her eyes, something she sought from me—approval. She wanted approval from me...

Her dad.

∽

Alicia

"I guess we figured you'd need dinner. You know, with the storm and probably not being able to get to the store and everything. You don't have a car and all."

Grayden himself stood at my door.

And he was drenched down to his kneecaps.

The top of his shoulders completely saturated, he blinked hard through his eyelashes, rain drops coating them as well as the thickness of his hair and dark beard. Upon seeing him, I hadn't been surprised he was covered head to toe.

He'd used his plaid shirt to cover Laura.

She currently stood before me completely dry as a bone, a casserole dish in her hands, which wafted the mouthwatering aroma of fish and carbs, two of my favorite things to eat.

Standing there awkwardly, shifting on his boots, Gray waited for me to—I assumed—say something, but I was currently taking a mental picture. I may not ever see such an amusing sight again and I was committing in all to memory.

Fingers up to my lips, I fought my amusement. They might take it the wrong way and who was I to do such a thing when someone brought me dinner with his kid. It'd been an entirely sweet gesture and I waved them in, standing back. Laura had the dish on an oven mitt, but Gray still took it from her when they got into the hallway.

He put it down on the hall's end table, helping Laura out of her raincoat before getting himself together. I figured he protected her because she had the food and no umbrella.

"We're not bothering you or anything are we?" he asked, always *concerned* to be bothering me so I hadn't been surprised by the question. After shaking Laura's jacket outside a little, he went to hang it on my aunt's coat rack.

I took it before he could, doing it myself while he got his plaid button-up shaken out. The thing was basically ruined at this point, so I took that too.

"Of course not," I said, going down the hall and opening the linen closet. Knowing my aunt's towels were in there, I pulled one out, tossing one to him.

He caught it.

"You know," I went on. "Because my door's always being busted down with callers wanting to bring me food with the company of themselves and their children."

His lips parted, worry creasing his brow and I figured he didn't get the joke.

Rolling my eyes, I told him it was fine again before taking his shirt. I planned to run it upstairs and hang it on the shower curtain rod.

"We'll just put this in the kitchen then," he said once I hit the stairs. I noticed him wave on Laura, the little one scurrying on behind him with his long strides and I shook my head.

That one is different, I thought, remembering Ava's words, smiling when I got to the bathroom. I shook out his shirt.

A smell of musk and extreme male breezed into the room and caught me off guard a little. I was used to the scent of Gray and his environment. I mean, the aroma wasn't necessarily bad but it did smell of work and sweat in general.

This smell was different, though, almost sweet with the scent and I smiled again, hanging up the shirt. I made my way downstairs and found nothing but a little miracle.

Saying I was so used to people being around was an understatement with Grayden and his workers, but I still never quite felt surrounded. It could be really lonely in my aunt's house. Especially after everyone left.

But no loneliness could be found now, as a little girl and her dad set the table.

A beautiful array, they had everything stationed from the butter dishes to the salt and pepper shakers, a place setting for three. They'd been putting the water glasses down when I came into the room, neither one of them noticing at first.

I watched them, lounging against the door. He handed her glasses, obviously knowing his way around the kitchen, and Laura placed them, obviously knowing her way around the task. The two had definitely done this before and that was a given.

Opening the fridge, Gray got the water pitcher and set it down on the middle of the table, his lashes going up and catching me.

Caught, I lifted my head, coming into the kitchen. I went to grab my chair, but someone got there first.

It'd been Grayden. He pulled it out, one hand on the back of the chair.

I told him, "Thank you." His slight nod was the only acknowledgment that he'd heard me. He even helped me push in, but his task apparently wasn't done.

"Little miss," he said, dipping his head and smiling softly at Laura before pulling her chair out. She didn't smile, and knowing her mannerisms for a little while, I knew she wouldn't. But she did have a little red in her cheeks when she accepted the seat given to her by her father. Pushed in, she waited until he had a seat himself to move.

He got her napkin, arranging it for her before doing his.

"This looks great," I said, a serious aroma going on in my aunt's kitchen. I bounced my shoulders. "And I definitely hadn't been able to get to the store so thank you."

Not to mention my meals lately consisted of usually frozen entrees and energy smoothies. I'd never been much of a cook back in Chicago and surely wasn't now.

A smile tugging at his lips, Gray grabbed the casserole dish.

"You actually have Laura to thank," he said, serving her first. "She made most of this."

Shocked, I jumped my brow in her direction. She wouldn't look at me, but that pink on her cheeks flashed bright crimson. Upon facing Gray, my look was more than curious. I obviously didn't know them in their day to day, but Laura really didn't seem like one to "help" in the kitchen. And if she had...

The pair definitely seemed... different tonight, the tone in the air different. I'd been around them for some time now and Grayden, when he wasn't running from me, put his focus either completely in his work or acting as a visual shield for his daughter. He surrounded her with this almost protective energy all the time. He was never casual, never at ease.

But he seemed so now, and then there was Laura, the little girl with the brown eyes who could never find me. She always looked down, away even when I played the piano.

I watched her, chin on my palm. She'd definitely opened up a lot in the passing days, letting me play for her and being around her now. She actually looked at Grayden when he said something to her, his comment surrounding how good her food was. He smiled at her, making her bashful again and maybe this was their routine. Like I said, I didn't know them too well.

Shaking my head out of my thoughts, I tried the food. It was very good indeed.

Dinner had been filled with a silence but it hadn't been a bad one. Peaceful, it almost felt like harmony, and like I said, it was nice not to be alone. I ate more food than I probably should have and, eventually, the baking dish was nearly clear.

"I'll take care of the dishes," Gray said, pushing himself from the table. He grabbed everyone's taking them to the sink, and almost instantly, Laura got up. She left the room, going into the living room and I spotted her right away as the kitchen and living room were connected.

Sitting at the piano bench, she placed her hands in her lap and I smiled at her.

"She wanted to come," came behind me and I turned, Gray.

Tossing a glance over his shoulder, he almost seemed dismissive, but the soft crease of his eyes told different as he washed dishes.

"She didn't say it obviously," he said, looking at me again. His expression warmed. "But she said it. She wanted to come. She wanted to see you."

She wanted to see me.

I didn't know exactly if he was right. After all, he did say she didn't actually say anything, but she was at the piano bench now and I was happy to play for her. I always would.

Tonight seemed different from the days I usually played, more pressure, *different* like so many things tonight, especially when Grayden came out into the living room.

His dish washing ceased, he sat on my aunt's couch. He didn't watch me, gaze distinctively placed outside the window but that didn't mean I wasn't aware of his presence. His focus soft, his stare ahead into the storm outside with his arm at the back of the sofa. He listened to me, listened as his daughter sat currently beside me.

Eyes closed, I knew this particular piece by heart. I figured it'd be perfect tonight, warm with the storm.

The room silent but for my keys, I played, the little body beside me I knew to be dutifully watching. That's what she did. She just watched, never played but I noticed something else different tonight too.

She sat up today, staring at my hands with her own in her lap. I had her full attention I assumed most days I played, but today? Well, I knew I had it if that made sense.

It made the pressure to play that much harder, but the attention around me kept me focused.

I played one song, then two, easily going into five before my hands felt the burn a little. I just didn't want to stop playing. I hadn't enjoyed it this much since I'd been a teen.

Literally *feeling* the music, I let go of the last note of the fifth piece, opening my eyes.

I found myself alone.

A little body sat with me no more, but that'd been okay.

Turning my head, I spotted Gray and he faced me, I assumed, because of the lack of sound. Under his arm was my previous companion, Laura with her eyes closed tight. She must have fallen asleep sometime during my playing and I actually considered that a compliment.

I'd been able to put her at peace.

I wondered about that sometimes when I snuck glances over to her while I played at the piano, if she truly was at peace or had the world on her shoulders like her father seemingly did. I knew nothing about the pair at all, but the stress around them when I was in the same room with them did seem evident.

This seemed non-existent now, a sleeping child under her dad's arm.

He looked down at her.

"I'm sorry," he said, squeezing her shoulder before looking up at me. "She looked like she was falling asleep so I grabbed her and brought her over here."

He had nothing to apologize for. Like I said, I took what she'd done as nothing but a compliment.

Moving, Grayden sat up a little. "Do you mind if she uses the guest room to nap for a little while or..."

Waving, I of course told him no problem, and adjusting, he got her arms around his neck before picking her up. Somewhere in her sleepy state, she must have known what was happening because her arms gripped around his neck when he put his hands under her legs, getting up from the couch. Nodding at me, he backed away, heading in the direction of the staircase, and I turned, placing my hands back on the piano.

I touched single keys, watching the raindrops outside above the piano. I'd never been one to be a composer, but there was as much music going on outside as in.

I played what I felt, stopping to listen for a little while. It was silent for a long time.

Until it wasn't.

Music blended into the room when I swiveled around on my chair, the sounds of a rich and sultry sax melody playing around the room. It was intense, vibrant and suddenly the most hypnotic voice sang.

I knew it was Billie Holiday immediately and I closed my eyes, losing myself in her sound. I had no idea where the music came from until Gray closed the glass housing of the record player, a record sleeve in his hand when I opened my eyes.

He took it, placing it on top of the record player's cabinet.

He put his hands together.

"I figured best to give your hands a rest. She's asleep upstairs now, can't hear you."

But did *he* want to hear me? I shifted toward the piano.

"I'm willing to take requests if you want to hear something too," I said, smiling at him. "I love playing and don't mind."

I found myself inspired tonight, playing pieces not just from my aunt's library but memory as well. I was happy to play for him if he'd let me. He seemed to enjoy it before, but perhaps, something changed.

He came into the light, shadows from the turbulent storm outside basking his robust frame. He looked like a man of the mountain, his plaid shirt dry and covering his biceps. He must have gotten it from upstairs.

"Alicia," he said, pushing his fingertips into the center of his palm. "Would you do me the honor of taking a well-deserved break?"

His hand went out then. I assumed for mine, and I accepted his invitation, letting him guide me to my feet. He had rough and weathered hands, that undoubtedly had seen things, touched things.

As soon as they were in mine, they left, the pair of us reconvening on the couch. He easily took up two cushions to my one.

"You play wonderfully," he said, eyes on me. "And I hope you don't mind me saying so."

A compliment just couldn't be a compliment with him.

A smile tugging at my lips, I placed an arm on the back of the sofa, resting my fingers against my forehead.

"Thank you," I told him. "I hope current unavailable parties enjoyed it."

"Feeling comfortable speaking on her behalf, I can tell you she did," he said, nodding. "And speaking on my behalf I can say I did as well."

Focused on me, no joke lingered in Grayden's voice. Not that he'd joke about something like that, joke about anything.

I placed my hands in my lap, not really knowing what to do with all that. A flash of lightning hit and somehow Ms. Billie combated it, her song like a roar cry for peace. Slowly the waves outside settled, the wind and rain soft against the windows surrounding the couch. The quiet allowed us to really hear the music, relax into it, if you will.

Pushing my hands along my arms, I rolled my shoulder into the couch, staring off ahead and into the empty room. I probably would have done that for hours and might have if not for Gray beside me. Something summoned me to look at him.

His eyes on me, I felt him all over and the instance itself had become something I'd come to recognize every time he looked at me. His attention on me had become more frequent in the passing days. In fact, pretty much every day since I started playing for Laura. The glance even accompanied a smile most days but not this moment, something in his eyes made me sit up.

"I suppose I wanted to apologize," he started with, his voice as serious as his blue eyes. His fingers coming down the scruff of his face, he turned toward me. "For what I said the day you started playing for Laura, or rather the tone in which I said it. It'd been inappropriate and you didn't deserve that."

He was referring to the confrontation we had about Laura's mom, and though I hadn't forgotten it, I had let it go. I felt I needed to, the line of questioning none of my business.

His lips moved. "Laura's mom has always been a sensitive topic. I guess that's why I snapped at you."

And regarding the details involved I didn't blame him, my hand coming down my arm.

"I shouldn't have asked," I admitted, my inquisitive nature only to blame. He was just always so secretive and Laura, well, she was different not much unlike Ava said about Gray. The whole town knew it but it was me who interacted with the pair on a day-to-day basis.

"You're only human," left Gray's lips as he turned, but he faced me when I moved closer.

"I still shouldn't have asked," I said studying every line and every etch of worry in his skin so tanned from his days outside. They'd been days he worked for me, labored and pained so I could have something to give back to this town and my aunt who, though I hadn't known well, I wanted to please.

He came here every day, worked and never once slacked in

the vigor and care he put into each revision he placed upon this home. If anything, the changes brought him life, a work ethic I'd only seen in myself and the care I put into my own hard work at the office.

He came here with passion.

He came here with heart.

His dark lashes drew downward, his eyes on the cushions between us.

"Things got so bad after," he said and it took me a second for me to realize he was referring to our previous conversation. It'd been a conversation that shouldn't have been started in the first place and one that wouldn't be pushed from my end again.

That didn't mean I wouldn't let him speak about it on his own free will, which he seemed to actually want to do now, his eyes closing almost as if...

Pained.

"She changed and I lost her—"

I stopped him with my fingers on the hem of his button-down, something I didn't mean to do but couldn't help. He sounded so awful and I just didn't want him to hurt anymore.

His fingers wrapped around mine and he guided them up to my chin. I didn't expect to feel something with the action. I didn't expect to feel anything, least of all something I hadn't felt in so long.

Even with Bastian.

My lips parted, Gray's too as he looked at me, his thumb brushing along my bottom lip.

"I'm bad at this," he said, hand pushing behind my neck. "I don't do this."

I didn't understand "don't do," but bad, I welcomed. I had good before. I had games and I was sick of it. I'd experienced more than my fair share of expertise. Maybe it needed to be simple this time.

Maybe it needed to be Grayden.

I sat incredibly still, as he made his move. Like a teenager waiting for her first kiss and the hum of his lip didn't disappoint.

Soft, he pinched mine between his, caging the back of my head in his large palm. If he really said he didn't do this he was lying. He'd done this, *was amazing* at this.

He forced me into a protective conclave, the wide spread of his body approaching me. Still holding my hand, he placed them between my heart and his. Mine might have been racing, but his was living.

The muscle pounded with a pure and unrelenting heat, his mouth doing a dance with every suck and taste. His hand releasing mine and moving down to my hip, he brought me closer and might have gotten to do more… if not for the creak on the stairs.

Our lips parted as if instructed, my fingers going to my warm lips and Gray faced away from me. He looked up and sure enough a little person was on the stairwell, sleep still in her eyes from what I could see. She rubbed them and more creaks took her down the rest of the stairs.

While we waited for Laura to arrive, Gray and I just sat there, the warmth in the air just as heavy as when he'd been kissing me. I didn't want to leave us and I guess Gray didn't want to leave either.

A little turn of his head and his lips were on my cheek, his eyes closing slightly and the short hairs of his beard brushing my skin. So quick, I might not have even believed he'd done that, but the tingle of his whiskered flesh embedded itself deep. I took my hand to it as he got up and went to Laura before she could really cross into the living room.

He bent down, his hand on her shoulder. He spoke light so I didn't hear him, but I assumed it was time to go when he stood, putting her coat on her, then picking her up by the waist.

Her arms around his neck, he faced me, some unsaid thing going on between us. I didn't think it needed to be said, still feeling it on my lips and cheek.

His eyes warm on me, he nodded, backing away and I followed the two to the door, catching a set of angelic, sleepy eyes on me along the way. Getting into the hall, I waved at her, smiling as her dad opened the door and walked out with her. She didn't do anything back, normal for her.

But then...

Her hand left her dad's shoulder, so light I doubt Gray even felt it. He didn't turn or anything like that, but I felt it, I felt the acknowledgement of that hand wave.

I felt Laura acknowledge *me*.

Thirteen

ALICIA

My fingers moved what seemed like dozens of music books, the multiple spines bumping under my fingers in the quaint Mayfield library. I had to find the perfect piece, something I remembered playing as if it were yesterday. Spotting it, I forced it out and the weathered cover blasted so many memories back to me. I'd taken a myriad of piano classes over my life, both myself and my brothers did. Something about the music senior people in my life enjoyed hearing and I hadn't gotten it at that time, not amongst the dozens upon dozens of classes and recitals I'd been a part of.

But after yesterday, I was starting to understand it.

I felt it too. I felt so much and after getting up this morning I had to seek out the competition piece that resonated with so many when I played it as a teen. I'd traveled to New York City and everything back then, invited to play with the orchestra there during their annual concert. Every year they allowed a gifted student to be featured along with their talented musicians, and though I never thought myself as gifted, I had been pretty good at one time. I won that year and got to play in Central Park, my entire family present.

I remembered the event as if it were yesterday now, but the notes themselves a little fuzzy hence my trip to the Mayfield Community Library. I wanted a book that had the classics, many of them and easy to be enjoyed. I had people that enjoyed them.

My mind spinning and still a bit confused, I fell into the influx of it. I honestly didn't know what was going on between Gray and me, why I touched him or why he kissed me, but whatever it was I found myself hard pressed to want to stop. I just knew the link, the link between all of us was the music and I wanted to play more, connect us more and make everyone happy.

I wanted to be happy too.

Smiling, I pushed the book under my arm, ready for checkout and so distracted I ran into someone, stumbling back with an "Oops" between the pair of us. With the sudden impact, I'd been surprised neither one of us managed to drop our stuff but we'd been okay. We held on. Even still, I felt bad and asked her if she was okay. To my surprise, she said my name.

"Uh, yes," I said not knowing this woman. I'd ventured to pretty much all the major stops in Mayfield in my time here but managed to miss her, and even though the woman was average in dress and demeanor, I felt like I'd remember her. Her dress quaint and her hair pinned, she gave the illusion of someone older or just maybe more distinguished and her smile on me definitely made me want to smile back. Some people just had that, a pleasantness about them.

Laughing a little, she pushed her hand back to her auburn-colored hair.

"I'm sorry, small town," she said, the many books in her arms jumping with more laughter. "I'm Jolene, Jolene Berry. I teach elementary in town and I guess we all know you're here. We all knew Jo well and loved her."

This had been the second person in town beyond Ava to say such a thing, and though Gray hadn't said anything similar, I didn't have to be an investigative reporter to know what type of influence my aunt had on both himself and his daughter. It seemed four individuals had both loved and respected her and I had a feeling the numbers went well beyond that if actually looked into.

I gave this woman my hand, my smile genuine.

"Nice to meet you," I said. "And yes, I'm Alicia."

"I didn't mean to bombard you," she went on, her hand going back to the bundle of books pressed to her abdomen. Her arms were nearly jam-packed with books and I wasn't surprised. She did say she was a teacher.

She grinned. "I was hoping to come across you. I've heard such wonderful things."

I wondered at first from whom, but like both she *and* Ava said this was a small town. I was sure everyone here knew about the long-lost niece who'd literally found her way back to Kansas.

"Well, thank you," I told her. "I'm glad I got to be here despite the circumstances."

The fact I was here in my aunt's place wasn't lost on me and that showed across the weight of Jolene Berry's freckled cheekbones.

She nodded. "We do miss her. She was a wonderful woman."

Something could be said about the jealousy I had for the people here. They got to know the woman who left so much for me. I now only got to experience her through others eyes and her personal possessions.

"That's what I hear," I told her, my sigh evident. "I was really young the last time I'd seen her."

Jolene acknowledged that, lifting and lowering her head.

"I hear you're fixing up her house," she said, the light returning to her eyes. She tilted her head. "Again, small—"

"Town," we said together, laughing at that. I pushed my hand through my hair. "Yeah, doing some revisions and prepping it and the property up for sale. I'll probably be here a few months."

Thanks to Gray things had been moving along, but I did still have a lot of time to root here. In the beginning that might have been a bad thing.

So much has changed.

I was still trying to figure it all out, my feelings and where I was going with them. The good thing in all this was at least I had some time, and because I did, I was going to allow myself to sort them out. I must have been smiling because Jolene's widened and like she knew, the next words out of her mouth were about Gray.

"I hear he's been heading your project," she told me, again not surprising me by her candor or knowledge. She hugged her books. "I hope you're getting what you need from him. From what I hear, he does very good work."

Because I could attest for that, I told her so, smiling. Gray really did know his way around a tool, a project. He had my full trust and more, so much more.

"And I'm sure you've—" Jolene started, pulling me out of my thoughts. Her lips closed and judging by the sudden change of her expression I ventured she was unsure about her next words. She wasn't smiling anymore and her books suddenly lowered.

Her head tilted.

"I'm sure you've met his daughter," she started, the words moving out slowly. Again, as if unsure. Her lips parted. "Laura. I used to teach her though our sessions concluded not long ago. Since I have the time, I tutor out of my home during the summers. Laura was one of my students. Gray's decided to do homeschooling with her during the school year so I guess I'm curious about how she's been."

I wasn't surprised Gray would be homeschooling his daughter. Her obvious special needs wouldn't allow her to be around many people no matter how sad that would be for her. I was sure that was incredibly lonely for her.

My smile fell like Jolene's had.

"I have met her and she seems well. I'm actually picking this up for her."

Her gaze traveled to the music book in my hands and as she looked clearly curious, I thought to explain more.

"I've been playing piano for her," I said. "She's over while Gray works and seems to like it while she sits with me. Up until this point, I'd been playing mostly from mem—"

"I'm sorry. You said she *sits* with you," she said, getting closer.

I moved my head. "Uh, yeah, but not all the time."

"But she does that," Jolene went on, a wonder in her voice I thought I understood. She'd interacted with Laura just as I had and one thing I was sure we both knew was that she didn't trust many people. It'd been something I was hoping to change with her by playing.

"She does," I said happy for the fact. Like I knew, she didn't trust easy.

Jolene stared off.

"And Gray, he doesn't mind it?" she questioned, her gaze returning to me. "He doesn't mind you playing and sitting with her?"

Her words saddened me.

"He doesn't," I told her and something about what I said changed everything and I felt that.

Especially with her smile.

Jolene proved to be such a nice person and pleasant like I originally believed about her. Before we parted, she made sure to let me in on all the community events, even going one further and inviting me to service on Sundays with the rest of the town, which I considered taking her up on. Before we left each other, me to continue on to check out and she her browsing, she did say something and it'd been something I hadn't expected.

"You should ask Gray about enrolling Laura in school," she said, kinda timid when she said it. "At least to take a tour. We can do specialized classes for her, small or even individualized. Laura's smart, Alicia. So very smart and I've seen it. I saw it every week I worked with her."

I believed that, that she was smart but I didn't think that was the issue, nor the reason why Gray was keeping Laura out of school.

I shrugged my bag up. "I'm not sure I should get involved and even still, Laura... she doesn't seem to do too well around many others."

In fact, not well at all and being around Laura herself I thought she'd know that.

She came closer. "I know she'd do well with others."

"How do you know?" I asked and to that, she simply smiled.

"Because I've seen it."

Fourteen

GRAY

"She did... what?"

The admission nearly made me miss driving the nail into the oak paneling. It'd been the final nail, the oak panels lining throughout Josephine's house. The others had been shotty, worn down and the revision went well with the new flooring I'd installed last week in the living room, the fresh floral wallpaper I put in even more. I pretty much had the whole crew in there to work quickly since that's the room Laura tended to spend the most time.

Getting down from the ladder, I found Alicia in complete seriousness by what she'd told me and the realization of that had me squeezing the base of my hammer to painful proportions. Jolene had no right.

But she'd done it anyway.

My anger was a cloud in the moment and something I couldn't easily will myself out of. What Jolene Berry had done was a complete violation of my daughter's and *my* privacy and had I known about it Laura would have never been working with her in the first place. I only went to her because Jo recommended her, and now, I was kicking myself because of the fact.

I actually had to put my hand on the wall to calm myself down, lost in my head and what this invasion could mean for me and my family, but something in the end, brought me out of it, an array of roses before the light touch on my shoulder.

Alicia in all her loveliness stood before me, a lacy garment covering her bare shoulders as she'd wore a tank top today. It must have been too breezy for her liking and the rich caramel color of it brought out the deepness of her amber eyes and smooth, honeyed skin.

Her hand came down my shoulder and to my arm, which currently shook. I hadn't kissed her again since last night but that didn't mean I didn't want to.

"She played with another child," she said repeating her words of only moments before. The difference was this time I didn't fall into a haze, something in her eyes having to do with that I believed. I was focused on them and I was able to see.

She had me sit, possibly knowing how this information was affecting me. During her story, she sat on a folding chair while talking to me. She had me take that, standing next to me.

"At least, beside another child," she went on, her lips lifting a little in the most beautiful way. Tucking a piece of her flowing hair behind her ear, she squatted next to me, holding her legs.

"They were together in the sandbox," she said. "At Jolene's house one day when Laura was there for schooling. Don't be mad, Gray. It sounded like the arrival of the other little girl was a surprise."

So she said, the girl Jolene's niece. Alicia said it'd been an impromptu visit and something Jolene hurried up quickly after explaining the situation to her sister who'd suddenly dropped in on her. They went to leave and that's when they found the girls. They'd found them out back.

They'd found them playing in the sandbox.

But this had to be a lie, not making sense. My daughter didn't play, and never, absolutely never, with others.

You'd never given her the option.

I ran my fingers over my beard, squeezing my mouth as I found Alicia again.

"Why wouldn't she tell me?" I asked her, but really, I was asking no one and not expecting an answer.

One seemed to come as Alicia looked at me, her head tilted as she studied my face.

"She probably didn't want you to get mad," she said, then stood, hugging herself and as she did I chose to follow her.

She took in all the revisions I made on the outside, the home really coming full circle with its new roof and siding. We still had a lot to do, but we were getting there. We were.

"It's wonderful, Gray," Alicia said, but almost sounded sad about that for some reason, which wouldn't make sense. Her aunt's home gaining closer to completion would make her happy. It had to have as it'd allow her to move on to the next step.

I came up behind her, unable to help indulging in her smell or the way the little hairs that escaped at the back of her bun brushed the nape of her neck. She had this way that always got to me, which made working hard. I think that was why I'd really been cross with her the day she first played for my daughter, not because she was distracting my workers.

But because she'd been distracting me.

I closed my eyes, a change in the air causing me to look at her when she turned around. I wanted to touch her, but it seemed she wanted something else.

"I think she should go to school," she said to me, another part of the story I'd heard. She said Jolene had led into that, which was how I found out about the woman's niece and her sister coming over.

I honestly understood the logic, both of them seeing

something that led them to believe Laura would be okay at a school. Things weren't that simple though. Nothing ever was when it came to my daughter.

I lowered my head, my fist touching the wall.

"That's not an option, Alicia," I said, looking at her, but constantly finding her eyes had me wanting to tell a story I never could, I let them go. Her enrapture of me was how she'd found out things about my life *and* Laura's she never should have in the first place. I seemed to want to tell all around her.

And that was dangerous to me.

Her hands coming around my arms were even more dangerous and soon I couldn't escape those eyes.

"Look at her, Grayden," she whispered and I didn't want to look. Mostly because I knew what I'd see. I heard the ball before I even saw it, but actually *seeing it*, well, that made it real.

My daughter *played*, kicking a shiny pink ball I hadn't seen in months. I had no idea when she joined us outside, but she had. She was here and she was playing.

A veil of her hair cloaked her face, and kicking the ball away, she looked up at us both, a look I'd seen before. It was a look of approval. She wanted permission.

I gave it to her, nodding, but I watched her as she scampered away, making sure she wouldn't go far. I always did, the tether never allowed to go taut. It'd been my way of protecting her, but as she moved, as she played I wondered if I really had been—protecting her.

"Don't you think she deserves to be able to play with others?" Alicia asked, the joy in her eyes brighter than any smile she could make. That came next, direct in my direction. I was lost in it, her hand coming to my cheek. Her smile widened. "Or at least the opportunity? If it doesn't work out and she doesn't like it, you could always take her out again."

"You don't understand," I told her and I knew in my mind

I wouldn't let her. I'd been keeping her at an arm's length as I'd done everyone I had come across in the last three years, even Jo. It hadn't been easy before but never as hard as this.

As hard as it was with her.

Looking into Alicia's eyes, I could tell she didn't understand and, really, she never would because I couldn't let her in. I just couldn't.

I enjoyed her hands on me so much that I couldn't push her away though, the softness of her fingers heaven amongst the weathered state of my neck from so many days outside.

I let her smooth her hands down my jaw, cupping my face and there was no getting away from her. There was no escape.

"I know you have a reason for everything you do when it comes to your child," she said. "I can imagine every parent does."

If only it were that simple. I wished it was. Laura and I came with so much baggage here, and because we had, it was easy. Hiding was easy. Her being withdrawn only cemented the fact that we had to stay away. We made no connections. We held no relationships. It'd been Jo to change everything and her niece to do one further and change *us*.

She had changed us no matter how much I didn't want to admit it. She changed me and I brought my arms around her, no longer fighting it.

We stared at my daughter, the little wonder never going far. I think we both could have stared at her forever.

"She seems happy, Gray," she said, tilting her head. "She is happy I think."

I believed she was right, but I supposed the only one who could really confirm that was my kid, but of course, she couldn't. Maybe one day she could though.

Maybe just maybe if I let her.

Fifteen

ALICIA

I WATCHED a man let go the following Monday morning. I watched a man *grow* beyond what I think even he probably believed he was capable of, allowing his daughter to go and experience something that clearly put him out of his comfort zone, but doing it anyway. Gray showed a bravery I'd never seen before and despite not wanting to get involved I supported Jolene's proposal, but not just because of what she'd told me about Laura and her niece but because of what I'd seen from Laura myself. The little girl was changing and I had no idea if that had mostly to do with me playing piano for her or something else, but whatever it was awoke something inside her. It was something I couldn't control and I think Gray understood he couldn't either. He had to let her go.

He had to let her live.

He asked me to join him during his tour of the school with Laura, something I happily did and would do several times over. Laura went in with the understanding that she wouldn't start that day or any day for that matter unless she was comfortable, something Gray emphasized ten times over her and that had only been on the early morning truck ride over to the school, well before many were up and attending their day. Jolene had arranged that, the kindest spirit and someone I truly did have a good feeling about. Some people one just knew had a genuine earnest want to help others.

And who wouldn't want to help that sweet girl after meeting her.

She went in with a bravery that was only trumped by her father, the man by her side as she held his hand and took in her potential new environment. Mayfield Elementary wasn't quite like the prep schools I grew up in with its fancy gadgetry and modern halls but something about all schools was they shared the same feel about them, the air the same and filled with a similar life, which told of youth. They had the construction paper hand cut outs and the bubbly letters displayed above them made up of cartoon figures and alphabet letters. They had the smiling faces of school children who showed merit or partook in group projects. The schools said kids learned there, *thrived* there and in the end that was all that mattered.

Laura's experience at the school itself would be different than the students who made their mark on those school walls, but hopefully only in the beginning during her initial transition into the new environment. She was going to be given an individualized learning program, which consisted of one-on-one teaching and limited immersion into group settings as both herself and her instructor saw fit. I think that set Gray at ease a little more but nothing about the experience itself would be easy for him. If anything, this whole experience would be harder for him than it ever would be for his daughter.

I knew when it was time to finally let her go.

Laura had given no indicator of anxiety or displeasure during her tour, but what I think made the final decision for her to attend that day had been her clear excitement while she strode those halls and *saw* those children on the walls. There was an actual skip to her step while she walked hand in hand with Gray and when she saw the pictures of other children she actually reached out to touch them. This had made me smile and even though Gray had as well it hadn't nearly touched his eyes.

I'd say not at all.

"You have your instructor call me the minute you don't feel good or something feels wrong, okay?" he said to her, his hands on her shoulders as he knelt down in front of her. He'd been letting her go for a few moments, reassuring her.

He pushed his hand over her hair. He styled it in two braids today, which I helped him with. She looked so pretty.

He smiled at her. "I'm not far away, kid, but even if I was I'd move mountains."

No truer words said and I saw that in his eyes. I bet he would move mountains if he actually could.

I wondered if he'd done so in the past.

I glanced away, giving the two their moment but I looked at them again when Laura forced her arms around Gray, her hold tight and steadfast. I had never actually seen her initiate a hug between them before or really Gray hug her. He'd pick her up or hold her hand but no hugs.

Well, they were hugging now.

It was a hug that, yes, she gave him, but it didn't read of fear. I'd seen fear in her. No, this was different.

This was her letting him go.

I think the hug in itself shocked Gray, but it seemed to be exactly what he needed as he relaxed and returned his child's embrace. He kissed her cheek, cupping it before standing back and I think I was so lost in their moment that I almost missed mine. I'd been here, but this wasn't my moment.

But she was making it mine too.

Laura came over to me and I didn't know what she wanted

at first. It was only after she opened her arms, wanting a hug too that I broke it down.

I wanted to *break* down.

I didn't though, holding her tight.

"You'll be okay," I whispered to her but like Gray's reassuring words I think these were mine. I'd be okay.

I'd be okay if she would.

I heard Gray's voice what seemed like only moments later, but it couldn't have been.

We were driving now.

"I want to take you somewhere," he said to me, my thoughts lost in a sea of emotions. They were lost reminiscing on moments I probably shouldn't let alone should keep. I shouldn't keep them because they weren't meant for me, this place not mine and neither was this man beside me.

A wash of dissipated clouds casted my way in the form of Gray's eyes, the ocean inside them settled and the usual storm behind them at bay. Gray had his hands on the steering wheel of his truck, watching me with a light in his eyes that eerily peaked of calm, peace. He should be careful with that.

He might grow to love it.

Dampening his lips, he faced the road.

"That is if you don't mind," he said. "I've been wanting to take you here for a while."

A curiosity filled me but something more lingered just behind that. It was something that made me warm, something that made *me* calm.

Sitting back, I trusted him and this journey. We didn't drive for long after what he said but it did seem as if he was taking me out to the middle of nowhere. I hadn't seen buildings for a while, only country.

And then that.

The country so familiar turned to fencing, rolling

meadows of prairie grass both kept and carefree. The only outlier was what occupied that land.

The various grays and stone of tombstones filled my vision and before I could fully get a grasp on what that meant, Gray had stopped, putting his truck into park. He got out without another thought, and when I turned, he was reaching for something in the bed of his truck. I noticed it to be a toolbox and, by then, I'd been so confused. I figured there was a reason so I turned, unbuckling. He opened the door before I could get out and had something so beautiful in his hands.

The roses could thrive in the worst light, their drive for life full and plentiful. He had dozens, looking fresh and wild with leaves of bright green as if cut fresh from a bush outside. He had them wrapped well in a thick towel, which protected from thorns.

He lifted them, staring at those vibrant petals.

"You'll need these," he said, handing them to me.

And then he gave me his hand.

He gave it without reprieve, unabashed, and roses cradled, I let him fold his thick fingers around mine, helping me out of the truck into a meadow of gravestones.

He took me for a walk through the paths, something definitely different. My questions tapered down only by sheer curiosity. Gray didn't do things like this. He never put himself out there or did anything out of the ordinary. If anything he was *too* ordinary, too safe.

Pulling me closer, he brought me in front of him and I realized right away this journey did not go without intent. He very much had a reason for bringing me here and that surrounded the life of a woman named Josephine.

Her grave may not have been one of the biggest or even the flashiest, but it had the cleanest script and the most polished marble one could see.

"I figured..." Gray started, his hand falling away from

mine. "I figured since you weren't at the funeral you might not have known about it, or maybe were too busy to..."

He shook his head out of that last thought, smiling at me with just his eyes and in a way that made my tummy dance. It made everything dance.

"Whatever the reason you weren't there I figured you'd want to at least see, visit with her sometime while you were here."

He'd been the first to offer such a thing and he was right. I *didn't* know about my aunt's funeral. I hadn't known about her death at all until several weeks later, and by then, her passing had been that of an afterthought. No one cared to tell me how she was in her last moments or even if she suffered prior. I was just the long-lost niece that a woman, however so kind, thought to think of when drawing out her will.

I stepped forward, chilled by the moment. I hadn't known what to do, the reality of where I was at and what was happening heavy upon me.

But I guess I didn't have to do it alone.

Gray came up behind me, his heat close but never close enough. He kept his distance, but I could feel him, his width seeping through me.

"Do you want me to leave?"

I shook my head.

So he stayed, touching the back of my arm and telling me things about her. He admitted he'd been the one to find her. He'd been doing work for her that day and she hadn't answered the door. My heart hurt that it'd been him, but was very grateful that of all people it was. She seemed to care about him and he definitely cared about her.

"She was good to us, Alicia," he said, soft behind me. "A good woman and her funeral was beautiful. The community made sure of that. *I* made sure of that."

I wondered how much of a part he did play in all that. I

bet as much as he could, as much as others would let him with him not being family.

Holding out the roses, I set them down, squatting ahead.

"Did she suffer?" I asked, looking up at him.

His jaw moved, his gaze shifting to the tombstone. "I don't think so. She never complained of anything before. Her body just gave out. It happened in her sleep."

I did know that, told by the people who ultimately found me.

Standing, I moved back and dared to stand back into him. He let me, his hands on my forearms. We never talked about our kiss the other day or even how he held me softly just yesterday. We never talked about why he let me be a part of letting go of his daughter today or even what led to this moment we currently experienced. We just did and I thought that's all we needed to do.

It just made sense for us.

"Laura used to spend a lot of time here," he said behind me, his hands warming my arms in wonderful ways. He squeezed. "I'm happy to say she doesn't anymore. I think she understands now. She understands and accepts."

I closed my eyes, falling back into the thoughts of how this would be for her, the little girl already experiencing so much in her life with her mom leaving. But he said she didn't visit now. Things were different now.

I turned, letting him know I was ready.

I was ready to go home.

We didn't do much talking on the way, not unlike how it'd been on the way out there, but something had changed, the tone of the world a little bit different. I didn't know what it was until Gray opened my door and I got out of the truck, but the moment I was in this man's arms again I deciphered it fully.

Gratitude.

Gray's broad body stiffened, his arms slack like he hadn't known what to do or how to receive the embrace I bestowed on him. He'd done the same with Laura not long before, surprised, and it made me sad that he didn't get many hugs. He deserved to be hugged.

He deserved to be loved.

I was showing him that, my love for him in our embrace and his hands slow, they moved into that warmth around him, his hold tight once I had it.

"Thank you for taking me to her," I said to him and he pulled a piece of my hair back when he brushed his fingers along my cheek.

"You have no idea my thanks for you," he said and might have done more if not for the streetlights.

Gray's hold went stiff on me again at the many cars that pulled in front of my house, but as one struck me as familiar I noticed his hold loosen. He must have recognized her too.

Ava's old beater was comfortable almost as much as her laid-back style, her smile wide. She was hanging out the side of her window, grinning from ear to ear at me.

"Join us for a good time at the lake?" she asked, laying her arms on her open window. "We'll provide the drinks if you provide the lake."

Letting loose in the middle of the day wasn't something I always did.

Maybe that's why I chose to do it in the end.

Sixteen

ALICIA

Ava's friends proved to be just as lovely as her playing, the girl coming fully equipped with her guitar to the lake. Had I known her skills we could have definitely gotten together with some sort of jam session, but I supposed that was for another day.

She had an ethereal sound about her tunes that paired well with the tone of the day, the world a dream for me since shortly after I woke up this morning.

It'd started with my view outside and into the wonderful land that I had somehow come to own. Standing out on the veranda, I simply watched the earth move until Gray had arrived, our journey to take Laura to school shortly after that. I felt I was living in a place of borrowed time and in a place that may have belonged to me on paper, but ultimately was on loan to me. Josephine Bradley's life was on loan to me and I was currently reaping the benefits of it from this lake with people enjoying it around Ava to the man that stood at the shore by himself, Gray a true wanderer.

He stood by the edge of the lake, the sun high and wide and cascading on his brawny frame. His stance tall in his t-shirt and jeans, he resembled a man who ruled the world, but I'd known different. He showed me just that day, a vulnerability he allowed me to see. I believed I was always fortunate because his daughter let me play for her, but a true gift came in the form of this man and his trust. He trusted me.

He showed me that today.

I saw that trust in his eyes when I came over, his hand dropping from his bicep and coming around me. The gesture felt natural and I caught an eye from behind him when he did it, Ava's over the strums of her guitar and I merely shook my head at her before finding the sun like Gray had. I used to have a boyfriend. I used to have a lot of things.

I used to have my heart in something only to leave it and used to wear an armor I quickly shed upon experiencing Mayfield, a town and a people that came to find me. I thought I was helping them but proved to be the one who needed the help. I felt that in Gray's embrace.

I felt that in his love.

Neither one of us had said it of course, but maybe like his arm around me we just did.

"Your friend plays so nice," he said almost absentmindedly. His fingers played with the plaid shirt I currently wore— his shirt. It'd been breezy today.

It smelled of him and I lost myself in it, only a soft sound escaping from my lips as I lay my head against his chest.

He allowed me to do so, cradling me more but something raised his heartbeat, his chest rising with more and more breaths.

I looked at him. "Everything okay?"

He said nothing, merely looking at me when he took a strand of my hair and tucked it behind my ear. Behind those light-colored eyes he seemed to be at war with something, a small storm creating behind his eyes before he spoke.

"What you did for me," he started, his expression fallen. "What you did today with Laura—"

"What I did, you did for me," I said reassuring him, as he seemed to be struggling with something. "You took me to see my aunt today. You've slaved over her house—"

"It's not the same," he continued, his hand dropping from my shoulder and I missed it immediately. He cradled himself, standing back to look up at me.

His expression stiffened. "You don't ask for anything, Alicia. You don't ask for money or even to be acknowledged. You just do. You *played*. You've played your goddamn heart out for Laura every day like Jo and—"

I followed him when he took a step back, not understanding. The group was still listening to Ava, something I confirmed visually before getting closer. He shook his head the moment I was in his personal space.

"I gave you nothing," he emphasized. "I gave her... Jo, nothing."

"You gave yourself," I said, not getting why he wasn't seeing that. "Now, I can't speak for her but I can speak for me. You let me in, be a part of your life, Laura's life? Gray, you—"

"But have I?" he challenged. "Have I really? I never told her much and I know I've never told you much."

I believed he referred to the conversation about Laura's mom again, the one personal thing he did tell me about the pair. I had been given enough information that day to stop my questioning, my inquiry invasive anyway.

I touched his arm, so warm and probably not from the sun.

"You never have to tell me anything you don't want to tell me," I explained then pushed my hands to his face, finding his eyes. "And again I don't speak for her."

But I was sure it was the same for my aunt. She found

something in him, the both of them and cared about them enough to respect their space as I have.

Gray couldn't keep my gaze, his eyes falling when he dropped his head.

"You deserve to know the whole story," he said. "My place in it. I made it sound like her mom is the only reason she is the way she is."

Is the way she is definitely stood out to me as that could mean so much. He addressed a clear problem here and one I didn't feel was my place to question.

He left my hands again in a breath, facing the sun and never letting him go I returned to his side.

His eyes narrowed.

"She wasn't a great woman, Laura's mom," he started. "But I wasn't a great man either. I met her at a party, fucked her at a party."

His crude language took me aback a bit but not because I was sensitive to such things.

It seemed to hurt him when I touched him this time, squeezing his arm.

His expression pained when he looked at me. "Alicia, we were strangers when Laura was conceived."

Not unlike Bastian and I had met, two strangers at a work event. It turned into something more after that first lay at his place that night and probably shouldn't have.

I rubbed Gray's shoulders, the guilt coming off him. "Gray, that happens sometimes. That doesn't make you a bad person."

His laugh was cynical and something I didn't like.

"No, what makes me a bad person comes later," he said, and though he didn't physically pull away this time he didn't have to, his emotions doing it for him. He panned to me. "You want to know what I did when she finally managed to find me and tell me she was pregnant? I didn't remember by the way. I fucked a couple of girls that night."

I cringed though I hadn't wanted to, so unlike him. But then again...

I guess I didn't really know him.

His jaw moved. "I told her two words: prove it. I said 'prove it' and even after she did, I didn't accept it. Not really. I gave her basic child support but that was it."

Even in all this, as graphic and hard to hear as it was, it was something that clearly changed him. Somewhere along the way Laura went from the result of a choice at a party to his daughter and I saw that. I saw it every day.

"Gray?"

He found me when I touched him, my hands moving up over his whiskers and up into the thickness of his hair.

"That still doesn't excuse what she did," I said, shaking my head. "Leaving Laura—"

"She left her because of me," he came back with, surprising me. His voice retched. "She left because she didn't have me, support from me..."

He stopped like there was something else, shaking his head.

"I cut her off from even the financial support eventually. I cut her off after finding out she had a drug habit, not another thought about it." His expression stiffened, visual tears glassing his eyes. "Who cared what she was using the money for? It didn't matter. It was support for our daughter. In the end, it was support for her."

"Gray—?"

"That was the last time I heard her voice, you know?" he said and I didn't take a step back at the sudden statement, though I wanted to. I was surprised, confused.

Somewhere in there, he found me in all that, after all that

and in my shock. His hands came to my hips, his head bowed in a clear shame.

"The day I cut Laura's mom off she'd been laughing in the background," he said, his throat jumping. "That was the last time I heard it, my little girl's voice."

My own tears stung my eyes and throat. Laura, she wasn't mute.

She'd spoken.

And he heard it, well, at least her laughter. Was it the same?

He didn't let on, his hand coming up to mine and squeezing. He pushed his mouth into my hand, his breath still labored.

"She left her shortly after that, Alicia," he said, his voice strained. He dampened his lips. "And by the time I'd gotten to Laura, literally *found her*, I was too late. I was *too late for her*." He cringed. "She was scared. She was alone... left alone completely."

And mute though he didn't say. He didn't need to. I got it. I finally got it.

The details in which Laura's mom left her stirred a taste in my mouth that I truly had to fight down to keep from doing something else. Gray had said her mom abandoned her but never in my life did I believe in the literal sense. How long was she alone?

How long had she been by herself?

Clearly, long enough to scar, and my pain for her, for this family fell upon me in waves, for this man and his guilt he felt so deeply.

After squeezing his eyes, he revealed them to be red, tears he was clearly holding back but doing a bad job to manage.

"Who does something like that," barely managed to be discerned from his lips, his deep voice thick. "Who—"

"Takes care of his daughter," I corrected, having a feeling

he needed to be corrected. From the start of this conversation, the direction of it needed to be changed, a conclusion he came up with and managed to believe so hard in had a need to be dissolved with the truth. He may have had a hand in what happened to Laura, but something he hadn't done was what her mom did. He didn't abandon her and showed her a love and care I personally had the honor of seeing every day. I cherished it.

Cradling his head, I brought him down to me, made him travel down to where I was and see the truth.

Our brows touched.

"You love that child... You *care* and *protect* that little girl in ways I have never seen, Gray. *Never seen* and don't you ever devalue that for mistakes you made in the past. It's not your present and what you're doing moving forward means everything, everything now."

He looked up at me, his eyes rimmed in red. All that disappeared from my vision when I kissed him this time, the hum off his body I felt throughout mine. The buzz warmed of a release, something he'd needed to let go of for a while and I guess finally found the strength to.

He kissed me back, heaven in the way his warm lips opened and closed over mine. Cradling the back of my neck, he tilted my head, taking over when he brought his other arm around me. Ava's music continued to play in the background, but even if it wasn't I didn't think we would have stopped. Like I said, we just did.

Eventually, we came away with no breaths and I lost myself in his lovely blue eyes.

"I think I'm falling in love with you," I admitted to him, but I lied. I lied so hard. I was already very much in love and had been probably since the moment he pissed me off in my aunt's bathroom. He challenged me and I'd always been a girl to love one of those.

My eyes closed when his thumb massaged my cheek, opening them to see his smile. He leaned in pressing his lips to mine again.

"I know I am with you," he said against my mouth, braver than I was. His arms going around me, he brought me in close, expressing that love with every kiss and every touch he so passionately gave me. It'd been a ring, which rang into the air that ultimately stopped him and a fear I think we both experienced. I didn't even need to confirm that by looking into his eyes. Gray's phone virtually never rang.

Least of all on the very day Laura started school.

Seventeen

GRAY

THE DOUBLE DOORS to the school would have busted off their hinges had I put any more force behind them and by the time Alicia and I located Laura's former tutor Jolene Berry, I already found myself in a place which I easily couldn't come out of. I was in a tailspin. My mind was *fucked* beyond belief and I just wanted answers.

I wanted to see my daughter.

"Her instructor turned her back for two seconds, Gray," Jolene said, sprinting down the hall with Alicia and myself. We met her in the principal's office, the former tutor the one to call me today.

I couldn't see. I couldn't *think* as everything rushed around me and Jolene guided me toward the location of my daughter. She kept saying Laura's instructor had been with her. She'd been with her all day and she had been doing so well.

The touch on my hand broke through the words and on the other side I found Alicia, her arm wrapped around mine and her fingers laced through the spaces of my own in a way that allowed me to fight through the haze in my head long enough to find speech, her eyes telling me everything was going to be okay with just a single glance in our hurried steps. I hoped everything would be okay. I needed everything to be.

My "what the hell happened?" left my lips not moments before I spotted her, my daughter ahead of me.

My daughter tucked away in a closet.

The images behind my eyes blasted away like flashes in a turbulent storm, errant and horrifying memories I fought so hard to keep away. They used to keep me up at night and did for literally *months* after that fateful day.

The day my daughter had become mine.

Stepping into the room now, drawing closer to my kid who cowered heavily in the tiniest ball she could make herself at the bottom of a broom closet, I saw her again that day.

I saw her neglected.

She'd been dirty that day I found her, covered in I didn't know what and the smell saying so much as an indicator. She'd wetted herself. The room reeking of piss and other things she'd obviously projected at some point on the bedspread. That's where I found her, locked in a room and all by herself. She'd been alone for hours, maybe even many days.

She had no voice to tell me.

Even after finding her like that, in that disturbing state that told so much of what happened even still I didn't have all the details, the unknown I wanted to know at the time...

But hadn't been brave enough to handle.

"She turned her back for a second," Jolene continued in this moment now, shaking her head at the sight. But she didn't see what I saw. She saw a scared little girl having another one of her spells. She didn't *see* what I saw, the product of nightmares from Laura's and *my* past.

Swallowing, she looked up at me. "It was an accident. I promise you. Her instructor turned her back for only a second."

And yet a second was all it took, a second to find this, my kid and...

I stepped toward her, Jolene beside me as well as Alicia, Alicia who never let go.

She squeezed my hand now as I took in my kid, lowering. Jolene lowered too.

"She must have been curious," Jolene let on. She frowned, her hands folding. "Curious about the other children. There was a music class going on next door. It must have been the sounds that made her wander in—"

My hand let go, empty.

Music...

It'd been that word to take me to another place, a place my daughter should have been as well as me. I think I lost sight of that for a while. I lost sight of a lot of things. I believed I was something I wasn't and somewhere I shouldn't be.

And I think I'd known that for a while now.

I couldn't look at Alicia as I eased my way toward the closet in which my daughter cradled herself. I only had her in my sight at the present, the way it always should have been.

"Laura?"

She arose after my voice, her shoulders relaxing at a sight ahead of her. It hadn't been me at first and I was aware of that, Alicia beside me. Even still, Laura eventually made her way over to me and once she had her expression nearly tore my damn heart out. It'd been the same expression she held when she knew she was safe back when I finally found her, when she knew she was loved and always would be loved. I never let her forget every day that she meant something to both the world and especially to me.

She crawled out of the closet and over to me and once she had it was over.

Picking her up, I saw sight of no one after that. I left.

I left.

Eighteen

ALICIA

He'd been quiet after we came from the school and left so quickly I worried if I'd even make it outside in time to go back with him. Something happened back there at the school and more than the obvious. I saw it in the way he let go of my hand and wouldn't look at me.

I saw it in the way he wouldn't look at me now.

Gray's hand squeezed his leather steering wheel, his right arm slack but only because Laura had it. She sat between us, her arms laced around Gray's like an intricately woven strand. In her few bouts of fear I'd experienced around her I had fortunately never seen her come to the point of tears. This wasn't the case now as the tears ran down her puffy cheeks.

Her face hidden, she pressed her cheek against her dad's arm, out of the worst of it now and I wondered in my heart how much her tears had resulted from actual fear versus the result of what her fear had caused, an uproar in her dad coming to console her once again. She'd been doing so well.

I obviously couldn't answer that for her, keeping to myself in the close-sitting cabin. Bumping along that silence remained but somewhere between the school and wherever Gray was taking us I suddenly wasn't alone.

A hand came out, a small one on the seat. Laura didn't look at me, but she didn't need to.

I took her hand without reprieve, watching it fold in mine and somewhere along the way her breathing evened even more than when she'd been resting against her dad. I brought her peace I guessed, my hand coming down and rubbing hers.

It's going to be all right, girlie.

It would be all right. She would get through this, but my stomach still turned by everything that happened.

Especially, when Gray noticed my handhold with his daughter.

He actually closed his eyes to it. Like it displeased him for whatever reason before opening his eyes on the road. I didn't understand it.

What had I done?

I wondered if he'd even tell me, but then, we were suddenly parked outside of my aunt's home, but no one was making any moves to get out.

I sat there, watching Gray continue his gaze at the open road despite the truck not moving. I wanted to say his name, something.

He spoke first.

"I need to take Laura home," he said and I noticed quite quickly his statement had nothing to do with me. It didn't include *me* at all.

I shook my head. "Gray?"

It was like my very voice caused him pain and I almost regretted speaking, my hand loosening from Laura's. Rising up slightly, she looked at me, confused too. I supposed I got some satisfaction in the fact I wasn't the only one.

I brought my hands into my lap, obviously realizing he

wanted me to leave for some reason but not understanding why. I didn't do anything wrong. At least, I didn't think I had.

I said his name again and this time he actually granted me the honor of his eyes. This man had looked at me in many ways since meeting me, not all of them joyous and uplifted, but all of them at least fair which this didn't feel like, his eyes narrowed at me in the ways of an enemy.

Not someone he'd just held less than an hour ago.

"I think you should go, Alicia," he said, my heart squeezing with every word. "I think you should let me figure this out with my daughter."

She panned from me to him, then back and sitting up, this conversation had her full attention now. She actually let go of Gray's arm in the transition, looking full on at me then him.

He swallowed like he knew.

"You push," he said, panning my way. "You always push so this time... This time try not to."

He said the words so seriously and their message for me crystal clear. He blamed me for today.

He blamed me for everything.

I tried not to let them affect me, his words. I tried not to *feel* anything about someone I just admitted my heart to, like I said, less than an hour ago. I thought he felt the same way too. He told me as much.

In all this, I could be strong. I could show no feeling and be about my way, but then there was Laura, the little thing so smart, intelligent like her teacher said. Her big, brown eyes told me she understood all about what her father said, his rejection right in front of both of us.

She moved on the seat when I vacated mine and pressed her hands on the glass window after I closed the truck door. I tried to steel my emotions like I had in the truck, but as I watched her turn in her seat and press her hands to the back window of the truck I couldn't help the burn in my eyes and throat.

I guess that made me human.

Nineteen

GRAY

THE SHADOWS DANCED on the walls later that day, the images produced earlier in the day unable to dissipate behind the lids of my eyes. They intermixed with the twigs and brush that blew outside, the heavy storm as if reflecting my headspace.

As if reflecting the heaviness of my heart.

I cradled my head in the living room of my trailer, our life piled around me in the form of a few bags. We could fit our entire lives in merely five and only one to two if the urgency was dire.

What am I doing?

Squeezing my eyes, I attempted to come to terms with what I was about to do again.

I was going to run. I was going to go when things got tough and things became tense. Upon coming home, I believed I did need to leave, a clear danger in staying but as it turned out the danger may have been less for the well-being of my family and more of something else.

She had my heart.

The images of deep-brown eyes and warm skin the tone of

honey and amber killed my insides. Especially as I watched her go away. I pushed her away, *blamed* her and now I was putting myself in a position to never see her again.

And all because I was scared.

I was terrified of Alicia. I feared what she could do, her potential to open me up and expose me in ways I didn't want to be exposed. I had already told her so much, too much.

What if she finds out the truth?

I'd have to lie to her every day. *Every day* would be a continued lie between us. She wouldn't accept the whole truth behind us coming here to Mayfield and her judgment, the potential lack of her love...

I couldn't handle it. I wasn't strong enough to see myself changing in her eyes so Laura and I had to go.

So why was I still sitting on the couch?

I sat for what felt like a short millennia and, eventually, I wasn't alone anymore. Perhaps, my daughter knew I needed her just like she needed me earlier that day, my little girl so brave.

She came into the room in her shorts-coveralls, the way she'd been since we had arrived home today. Going right into her room to take a nap, calm down, I sat with her until she closed her eyes, rubbing her back and telling her everything was going to be okay. I wanted her to get one good sleep in, one more before I made sure our lives changed again.

Her arrival in the living room put me off at first as I'd just laid her down what felt like not too terribly long ago and I confirmed that when I looked at my cellphone. Even still I welcomed her, smiling at her. Like I said, I needed her.

"Hey, kiddo," I said guiding her to me. She leaned against my knee, a red to her eyes that let me know she'd been crying again. She didn't cry a lot but when she did it destroyed me in the worst way.

I should have listened to my instinct. She wasn't ready.

My kid was so brave but it was all too much too soon. I should have known that. I should have trusted myself.

You trusted her.

And I still did despite myself. I couldn't help trusting Alicia. I couldn't help loving her even more.

The ache in my chest suffocated like a cellophane bag over my head. Even small breaths weren't easily managed. I asked Laura if she wanted some peanut brittle as when she did have these rare times of unease she enjoyed sharing a box with me. It was one of my favorite things to eat and our shared love of the snack let me know we did share DNA. She was mine, a product of me and who I was.

After cupping her face, I got up, heading over into the kitchen. The food was all still in there because in my panic I felt it best to just rush out and start from scratch after Laura woke up. I didn't want any more baggage than needed I supposed.

I heard steps behind me when I reached up and grabbed the brittle, but I dropped the box to the floor as I heard a sound.

A voice.

"Daddy...?"

The word repeated, the word that didn't exist and I turned around, the only one in the room my kid.

And the tears had returned to her eyes.

"Dad?"

The word I actually saw form from her lips this time, a light sound and rasped like it was new, newborn, new... everything.

I crossed the room to my daughter, on my knees as the afternoon storm crashed and descended on our small trailer like we truly were in that fairy tale, Dorothy in Kansas.

The shake hit my hand like a tremor, my reach to Laura unstable.

"Laura?"

Her tears moved down my fingers, her face cringing as if she was in pain, but she'd said my name. I heard her.

She broke down.

"Daddy, please don't be mad," she retched, the words straining from her lips. "Please, Alicia did nothing wrong."

The words shocked me as much as their existence, but so happy...

My other hand came to her face, looking in awe at my daughter, my kid.

Her voice...

It took me so long to realize this was happening, maybe too long to establish this wasn't a dream or some cruel trick someone was trying to play on me. It took me a moment to realize this was *real* but once I had I couldn't let go.

"Alicia, honey?" I questioned, my heart, my *soul* so damn happy. I wanted to wipe my eyes, hard to see clearly all of a sudden, but like I said, I couldn't let go, only getting closer.

Laura shook her head in my hands, her tears dripping down to the kitchen titles.

Her face scrunched up.

"Alicia... You're mad at her. Please, don't be mad at her. It isn't her fault. I wanted to go to school."

She was... defending Alicia. My little girl, my child who hadn't spoke in so long opened up her mouth, her voice to go out to someone else. Alicia had brought this out of her.

Alicia had brought her back to life.

Dampening my lips, I swallowed down hard.

"You weren't ready, Laura," I said, this moment so surreal. "She overstepped and had Dad not listened to her—"

Laura's head shook with vigor, her eyes red and nose puffy.

"But I was," she challenged and so, so adamant. She was so brave and stronger than I ever knew. Her arms came around me and like earlier I'd been surprised. She'd never been one to hug. She'd never been one to do anything.

How much had changed.

I held her, closing my eyes as she continued to plead, plead she was ready, plead this wasn't Alicia's fault, and plead I shouldn't be mad. She pleaded I should forgive. She pleaded I should be as brave as she was.

"I want to go back, Dad," she said to me, the determination her voice teaching *me* something. She wanted me to take her back to the school and finish the day. She wanted to face her fears and maybe if she could?

I could face mine.

Twenty

ALICIA

The wind drummed hard on my aunt's door, but the slams of a persistent knock still pulled me out of bed. I had lain down for a spell, stuck in my head, and the sound at the door I feared at first as it'd been so rushed and almost angry.

The storm-clad figure on the other side of the door matched the sound, the air dusky around him with the fray outside and his body rising and falling with rapid breaths.

I saw Gray well through the translucent glass, and upon realizing my visitor was him, I shut the curtain right away.

Breathing, I didn't know what to do at first, but one thing wouldn't be to lose my nerve to him. He'd already made me feel weak enough, so bravely I unlocked the door and tugged it open.

He was on me in the next breath.

Lips pressed steadfast to mine, Gray swept me away in a breathless kiss, causing me to let go of the door and fall back into it, his arms wrapping around me and tucking, snuggling underneath my bottom.

"Gray...?"

I couldn't get it out, his mouth, his hands...

His fingers skated up the back of my thighs and into the underside of my nightgown.

"Gray."

His name a moan on my lips, I dizzied. Gray reached behind and freed me from the door. He cupped me in a single strong hold, closing the door with his foot and carrying me over to the wall.

He pressed me against it, using his big body to lock me tight and I didn't understand.

I braced his arms.

"Gray?" I forced into his lips, his name very much a question again. "Gray, where's Laura?"

She'd been the reason for him pulling away, as well as the reason for the coldness he'd encroached on me. She had been his main concern, but at the present, no unease was in this man.

Only our lips, his lips as a smile slid across them when he guided my mouth open.

He cupped my head.

"She's fine," he said, the words so soothingly true. She was fine. I heard it in his voice.

I felt it in his kiss.

His body encompassing mine, he mentioned his daughter was with someone, that she was *safe* but the urge to still stop him, *stop this* rang at the forefront of my mind.

Until it wasn't, until I fell into him in a way I always had, and like the moans of his name my hands fell into the same dizzying trap, the vice of Gray and everything that he was the continued culprit. I loved this man.

I just couldn't help it.

Even though he'd hurt me beyond belief I still loved him, actual tears stinging my eyes as his tongue fell softly upon my neck.

He was even softer with his hands, his fingers a secure grip but touch as distinct and precise as if he was doing something as finely as opening a delicate bar of chocolate, his hands working in a similar way with every lovely and beautiful revision he did with his hands. He knew his hands. He knew how to use them.

He knew how to love with them.

He knew how to love with his mouth, his lips opening and closing on the underside of my chin. He was speaking to me, undeterminable words at first since he was so in the moment, but when I heard them, I felt them.

The first "Forgive me" he slid down my neck and the second pressed to my mouth again. He pushed them into me, made them a part of me as he lifted my arms and pressed his erection between my legs. It was like he was trying to fuse himself with me, both his words and his body.

The hardness between his legs hit again when he lifted me by the back of my thighs. *He* was trembling now, holding onto me just to be still.

"Please," he begged and tears were in his eyes as he kissed my lips, not fallen but glassy none the same. "Please, Alicia. Please forgive me."

He sounded as if he was in agony, unable to move forward until he heard from me and I accepted him. What had happened to this man to make him feel this way, what did he have inside him to make him feel unworthy of me, unworthy of love?

I'd felt that for a while with him, a hum in the air that hovered over him like a dark cloud. He took it with him everywhere and I wondered if it went back to that guilt he expressed to me at the lake, still holding onto that.

My arms wrapped around him, I kissed him back, expressing my acceptance as I opened my eyes and skated my lips along his.

"Yes, Gray," I said, my hips pressing to his. My thigh wrapping around his, I eased up my silk gown, causing us both to moan when I pressed my heat against him, my panties thin.

I breathed. "Please, yes, Gray. Yes."

I'd forgive him forever. I'd forgive him always. I just wanted him to touch me now, give himself to me in ways he never had before, and after I removed my robe, then reached down and slid my nightgown off, exposing myself to him, he did the rest.

Two fingers pulled my underwear down from behind, the material sliding down my thighs when he lowered them. He didn't start at my breasts like I believed he would, simply pushing hot breaths across them before going straight to my core.

My legs pushed open, he pressed his mouth between them, reaching up to cover and grip me with his hand. He loved on me, his tongue spreading me open and mouth tunneling and accepting my taste. He flicked like the best of them, and like his kiss, he'd done this before.

But maybe he hadn't done *this* as it felt so different to even me, so much more intimate, my body completely exposed to him and in the open air. His dark head between my legs, I gripped him, widening my legs as I ground against him. He hadn't shaved down the scruff of his beard in a few days and it only proved to stimulate me more, my mouth falling open.

His fingers pushing inside me, he said my name as his unruly whiskers brushed raw against my sensitive lips. My thighs aching, I couldn't spread any wider for him.

"Gray, I can't."

It felt so good, and able to contain it, I gave into it, Gray holding me up while I spilled into his mouth.

Using his tongue, he accepted each taste as if it was the sweetest gift and, perhaps, it was to him. He stayed for a little while even after I stopped, spending time to kiss me and ease some of that burn between my legs. Upon standing up, he took me with him, wrapping my legs around him as he took me up the stairs. He kissed me the whole way, even partially undressing as he kicked his boots off in the hall and ripped away that plaid shirt he often wore over his t-shirt. Holding me by the waist, he took me to that large bed in the master, hovering over me as I climbed to the center.

His dark hair hanging over his eyes, he simply watched me as I got acclimated and like downstairs didn't do anything for a moment even after I got situated, his gaze traveling over my body from my head to my toes. He didn't spend any particular amount of time over any of it I noticed, like no sight was better than the rest. It made me feel some type a way under his gaze.

Especially when he pushed his lips between the valley of my breasts.

He smiled when he did this, like he was so, so grateful for this moment.

Like he was grateful for me.

The tears came in what seemed like a river and he stopped when he noticed them, his mouth lifting from my cheek. I'd actually become one of those women who cried during sex and couldn't help laughing through my tears when his finger curled underneath my chin, lifting it to look at me.

"I've just never been looked at that way before," I admitted to him, pushing some of those tears away. Because I never had, not once.

The wrinkle always hard in the corner of his eyes softened, his lips coming down to the shell of my ear.

"If it'd been me," he said, pushing his hand over my shoulder, then down between my legs. "If it'd been me every time..."

I wished it had been. I wished it always had been this way, but then again, if it had I might not have been able to value this the way I was. I wouldn't be able to get the full experience of it or him.

His large hand touched and fondled my breasts, his tongue flicking and pulling my nipples into his large mouth. Pinching my lips below, he got a rhythm with his fingers in me, my hands tugging at his t-shirt before he pulled it off.

The broad, muscled physique of a man exposed himself to me, dark hairs smattered along his pecs and down his abs. No gym saw this man, pure, unabashed labor the result of his impressive form. He was giving it to me, allowing me to have it when my hands explored down his chest. Undoing his belt buckle, he let his pants hang at the base of his cock, coming over to me and kissing my neck.

The bubble of his ass hung out the back and I shoved his pants down, letting him rub himself against me, my thighs falling apart and searching for him to be inside me.

"Gray..."

He cupped the back of my neck when he kicked his pants off and grabbing his cock, he explored, finding his place and once he did...

He filled me, his name seeping into the air at the welcome release of this man finally between my thighs. Slow at first, I knew he was holding himself back, as if almost scared to do what he wanted and *feel* what he wanted to feel in me.

"Please," I called to him, my fingers in his hair and face buried in his neck. "Please."

I wanted him fully. I wanted him to have what he wanted to have.

My words like a grant of permission, his powerful hips drove, smacking and hitting with the force of a wanton hunger. Caging my cheeks with his thumbs, he watched me, studied and gave a give for every one of my takes. He worked with me, taking no more or less than he felt he should. Upon kissing me, he pressed his abs against my tummy, going as deep as he could until he couldn't anymore.

Until it was too late.

We both expelled, his seed spilling inside me and my body milking around him. The fact he hadn't worn a condom became an afterthought in my mind, Gray raw, Gray inside me.

I grabbed his hips, keeping him there, wanting him there forever and his mouth on mine, he apparently thought to do the same. He didn't fall out when we finished and instead he remained inside me, his hips moving slowly while he pressed soft kisses to the underside of my jaw.

"We didn't use protection," he said at one point, peeling away. Searching my eyes, the air of concern was in them.

"I'm sorry, Alicia. I don't have anything. I..."

He didn't have to say it again like he had that first night he kissed me. He never did things like this and I got that, but I had thought about it and I smiled before I kissed him.

"We're good," I told him, knowing I was on the pill. "We're good."

He took that for what it was, only taking seconds to clean up both of us before he was pulling me on top of him.

"Ride me," he said, closing his eyes and pressing his unruly hair back into the bed. "Ride me."

Massaging my hips, he held me to him, letting me give him pleasure, which he took. At one point, he braced me from underneath, loving me from below and I pressed my hands into my hair, unable to discern all the feelings I had. I singled them all down to love. I was in love and being intimate with someone I was in love with—felt different.

It felt amazing.

Eventually, I found myself in my aunt's bathroom, cleaning up after our second time. Gray joined me when I took too long, his beautiful body standing behind me.

He wouldn't allow me to see him completely, his body behind mine in the mirror.

His hands on my lower back, he pushed up, forcing my

breasts out, my dark nipples peaked in the cool air. Bringing his large hands over the tops of my shoulders, he kissed my neck in the reflection and I watched him, his hands so gentle, intimate.

"I want to talk to you," he said after awhile. I was tugged away and got to see his perfect, muscled ass with every step, his legs thick and firm like his backside.

The floor creaking with every step, he made his presence in the room known, lounging down to the bed with his beautiful cock between us. He sat back against the headboard, pulling me into his lap and allowing me to experience yet another thing I hadn't.

I'd been snuggled, but never held. I sat in his lap with my legs over his and his strong arms around me. He was like a cloak of protection, security to the utmost extent.

Covers around us, Gray massaged my shoulders beneath them, his large hands roaming over them.

"You smell warm," he said, leaning forward and pressing a kiss on my neck. He squeezed his arms around my waist. "So warm."

I smelled of him and I told him, his lips smiling against my skin.

"Can I ask you a question even though it might seem silly?" he asked, the nature of his question using the humorous word but his expression completely serious.

Breaking all that down, he grinned a little. "What's your last name?"

I supposed I hadn't told him mine, nor received his and doing so at this stage was only a formality for me. I didn't need to know his last name to know that I loved him and the fact he'd proceeded to believe the same by telling me back just showed me what was more important, not names or formalities.

Even still, he wanted to know so I told him, my last name

Davey, and was surprised to find his to be Davenport. I knew a few in my work back home, but that was far away from here and in another world, somewhere I found myself letting go more and more each passing moment.

Especially, being in his arms.

He told me other things too, like his age, thirty-five, and like his name I'd been surprised at that too but in a different way. He looked several years older with the gray in his hair and age around his eyes, but knowing some of his history now I gathered the truth behind that. This man had been through something I'd been blessed to say I hadn't experienced, nor knew anyone who had that admitted the fact to me. He'd been hurt, both Laura and he did and it'd been after I told him my age of twenty-eight, his daughter's eyes found themselves in my memories, as well as the reason, which separated us earlier today.

The storm lifted behind Gray's eyes as I asked him about his daughter and the smile that revealed across his expression sent my heart soaring in ways I didn't believe was possible. I'd never seen him so happy, joyous and he kissed my brow when the sun came out over his face from my aunt's veranda.

"That's what I wanted to talk to you about," he said folding his arms around me. Still naked, he was as warm and at home as he described me to be only moments before.

His fingers brushed the side of my arm. "She's at school, Alicia," he said, the location causing me to rise and look at him.

He used those fingers across my cheek. "She wanted to be there."

"Wanted to?"

His nod had that smile going to himself. He dropped his hand and twisted his fingers up within mine, his eyes closing as he kissed the back of my hand. "She wanted to be there," he repeated and when I asked him how that was possible, or how he even knew he told me something I believed had occurred in my dreams, but only proved to be sweet reality.

"She spoke?" I breathed and my awareness of my tears came at the touch of his fingers to my cheek again. He took them, brushing both sides away with the tip of his thumb.

He proceeded to tell me the story, how she'd come to find her voice and how she somehow found it for me, to *defend* me of all things to a person she and I both loved. She vouched for me and my tears didn't scare me. They didn't put me off or make me feel like a place with him or *her* wasn't mine to have anymore. My heart had known the truth. It always had.

"Can we see her?" I asked Gray, smiling through my tears now. They weren't of sadness, but of a pure joy I myself hadn't experienced in so long. It was true love and a feeling for a family I had somehow gotten the honor of being blessed to know and love.

I supposed I could thank a woman named Josephine for that.

Hands folded behind my neck, Gray kissed my brow, saying he loved me and it was time to go now.

We had to pick his daughter up from school.

Twenty-One

ALICIA

"It is with great honor that I proclaim this establishment and once home to a dear resident of our community a recognized landmark to the township of Mayfield, Kansas, always to be seen as and will be from this day forward."

The mayor of Mayfield cut the ribbon in front of my aunt's home, a stout man I'd come to see around town on more than one occasion. One saw everyone here. They only had to be a part of it all and as I had been for the past six months I saw it all. I was a part of everything.

Grinning, I couldn't hide the expression, the mayor placing his hand behind my back and presenting me, as well as the home that'd be cemented in time now. I still owned my aunt's house for the time being and what an honor with the home turning out as beautiful as it did.

A flourishing display with new siding and a fresh coat of paint, my aunt's home had a transformation, now powder-blue in tone instead of the faded green color of before. The roof ripped off and replaced, the shingles shined bright in the afternoon sun and with the flower arrangements planted throughout the landscape a wonderland was created, the outdoors just as magnificent if not more than the internal house revisions. Those had been in influx, everything replaced and shined for the day, this day.

I hope it makes you proud.

I actually talked to my aunt a lot since I visited her, found her, or I guess since she found me. She'd always been here it was just now I could actually visit her, which I did every week. I brought pictures and even flowers from the garden, her beautiful lake just as picturesque. We hadn't gotten too much work done out there and frankly it hadn't been needed. Trees trimmed and brush managed, an environment had been created that this town could be proud of, a bright star in a sea of country land.

Squeezing my shoulder, the mayor handed me a plaque, which he instructed to the press would be placed inside the home for all to see. The photographers in bounds, they took pictures with the two of us, the plaque the forefront. The sun high today, half the town was here, many people I got to call friends amongst those pleasant faces. They whistled for me, throwing their hands up and clapping. All this meant something to them.

I knew the feeling.

Laughing, the glee overwhelming, I stepped back, taking it all in. After a pat, the mayor left me and I was on my own for the questions about the property and my plans for it. They came in droves, but I answered every one. I told them I was still in talks, which was true, but in the end, the home and my aunt's land would be priority.

After they were done with me, I was rightly out of breath, and then came Ava, her arms thrown around me.

"Oh my gosh, how are you dealing?" she asked, laughing a little. She brought a few of our friends with her, local guys. I'd come to know Ava definitely as a tomboy. I seemed to be the only one she made an exception for.

I shook my head. "It's a lot," I told her, placing the plaque under my arm. She wanted to see it, so I pulled it out for her.

Her expression changed after seeing it, softening before staring up at me.

"She'd be proud," she said. She said that a lot. I knew my aunt Jo would be. I hoped I could do something for her and this amazing town I suddenly saw myself a part of. It was the least I could do after she gave me such a gift.

Squeezing my arm, Ava stood back.

"So now that's done, we drink," she said, conferring with her friends. "We're going to Brown & Hobs and I'm buying."

Brown & Hobs was the town's hotspot outside of the bar Ava worked at, a place where drinking, eating, and dancing were the standard fare. But it hadn't just been any drinking and dancing.

This girl—i.e. me—had actually added line dancing to her arsenal and no one had been more surprised than myself. It wasn't my favorite pastime, something I'd only done a handful of times in the past few months, but I always enjoyed myself when there.

I told her no problem, but I had to ask Gray first. I lost him sometime between the beginning of the speech and the end, not surprised. He was a pretty good sport when it came to being around people. He often joined me in my ventures out with Ava and friends, but literally half the town and more had been here today, something I knew would put him completely out of his element.

I was coming to learn a lot about him, how he flowed and how he worked. He was different, but then again, maybe everyone else was. He had a good heart, a good soul, and his kindness battled the unusual. He was an amazing human being, man or otherwise.

I could go on about him all day.

And would most days if he let me, if Ava let me. As it

turned out Ava knew exactly where Gray had escaped to, on the other side of the house with the rest of the wallflowers I imagined.

I went over after hugging Ava goodbye, figuring he wouldn't be hard to find with his size. I knew exactly who I was looking for, his distressed jeans and crisp white t-shirt the standard with him. He dressed up a little today by wearing a collared shirt and I looked for that toward the front of the house. I found a few friends, more smiling faces of the city. They'd been enjoying the refreshment table in the front, but no Gray.

Hands coming down my shoulders told of his location, his thick fingers embedding deeply into my skin. A daisy pushing in front of my eyes, he used a free arm to crane around me, his lips pushing a smile into my neck.

"Congratulations," he said, pulling away and I got that daisy in my face when he presented it with a bow of his head.

I took it like it was the most valued treasure, smiling as I kissed it against my lips before bringing an arm around his broad frame.

He didn't have to say anything about where he'd been or why he'd gone. It didn't matter. He was here now.

After pinching my lips between his, he pulled back at the call of his name, but it hadn't been me who said, "Dad."

A light shown around a perfect ponytail drawn back with a few braids decorating the sides. She'd let me do her hair today. I'd do it every day if the girl calmed down enough to do such a thing. She was always running around.

She was always laughing.

An excited and jubilant, "Dad!" Laura tossed in her father's direction once more, pressing her face into his side before throwing an arm around me too. I'd never get enough of this girl's hugs.

I used to wish, once upon a time, that I'd been there the

very first time. I wanted to enjoy the moment of hearing her voice, but that hadn't been for me. The moment had been between a father and daughter, a long time coming for them, and me, I got the best of both worlds. I got the glee and excitement of it all after.

Her joy heavily displayed today. She let go of me and tugged on her dad's t-shirt.

"Slow down," Gray said, his child literally lunging at him. It made him smile, *smile* in the most desperately handsome way. His hand on the back of her head, he dipped a chin down at her, his kid's words a mile a minute now that she'd found them. I deciphered her asking to go to her friend's house, a lot of friends she'd made over these past few months since attending school. It was slow at first and only one friend at a time. It took some time for her to brave and no one rushed her.

Gray's Laura wasn't to be rushed.

She was like her father in that way, comfortable with change if only not pushed. I learned so much since being around both of them, blessed to be able to.

Laura went on about going to her friend's house and eventually, Gray's lips turned down at her.

"And what does Jasmine's mom have to say about that?" he asked her, rubbing the back of her head. He'd referred to her friend who'd come to be her best friend over time. She also happened to be Jolene's niece, the first one she initially shared her beautiful spirit with.

"She, she, she, her mom said she didn't care," she spouted, jumping and tugging on his shirt still. Again, she had so many words and excitement bubbled up within her she couldn't seem to express them fast enough for her newfound voice to catch up with. She grinned. "She said she didn't care even though it was a school night."

"I highly doubt that," Gray exclaimed, tugging on one of her braids. He smiled. "She really didn't care?"

"No, no. She didn't. Can I go, please? I'll be back before dinner."

"Oh, I *know* you'll be," he said, coming down to her. He grabbed her shoulders, shaking her playfully and I knew his answer. They'd been the same answer every time she asked something from him, every time she needed something.

And I think it made him just as happy to say yes as it did for her to hear it.

Twenty-Two

GRAY

She was wild today, which excited me, but I'd never admit that to her. We'd had a picnic down at the lake since we'd been Laura-free today, the spot we picked far enough to drive to. Alicia had wanted to explore, see all of what Josephine's land really consisted of which I showed her. It'd been after all the fanfare and away from all the press that seemed to constantly be around these days. As the project of Josephine's home gained toward completion and word about the plans for the development got out more and more people seemed to be stopping by. They were excited for it, the town more than.

It'd been a whirlwind, but we'd made it, a house, a story I'd been proud to be a part of. I got everything out of it in which I intended. I honored a woman who had been so good to me and my family.

I also got something else.

Alicia ran from the lake and in the general direction of my truck, picnic basket thrown over her arm. Out of breath, she sprinted from me, but I honestly could have caught up to her in maybe a stride and a half if I tried. My legs were quite extensive compared to hers, and in her short dress and sandals, she wasn't gaining a lot of traction on the sand and then later through the woods, as she headed out toward my truck parked just off the side of the road. The one handicap I had was the rest of our picnic gear, but that really hadn't been a handicap at all. I could have easily caught her, a finger brush, then grab away.

I just liked chasing her.

I enjoyed the chase *of* her, a constant game I'd been playing in so many months. I didn't know my life without that game, without her heavily embedded in all aspects of my wonderful life.

Gaining on her, she'd reached my truck, spinning around and the bell of her dress whipping in the wind and exposing her beautiful brown legs. Dropping our stuff to the ground, I wanted to see more of them, bunching up her dress and pressing my mouths to hers. She teased me though, not making that easy. Dropping our picnic basket, she threw her arms around my neck, backing us both into my truck with a slam, tossing her hips up against me and spreading her legs. Her sweet heat between us, she rubbed steadfast against my jeans and I pressed a hand against my truck.

"Alicia..." I groaned, her hands exploring, undoing my pants. "Alicia, no."

I wasn't as adventurous as her. She'd kept her hands to herself for the most part at the lake, mostly because I believed she'd been afraid one of the people down at her house would somehow make their way to where we'd been. *I* knew there really hadn't been any possibility of that considering how far away we'd gotten, but I let her believe the fact. If I hadn't, she'd be doing what she was now.

Testing my resolving in the worst way.

Mouth parting on mine, she eased my cock out of my jeans, massaging me and guiding me to pump into her hand.

The stimulation was something I could easily give into, her hands like fire and the space between her legs just as tempting to fill. Enraptured, I took over her lips, nibbling and bruising them between my teeth. Eventually, her hand left me and went to the skirt of her dress and the moment her arousal hit the air I was done for.

I was giving into her.

Opening the door of my truck, I pulled her to me, her body trembling and my hardened cock against her back. I rocked my hips, pushing the door wide then guiding her forward. Bent over my seat, I shoved her dress above her ass, her supple bottom exposed when I tugged her panties down.

She made me this way, insatiable for her. Her honeyed flesh pooled between the spaces of my fingers when I gripped her tight flesh, a mew sound eased from her lips.

Corkscrewing her hips, she rubbed her sweet pussy against my seat, trying to get some relief I imagine, but if I wasn't getting any she wasn't.

I created a barrier between my seat and her mound with my hand, bracing the warmth and thrusting forward a little. I watched my cock smooth between the slit in her backside, my pre-cum on her ass and sliding between her cheeks. She called my name when I did that, a soft and aroused, "Gray," which toyed at my soul. I wanted to tear into her, ease myself inside and claim her until she was mine, until she *knew* she was mine. So many things were up in the air with us, time, distance, and space were all ultimately against us. The topics had been something we never discussed because neither of us had the answers. We just had this, Gray and Alicia.

We got this.

Sliding on a condom, I eased her legs apart with a tap of my boot to each of her ankles, the protection something I'd invested in. We hadn't had unprotected sex since our first time together, my error, and even though she'd said we were okay I wanted to make sure of that. It wasn't because I didn't want another child. I just didn't want to leave *her* vulnerable, the possibility of having a child placed only on her when I was in this too. We were two people and shared responsibility.

I loved her.

And I told her that at the first fill, easing up and burying myself inside her. Being cautious of my weight, I pressed my body on hers, gripping her hip while I got good traction by placing my boot on the step of my truck. Getting a rhythm, I tunneled in, my hips slapping against her bottom and creating the most beautiful, audible arrangement amongst that of the nature and trees.

She grabbed my hand while I slammed into her, holding it to her hip.

"I love you, Gray," she said. "I love you," and I came. I came so hard inside her I felt it in my toes, my balls drawing up and my core tight with the release.

I filled the condom, her, and enjoyed the high of feeling her pulse around me as her pussy pulled me in. She gave in right after I did and I watched her, held her through each gorgeous second. After she finished, I smiled into her back, kissing the warm brown skin above her bottom.

"I can't believe you got me to do that," I said, laughing against her skin. I drew my tongue down her back, and when she pressed her bottom into me, I knew something else.

She was about to make me do it again.

So many times this woman got me to go outside of myself, to *change* and each time had been a welcomed relief.

I watched her change too; free herself in the ways she hadn't been upon coming to this town. Alicia was the type of class to see me on the street not even a year ago and pass on a glance my way, no time for her or her attention. She was a woman of the world, myself far from.

But she was with me now, *here* and now, her beautiful

breasts bouncing above me while her hips tightened down below.

I eased the straps of her dress and bra down, wanting to see her completely as she rode me in my truck. My hands on her breasts, I massaged, her nipples dark and dimpled between my fingers.

I pulled, tweaked, and sucked each one, her lips calling my name, her hand on the back of my head.

"Gray, Gray, Gray."

That meant she was close, her hand coming down to grip my frame. Her fingers created a white heat in my side, my abs tightening and pulsating with her hand beneath my shirt.

Guiding my hands to her thighs, I drove up, my boots securing themselves to the floor while I thrust my hips. Her hands instinctually went up to the top of the truck's cabin, the space tight, but big enough.

My thighs slapped her, hard hits, which burned with every retreat. I could imagine it was the same for her, a call from her throat with every retreat. Eventually, our labor exhausted us and I saw it on her face the moment it happened.

I brought my hand to her cheek at the very instance, wanting to feel her beneath my fingers when I brought them down her mouth. She was so soft, so perfect in every way. I had no right to be with this woman and only in this universe would it work.

But I took it. I fucked her. I *loved* her with my entire being.

I cleaned her up right after, knowing we wouldn't have a lot of time to just be together. We'd been out all afternoon, reality and obligations coming back to us.

I held Alicia in my arms in my favorite way, her nestled on top of me, my truck door still open and allowing her feet to hang freely. She lost her shoes at some point. I hadn't been surprised I guess.

Using a few strands of her hair, I stroked her cheek, watching her eyes and a little noise left her lips in response to my touch. I could watch her all day like this. I did watch her on a lot of fortunate nights.

"Everyone seemed to enjoy today," I told her after awhile, her eyes opening on me with a smile. I smiled back, cupping her face. "I think you made the town really happy."

We'd seen literally everyone there in a matter of weeks, people stopping by to wish their warm regards and give their blessings.

It was little things like that... *thought* for people and the place they called home that meant something to them. Alicia and I both were foreign to this place, but she thought about them, their town.

Her eyes creasing in the corners, she tilted her head at me.

"You think I made her happy?" she asked after a while. She cupped my hand on her cheek. "That's what I want."

Leaning forward, I kissed her nose, enjoying her scent and feminine heat.

"I know you have," I told her. "She would have loved this. She would have loved this so much."

Josephine loved her house and to know, at least in all this inheritance business with Alicia and everything else, that *this element,* in it would be preserved a huge blessing. Alicia didn't have to do any of this, the woman basically a stranger to her.

But she had and did so graciously, using her own money at that too from what I understood.

I had no idea her future plans for everything and, basically, had put all hopes aside. I had no hopes.

Mostly because I didn't know what I wanted either.

"Do you know what you're going to do? With the rest of the property I mean?" I actually asked her, questions so forbidden before. Truth be told, I didn't want the answer with every passing day because each one meant the possibility of her leaving.

Her expression changed with the questions, her shoulders shrugged, and she brought a shawl she'd taken with us up and over her shoulders.

"More and more offers for me to sell have come," she admitted. "With the press and everything you know."

I did know, clasping her hand. I could imagine the land was a hot commodity. Especially with the revisions.

Nodding, I let her know I understood, playing with the material of her dress on my lap.

I didn't know what to say to her. I didn't know if I *could* say anything when it came to whatever decision she was trying to make. When she started this project, I'd gone in myself with a finality, this town in my rearview mirror once the development of this property and my duty to a kind woman named Josephine ultimately fulfilled.

But with each passing day, each laugh, each moment experienced in this town not just with Alicia, but my daughter...

It was hard not to deny the power of this place and what it was starting to mean for my family. We'd found something here.

We had security finally.

I was tired of running. I was tired of fighting for something I already had. I hated moving my daughter to a new town every time I felt we'd been there too long. I hated uprooting and changing our lives due to mistakes I'd made in the past. I was tired of worrying about the if. *If* something would happen if we stayed somewhere too long.

I was tired of paying for my mistakes.

I was punishing my daughter in response to them too and something I knew heavily. I'd been punishing her since she'd made her way to me and even long before that. I had my fair place in the sadness, which had occurred in her life, the tragedies placed upon both her heart and mind. Her mom had a good grip on the responsibility of it, but I'd been the catalyst for what had ultimately ended up happening to our daughter when her mom abandoned her, the details of it...

As well as what we'd had to do in response.

We'd been running for a long time, my kid and me. It'd been necessary and something I hadn't regretted in the slightest. Running kept us hidden, kept us *safe*, but the toll it took on my kid was undeniable. Her mental state did nothing to recover from what her mom had put her through when she initially abandoned her, the running only further burying her within herself. She closed off, clamped up even worse than when I found her.

Then when I *literally* found her, my little girl by herself.

I had no idea how long she'd been alone. I just knew after that day I never heard her voice. It'd been a day I established my responsibility in her life and role I had pushed on with to this very moment. I did what I had to do to protect my kid, but somehow in my crusade, my protection had the reverse affect. My mistakes were starting to punish Laura, my sheltering of her keeping her from experiencing life. She hadn't been able to make friends or really do anything. At least not until this town.

My daughter had found something here against all odds and that went beyond that of her voice. She'd found happiness, true happiness within herself and she wasn't the only one.

My thoughts peeled away to Alicia, my happiness so close to me. It wasn't fair of me to love her, but I couldn't stop myself.

I didn't want to stop myself anymore.

"Since Laura's in school now," I started pushing my hand over Alicia's cheek. Her smile sent my heart in places it shouldn't be, but since it was, there was no more fighting it. It was time to take a look around and see what was reality.

It was time to wonderfully accept it.

Kissing her forehead, I told her about the jobs I was going to take on now that Laura was in school and I'd finished up with Josephine's project. I was going to root myself and find my way here like my daughter seemed to have.

"And I'll get Laura and me a house eventually," I said to her, a house... A *life*. I never would have dreamed it in my best ones.

The heat in Alicia's hand embedded within me and I only opened my eyes when I believed I missed what she said. She mentioned her aunt's house.

And she mentioned me living there.

"You want to sell it to me?" I asked her, shaking my head. "You want to sell Josephine's house to me?"

She stared at me long and hard. Taking back her hand, she rubbed it against my chest.

"You'd be the only one it would be for," she said and the sadness in her voice I didn't miss.

Her gaze reached me when I cupped her jaw and I took her lips between both hands.

"It'd only be for *us*," I corrected her, pulling away. I scanned her eyes. "We are the only ones."

She watched me, her eyes opening up in the most beautiful way. Her smile played with me when she reached forward, her hand touching my lips.

"We," she started, the word in awe on her lips. Her eyes creased hard and she shook her head before saying, "I'd have to change so much, do so much to make... to make that happen."

She would. She'd have to rearrange her entire life. I didn't know exact details of her world, but I did know she'd have to change them. She'd have to give up who she'd been.

And choose who she was now.

It'd been a change I had to make as well, and though our journeys were different, I knew her struggle had to be just the same.

I didn't want her to respond right away to what I proposed. I just wanted her to know it was there, an option.

"It'd be everything," I told her, her hair brushing along my fingers against her cheek. "I'd make sure it was for you, for all three of us, I'd make sure of it."

It was the first promise I'd ever truly made to anyone.

Including myself.

Twenty-Three

ALICIA

Gray lingered by my door that night.

But not because he'd had a choice.

He'd made several weak attempts to leave my lips, our kiss, and each time he gave in, his hands on my hips and his mouth on mine.

Pressing me up against my door, he hummed, "Alicia," against my mouth, his fingers bunching the material of my dress at my thighs.

"Alicia..." he repeated, a sigh this time on his lips as he smiled against mine. He pushed me back by the hips. "I have to go."

He spent a lot of our time together resisting and I couldn't rightly blame him. I had my hands all over him most of the time, unable to be helped.

He was just so powerful, all encompassing in the way he made love. He touched me like it would hurt him not to, then held me after like he never wanted to leave. The feeling was addicting and something I wasn't used to. I'd made love to enough men to know what I felt with Grayden was different.

I pushed up on my tiptoes, my hands pulling down over

his shoulders. He already told me he needed to leave, that he had to get Laura and wouldn't be able to join me and the others tonight at Brown & Hobs. It was still early and he never drank anyway, but asking again would be futile. He'd want to go. He was just too responsible.

I adored him for that.

The exact reason he was leaving was why I couldn't keep my hands off him, my arms around his neck allowing me to pull my body against his. He indulged me again, hands working my ass, but his hand pressing against the door told me he wouldn't be doing so for long.

"Alicia..."

One final kiss from his lips and his mouth pulled away. Bruised and out of breath, he licked them, stepping forward in his boots one last time to touch an innocent kiss to my cheek. That was the way he always left me, his hand in mind before he put distance between us.

I lifted my hand, still feeling his though he'd made it to the porch steps.

"Give her a hug," I said, pulling my arms around myself. I adjusted my shawl. "And a kiss for me too."

He did every night, the two of us always parting eventually. They were always invited to stay here, both Laura and him but, eventually, I stopped asking. He told me once he didn't want to confuse her about what all this was, what *we* were, and I got that.

Mostly because the two of us were the most confused.

I didn't know what we were, just that I cared about him and he cared about me too. Sex... love had always been enough, and after this evening, I knew he wanted more. I think I wanted more too. In fact, I *knew* I did.

But this was all so very complicated.

His hand lifted on the stairs, his smile that of my heart. It created wings whenever I saw it, fluttering bright within me.

This man was so very dashing, *good* and sometimes I wasn't quite sure I deserved whenever he smiled at me. He looked at me like I was the only one, like I was everything.

"It'd be everything," he told me. *"I'd make sure it was for you, for all three of us..."*

I knew he would. I knew he'd change my life.

If only I let him.

"Grayden?"

He faced me at the bottom of the stairs, one boot lifting to a step as if he'd return. Hesitating, he stood, waiting for me and I knew, *I knew*, he'd wait for me forever.

"I love you," I told him, nodding with it. I loved him more than I could express.

He did come back then, and reaching, he folded his fingers behind my neck. He kissed me again, bringing me up on my toes.

"I love *you*," he told me, his emphasis I felt in my soul. It'd been rough-edged, and his brow creased when he said it. I had a feeling he didn't tell that to a lot of people. I guess I'd just been lucky.

Pressing his mouth to mine one last time, he closed his eyes, squeezing me before pulling away. I watched him head toward his truck but didn't stay to watch him drive away. I hated that part and didn't want to see it. Instead, I chose to go inside, clean up and try to recover if not a little bit from the day. A lot had happened.

And a lot of decisions needed to be made.

I knew my love for Gray and his daughter wasn't one of those, though. They were in my heart. They were there to stay, but what I was going to do with that became the ultimate question. Leaving this town, this *home* unscathed would be impossible. Everything that happened here would always be with me.

You knew that would happen, didn't you?

I could feel my aunt's spirit upon closing the door as I mentally spoke to her, shaking my head to myself. I intended to go upstairs and shower from the day, but shortly after I touched the stairs an engine's rumble had me coming back, an automatic smile on my face.

He must have forgotten something.

The smile reserved on my face for him, I opened the door, but in the end, the expression didn't last. Not many good things in my life did. I was always so busy, never had time to be happy.

That's how Bastian had worked his way in.

He'd been easy, no time like me. We'd been... perfect for each other. Little did I know perfection came in a man who couldn't ultimately commit. He'd casted me away and in that time, I tossed him in return.

It seemed he didn't want to be tossed.

A CEO stood at my door, a man of power and prestige with his hand pushed inside a single side pocket. Pants dark and pressed, they hugged the slim build of his muscular thighs, the seams of the jacket he paired with it hitting the various dips and curves of his shoulders and biceps. He looked ready for a day at the office, a smoky button-up shirt beneath his suit jacket that brought out his dark eyes and the waxy shine of his black hair. It cut the evening when he lifted his head, blades of perfection he styled and parted to the side. Cheekbones high and lips full without even being pursed, I fell for this man, his looks not even being part of it. He'd exuded a power I enjoyed and found myself lost in at the time. I just wanted to be around it, his energy and drive I felt were always elements in myself. We'd been like-minded and passion-focused.

Bastian stepped into the light cast off by my porch light, his skin the glow of a natural tan. He was only half Japanese, but the Brazilian side caused him to be just as honeyed.

"Hello, Alicia," he said and how I used to enjoy the depth in which he used to say my name, how rough and deep the timbre could get when he was really feeling it.

When he was really feeling me.

As good as it had been back then, as good as he made me feel, the previous effects of his voice couldn't be created now. I didn't feel *good* in his presence now.

If anything I felt naked. I felt vulnerable him being here and unannounced.

We hadn't spoken in months.

He passed me a few texts after that last conversation we had, ones I responded to and let him know I was staying in Mayfield for an extended project. He had few questions for me, which let me know the truth about us even more than what he told me that sent me into a drinking binge. He was okay with me putting distance between us. He was okay with me doing my thing and him his. He was a busy man and he had plenty going on with himself outside of me.

Maybe I'd been wrong.

"Hey," I said, creeping outside a little. I dampened my mouth. "You're a long way from Chicago."

A long, *long* way.

Dipping his head, he confirmed it, a smile on his face I used to love. He only made it when he was pleased, always so serious.

His gaze dashed left and right of my aunt's porch, I could imagine taking it all in.

"Are you going to invite me inside?" he asked after a while and because I had no reason not to, I stepped back, holding the door open.

He crossed me with three steps and left a musky scent in his wake I also used to enjoy but now found overpowering. It could stand to be more natural, more Gray.

The thoughts had me closing my eyes as I shut the door behind him, the man really in my house.

"What brings you?" I asked him, knowing this was unusual. I'd invited him just that one time, but back then he expressed no interest. Even more so when our correspondence started to fade. I literally hadn't spoken to him since that last conversation in which he let me know our reality as a couple, our texts few and far between after that. He knew I was here in Mayfield to see through a structural development project I started prior to the sale of my aunt's property. He knew all that because he wondered why I hadn't come home when I said I'd be there. It actually took me not being in town for him to realize he hadn't spoken to me in weeks. Knowing I had to give him something, I told him the truth. I'd be gone for a while and because he was a business man he understood and respected that. He left me *alone* after that.

I guessed not quite.

"I wanted to see," was all he said, standing in the living room now. Walls of fresh paint and polished lacquer set over hardwood floors took his vision, the home truly beautiful with all the work Gray did. Something of appreciation was in his eyes when he turned around and I hadn't been surprised. He knew a project done well, in real estate himself.

"It's a fine place, Alicia," he said, the words actually meaning a lot from him. Like I said, he knew good work.

I was standing in the entryway at this point, my fist touching the arched wall.

"Thanks," I told him. I moved my shawl around me. "We put a lot of work in."

"I can see that," he said, approaching me with his long strides. This man towered, a full head taller than me. Stopping in front of me, he touched the same wall my hand had been on, lengthy fingers moving down with an air of a caress.

"It'll sell quite nicely," he went on, speaking of things both of us knew he wasn't involved in but that didn't stop him. I could imagine he felt he had the right, his knowledge of property and business vast.

His knowledge of me extensive as well.

He knew I wouldn't challenge him and I didn't, standing there. A sound behind me had us both turning, the door opening for some reason. I thought at first I might not have closed it, but then I realized only two people just walked into my aunt's house unannounced.

A flash of Grayden's dusky hair pushed into the room and then Grayden, his focus on the door as he closed it behind himself.

"Alicia, you forgot your—"

My purse was in his hands, the chain wrapped around his thick digits. The chain un-looped itself, hanging from his fingers when he got inside the house.

"You left your purse in my truck," he finished, picking it up and palming it. The sparkly bag looked so small in his hands and I often did forget my bag in his truck. He usually just waited until he saw me next to give it to me. He would have if this had been any other day.

The two men stood in my aunt's entryway, myself the single body between them. That didn't say much. I took up little space in comparison and with the small size of the foyer to my aunt's home, they basically filled it up, two large mountains of never-ending male. Bastian wasn't as big as Gray, but he was taller.

I could easily compare with them both being here and struck silent at first, I didn't introduce them right away. It took Gray standing there, the bright blue of his eyes squinted on Bastian for me to get my thoughts back.

"Hey, this is Bastian. He's from back home."

He was from back home, so that's how I introduced him.

The sharp crease in the sides of Gray's eyes lifted after that, easing as if that was okay and, instinctually, he put out his hand.

"Grayden." He introduced himself as *Grayden* when this whole town knew, *I knew* he was just Gray.

He squeezed his hand down on Bastian's, the man's hand lost in his if not for the length.

"Bastian," he said, taking his hand back. He returned it to his pocket. "Alicia mentioned a Gray."

"He headed the development," I reminded him, remembering I had told him that too. He'd been so inquisitive in his few texts when they actually came, wondering *why* I needed to be here and for so long. I had to give him something, so again I told the truth.

"That's right," Bastian went on. He lifted his chin. "Tell me, Grayden. Have you ever seen yourself in Chicago? I feel like I've seen your face."

His line of questioning placed a surprise in me, but not for Gray as it seemed.

His head tilted as he palmed my purse, his unruly locks cutting the air with the shift of his single headshake.

"Couldn't have been me," he said, lifting his head a little. "But I'm told sometimes I have one of those faces."

"I suppose so," Bastian went on. His eyes smiled as he slid the other hand into his pocket. "I interact with a lot of people on my day to day. I guess I just have you mixed up with someone else."

The smile didn't quite reach Gray's eyes when he said this, and turning, he handed my purse to me.

"You forgot this," he said, stepping back a little. "And I've changed my mind about Brown & Hobs. I'll call Jasmine's mother on the way. See if she can watch Laura a little longer. It's still early. It'd be a shame to waste the rest of the evening considering how well everything went today with the house."

He faced Bastian. "Alicia's home has been proclaimed a

recognized landmark. Friends are wanting to celebrate downtown with drinks. You should come."

A lot was happening here I didn't quite understand, Bastian coming here, Gray *coming back*, Gray referring to my aunt's house as *my* home and, now, suddenly wanting to be social when he never wanted to be. It just didn't feel right. Something was off about all this.

I looked at him. "You're sure—?"

"That sounds like a good idea actually, Grayden," Bastian said to me, my words all but gone to Gray. He smiled at him. "You can tell me what she's been up to while she's been here."

Twenty-Four

GRAY

He'd been right. His face *did* strike me as familiar, but for the life of me... I couldn't place the man who'd suddenly arrived at Josephine's house.

His face blurred as if lost in a never-ending sea. I'd known a lot of people over my lifetime, interacted with them in my "day to day" as he proclaimed as well, the man displaying an air of uppity-ness that I too had exhibited once upon a time.

It seemed like a lifetime ago.

I sipped my seltzer water, eyeing him over the many heads and faces of Brown & Hobs. He was over at the bar, selecting something as the pitcher that had been brought to our table wasn't to his liking.

Where have I seen you?

Or maybe I hadn't, just felt I had. Like I said, I came from a world, one he looked to fit right into. My old job, my old life had kept me around a lot of influential people at one time and that guy by the bar definitely fit the type. He wore a suit just because it was a Tuesday, didn't matter the occasion.

Shaking my head, I peeled my vision away from him. I'd fought hard to scrub my memories of the past, not my reality now and not the point. He must have just resembled someone I knew and my face the same to him. Like I said, I used to come from that world.

And thank God no more.

More pressing issues arrived in the form of Alicia and how weird she'd been acting since this guy showed up. She rode with me to the country-dance bar featuring line dancing, but she'd been rather close-lipped about her friend. She said he was just a guy she knew from back home. He'd come to check up on her and how she was doing down here being gone for so long. I took that for what it was until they were in the room together again, the guy driving over in his expensive rental that stood out in this small town. Red and polished, he'd parked it right up, arriving before Alicia and me. Opening the door for her, he placed his hand behind her lower back. Not really... *that* weird if he was just a friend.

But usually one wanted to interact with their friends.

She stayed close to me, one- or two-word answers to him and our group of friends, which crowded around us when we arrived. She'd introduced her friend Bastian to the rest of the gang, but then, she faded off from him in conversation. She let the group lead on, which wasn't much like her since she enjoyed being social. She enjoyed *talking*, but tonight, she remained rather passive. Even her friend—the guy—had actually been talking more than her, inquiring about the town and everything about it. He was quite eloquent, obviously of the city as Alicia herself.

Nursing my drink, I watched Alicia now, the woman involved in a rigorous line dance. Her friend Ava had brought her in shortly after arriving, the bartender not taking no for an answer, and Alicia, she was usually quite receptive to the dancing though she'd just learned while she was here. She liked to have a good time and always was a good sport about dancing with her friends.

But tonight she wasn't too keen on doing that. In fact, she fought Ava pretty hard before giving up. She'd used me as an excuse, saying she didn't want to leave me sitting at the group's table since I didn't ever dance. I told her I'd been fine. The group knew I never got out there, my lack of dancing never an issue. I urged her to go and she eventually did, her friend Bastian leaving from the table around the same time to get an alternative to the beer we had.

Alicia could dance like the best of them though she claimed this wasn't her thing, a Stetson hat placed on her head by Ava while she joined her hip to hip. The pair was sandwiched between a couple of our other friends, Jordan and Taylor. Arms hooked, they danced with glee and the smile on her face made me feel like I was out there with her. We all had our spheres and though dancing wasn't one of mine, I enjoyed watching her. I could watch her do anything.

Catching her eye, I tipped my chin at her, her grin strong when she spotted me too. She waved before the group spun, her position switched and her legs having to reroute because of that. Stumbling, she ran into Ava, which caused them both to crack up in laughter, Alicia throwing her hair back and grabbing her stomach. Smiling, the situation had me laughing too. They all got back into it, Alicia laughing again, but her lips straightened a little when her gaze panned to the right. The laughter suddenly left her lips completely and she turned, going back into the dance, but I moved my focus over to where she'd been looking.

The man of before, her friend, had his hand raised in her direction, his drink of choice, a brown liquor, in his hand. Closing his fingers, I assumed he just got done waving at her, his gaze panning. Stopping on me, he strode in my direction.

I lifted my seltzer water, going into a drink and putting my focus back on the dancing. As I was the only one sitting at the table still, our friends all out on the dance floor, only Alicia's friend and I sat there, the man taking a seat on the other side of the table. Bringing his arm around the back of the chair, he gazed out toward the dance floor, lifting his hand again.

Alicia spotted him immediately, reciprocating the wave. She tugged her arm as if to leave the dance and come to us, but Ava pulled her right back in.

"Not a dancer, Grayden?"

His attention in my direction, Bastian danced his fingers on the wooden table between us with soft clicks.

"Not much of one no," I told him, taking a drink before pushing it down with a stiff swallow. I tipped my drink at him. "You're not either?"

A headshake followed what I said, his gaze shifting toward the dance hall.

"I prefer to watch," he said, his gaze one of appreciation on the dance floor. His fingers flat on the table, he watched out there like he said, his vision lingering in the direction mine had all night.

Ava had Alicia in the throws of a spin, Alicia smiling in her arms and Bastian made no qualms about staring at the two, his fingers sliding up the table before grabbing his drink and taking a sip. The action caused me to grip my own glass, my eyes cutting hard in the corners before I took my own sip.

Clicking his teeth, Bastian placed his glass down, grinning a little too much at me for my liking.

"Alicia speaks very highly of you," he said, sitting back. "The work you've done for her? In fact, so much, I had to see for myself which was why I came down."

His words brought me amusement for some reason, my ice clinking my glass in my fingers. She may have spoken to him about me.

But not once had I heard a word about him.

"Well we put a lot of work in," I told him, hoping she might have just overlooked the fact in our time together. "And

I'm surprised she mentioned me as this is the first time I've ever heard about you."

This was fact, nothing more and no concern had been given by me prior to this moment. Alicia had a life. She had one before this place, Mayfield, and I got that.

My words sent a curiosity skating across his expression, his lips hiking up slow in the corner.

"Interesting," was all he said before our party was no longer alone.

Alicia joined us, her friend Ava and a few others in tow. Out of breath, they all dropped themselves around the round table easily large enough for twelve. They all found seats and Alicia positioned herself beside me, Bastian on her other side. She went to sit, pulling out her chair, but before Bastian let her, he grabbed her.

A side kiss touched her cheek, one of those French ones where his lips didn't quite touch and I didn't know what to make of it.

"You looked gorgeous out there," he said to her, letting her go by the fingers and allowing her to sit beside me. He crossed his legs. "Though, I have to say, Alicia, the style isn't quite your forte."

The comment had all of us at the table looking at him, the randomness of it and how unnecessary it'd been. He basically told her she looked foolish when he himself hadn't even had the ambition to try.

Dampening my lips, I felt words on my tongue I didn't want to say. It'd make things weird and may embarrass Alicia even more than this... friend did.

She spoke before I could.

"Well, it's just for fun," she said, dipping her head a little before placing her hands on the table. Bracing them, she wouldn't face either of us at the table, no rebuttal to what was said to her.

I sipped again, keeping myself occupied and only came out of it when Alicia squeezed my leg slightly. It'd been quick, nothing more than a swift movement of her fingers but it'd been enough to let me know she was okay I supposed.

I wasn't though, a few things this guy had said not sitting well with me. Alicia had looked gorgeous tonight, but I didn't appreciate him saying that and doing so vocally to her.

Knowing I didn't know the details in regards to the comfort she had in their relationship, I stayed silent, letting the conversation move. One thing I learned about Ava in these past few months was she was good at attempting to make people feel at home. She engaged the man, actually sounding like she genuinely wanted to know more about Alicia's friend.

Needless to say he indulged her, almost to the point that revealed himself as his favorite conversation topic.

"Actually, I work in development. Not much unlike your Grayden here," he said, nodding at me.

This man and I were far from the same, but I stayed silent, doing so a virtue all of a sudden.

"That's actually how Alicia and I met," he went on, dropping his arm behind her chair. He spoke to the crowd. "She represents my firm, the best at what they do and definitely worth the billable hours."

Alicia's smile was only slow to move over her face, her fingers reaching and scratching the back of her neck. Shifting in her seat, she moved forward a little, Bastian's hand on her chair suddenly distant from her. Again, I didn't know their relationship, but this seemed off.

And definitely not reciprocated.

I leaned over. "Alicia?"

She barely looked at me, shaking her head before following along with what Bastian went on with and I sat back, put back. Tapping the table, I lost the train of the conversation and, really, wasn't seeing my place in it anymore.

Working my jaw, I checked my phone, going to get my kid an easy excuse.

Until I heard what I had next.

Alicia had been standing when it was said, her friend Ava next to her and tugging her for another dance. Alicia looked like she didn't want to go, but again, she was going to go.

And then came Bastian.

"Don't, sweetheart," he said, his hand on her wrist. He squeezed. "You'll just embarrass yourself again."

I remember a, "What is your problem," coming from my lips, his hand not leaving her arm fast enough. He stood first, but I'd been the one to engage, drawing Alicia away from in between us, which he took the wrong way. I just wanted his hands off her.

I just wanted her away from him.

He pushed, nothing but a tap on my arm, but it'd been enough for me to rear back.

It'd been enough for me to send him down with a single blow.

He was on the floor and suddenly everything was a blur, a crowd around us. Some had been our friends, some hadn't but the reaction was just the same. They all stood, silent and even the music in the background seemed to have stopped. Everything struck silent, a man's fingers to his lips as I cracked my fist right there. His mouth bleeding, Bastian let his fingers fall away and I'd never forget the expression on his face.

The smile moved slow across his mouth, the woman between us not going to me...

But taking care of him.

Twenty-Five

ALICIA

"Alicia?"

Bastian's fingers skated across my cheek and my stomach twisted, my body instinctually backing away from his touch.

His fingers lowered into the calm light of the room, my aunt's end table lamp in the living room the only light to see by. We came back here together in his car, not saying many words at all along the way.

The reason why in my hand, I lowered the damp towel I'd been tending to his busted lip, the edge a deep and angry crimson. Gray had gotten him so very good.

Dropping the towel into a basin of warm water, I squeezed it out and brought it to his lip again. It'd swollen pretty good on impact, but the size seemed steady at this point. He had the indentation of bruises as well above, the print of thick knuckles embedded in his skin. Considering his injury, Bastian said nothing of pain, simply sitting there while I cared for the wound in my aunt's living room. I guessed I felt it was the least I could do or something. I didn't know why.

Why are you doing this to yourself... again?

The question circulated my head, Bastian's and my history

playing out before me even in the dull light of this room, him and his dominating presence and me, who always seemed to find my way back to this place when it came to him. It all started in a world outside of this one.

It seemed it found me again.

It found me in this place I discovered an unexpected peace within. It'd been one I hadn't searched for but welcomed anyway. I loved it anyway.

My chest caving, I pressed the towel to Bastian's mouth again, not a word of discomfort on his end like before, but when his hand reached for me once more, my blouse this time, I took my own extremities back.

He simply stared at me, questions in his eyes, but I had my own. I had so many.

My hand squeezed the towel and "What are you doing here?" fell from my lips. This had been the main question that circulated my brain since he arrived. Why was he here?

And what did he want with me?

The man sat back on my couch, his suit jacket gone and his gray button-up rolled over the thickness of his full arms. Considering Bastian had been in a fight tonight, the only indicator was a slight tousle to the wave of his spiky hair.

His head tilted, his chest rising and falling with a single breath. Bringing his hand down from his mouth, he leaned forward, arms draped over his knees.

"I feel like the real question is why don't you want me here?"

He reached forward again, fingers intent on my chin but I pulled away once more, not letting him touch me.

His mouth closed.

"As well as why can't I touch you?"

He lounged back with those words and I shook my head.

"You said you wanted to take things slow," I told him, the word reverberating in my head like they had that day. He *wanted* to take things slow. He wanted to do his thing and let me do mine.

His fingers gathered at the top of his hair, and when he dropped them to the couch, his lips turned down.

"Yes, I did say that," he said, moving closer to me. "But I think we can both agree we've been taking things slow."

Swallowing, I panned away.

"Well, you can't have it both ways," I said and when I lifted the towel with intent to his lip, which started bleeding again, he grabbed my hand.

He brought the towel to his mouth, helping me wipe down his lips. The gesture was very intimate and I...

His hand replaced the towel, it dropping between us. He leaned forward and my only reaction was to move away.

"I don't want it both ways, Alicia," he said, drawing his body toward me. His hand touched the couch beside my hip and it would be too easy. It always had been easy.

But easy wasn't what I wanted anymore and that wasn't why I brought him here either.

Standing, I tried to find the reason, the bowl in my hand I placed on the end table near the lamp. My back to Bastian, I heard his breath behind me, a "You're different" causing me to turn around.

He had his arms hung behind the back of the couch, his gaze appraising me. It was as if he was looking for something, but I knew if he found out just what that something was it'd be the last thing he wanted to hear. He'd find out I had moved on from him, that slow was exactly what we should have been doing. We'd gotten together in a way we shouldn't have, his separation from his wife more than fresh when we initially hooked up.

It took time away from him to make me see that and that went beyond this place, beyond what my heart ended up finding.

He stood, his fingers touching his lips, and when he came away, blood coated his fingers.

"I suspected," he said suddenly, tongue touching down where his fingers had been. "That you were being unfaithful but I honestly didn't believe you the type."

"Bastian—"

"You're sleeping with him, Alicia," he said, the words no less a statement than me standing before him. He lifted his chin. "You're sleeping with that Grayden. No man reacts that way unless he feels what's his is being messed with."

He said it so calmly, so... cold and I wondered if he even cared.

But then again it'd make sense that he didn't.

Turning away, I intersected his hand, touching me and moving my chin in the direction of his gaze. I moved away and he only smiled, his hand coming down on the wall behind me.

"Like I said, I didn't believe you the type," he said, looking me up and down. "But don't be ashamed. I've been with others as well."

Of course he had.

I'd be surprised if he hadn't.

But still my lungs felt too small in the cavity that contained them, his hands on me drawing me in. He stared at me, the epitome of collected and I had no idea how I didn't see.

I had no idea why I felt I deserved this.

In all honestly, it took how it could be to make me see, know what it could truly be like to be cared about by someone. Gray had punched someone in a bar tonight. He punched someone to defend me.

And I went home with the man he was protecting me from.

I'd defaulted to old ways, disappointed in Gray being so

reactive when all he'd done was the right thing. All he did was love.

Bastian's hands smoothed down my arms, a squeeze in his hands before he brought them down to mine.

"We've gotten it out of our system," he said, moving forward. His strong smell stimulated my gag reflexes now. He looked down at me. "And once you come home, once you put this place behind you..."

He reached forward, again wanted to touch me, *brand* me in the ways he always had. One man never felt the need to do that in my life.

He'd been sure enough of himself where he never had to.

My hand cut him off this last time and I shook my head when I backed away.

I wouldn't put this place behind me because I wasn't coming home.

I was already here.

Twenty-Six

GRAY

I WAS LOUNGING against the front door of my trailer that night like I knew she'd be there.

Like I knew she'd come back to me.

She'd left with that guy, almost like he'd been an out, a means by which she could rid herself of this place and all that happened here. He was her familiar, her link to her world that didn't involve this town or me for that matter. He'd taken her away, no other words said after I hit him.

I'd hit him again any day of the damn week.

My shoulder fell from the doorframe as I watched Alicia come to me, the night around and her steps fast. I didn't know what to say to her, if I should apologize for hitting that guy or what. My guilt when it came to that issue was limited, but I didn't want to hurt her.

I wanted to lose her even less.

She stood in front of me, her rental car she currently drove in the distance, and she stood out of breath, her breasts rising and falling in her top. I supposed the apologies happened at this point and I would have no matter how little I regretted what I'd done. I would have done that for her if she needed it though, tail between my legs and all. Pride was only for that of foolish men and it took me learning that the hard way a long time ago to figure it out. I didn't have time for pride, life limited. Even still, I wasn't the first to engage her, truly not knowing *how* to act. After all, I may have hurt her by what I'd done to the guy she brought into all our lives.

But she cut me in two as well.

Holding herself, her shoulders shaking I nearly broke down and grabbed her, but then she stepped forward, dipping her head before pushing her arms around my torso.

She fit right in that perfect place, just below my neck and shoulder with her height. Her fingers into my open plaid shirt, she found her place, her energy and soft heat flowing through me.

I lifted an arm, accepting her. I didn't know what brought her here, but I wouldn't turn her away.

I guided her inside eventually like a man would his woman. Though, I had no idea what that meant for us. I remained hopeful and did what I normally would when it came to her.

Her vision panned once inside, her jacket sliding down her arms.

"She's in bed," I told her, assuming she was looking for Laura. By the time I got to her it had been late and I probably should have picked her up sooner.

Alicia's hands came together, her head nodding, and I invited her to sit on my couch. I'd been sorta watching television before she came over, not really.

We sat and, instinctually, I lifted my arm, welcoming her to come over.

Sliding right away, she gathered her legs underneath her, her hands on my chest and I listened to her breathing beneath the soft sounds of the television set. She remained silent for a long time, but the first words she said were "I'm sorry."

My eye closed softly to them, my arms sliding around her shoulders.

"I shouldn't have hit him," I told her, but then she looked up at me, smiling in her special way that made her curly lashes peek up at me.

"I wish I would have," she admitted. Not knowing what she meant by that, I pressed my fingers to her cheek.

"He didn't..." I started, vision clouding before my very eyes. I shook my head out of it. "He didn't touch you."

The fact I actually let her go tonight with that son of a bitch struck me hard, my shock the only reason I had. She'd looked at him in the way of showing sympathy tonight, and as I'd been the one to hurt him, I could react in no other way than to step back, give her space.

But if he'd hurt her...

"No, nothing like that, Gray," she stated, soothing me by pressing her fingers into my chest. Her lip was chewed with her next words.

"We were lovers, Bastian and I."

Something I suspected. Though, I hadn't been entirely sure.

It hurt no less.

The cave in my heart settled in, a slow collapse of the walls already vulnerable to her. She had a means to destroy my insides if she wanted to, something I'd allowed her to do over time.

Her gaze searched my face and slowly she was on her knees, her essence, that power before my eyes in the most beautiful woman I'd ever seen. Her lids closing, she moved her body forward and kissed me in a way that pulled all emotions to the forefront, her body languid against mine. Her lips pulled at my mouth, her teeth tugging my lower lip and I massaged a hand to her hip, unable to help myself.

"Alicia..."

"Gray."

Guiding a hand around her thigh, I brought her over my waist, pressing a kiss to her stomach.

The flesh beat with intensity under my mouth, her tummy quivering through her shirt and shaking beneath my touch.

"You're in my bed tonight," I told her, then took her there, my hands around her hips and her thighs locked to my waist.

We exchanged words tonight, ones I had no idea where they would lead or what they meant for us. A lot happened this evening, and for all I knew, she had that guy waiting for her when she left tonight.

But in my house, in my bed, she was mine. She was mine, as I pushed myself between her legs, kissing her folds and making her body sweat and shake. I was hers as she drove her nails into my back, branding me with red welts that'd be there long after she left me. She'd always be with me. It didn't matter how long or by what means I tried to forget. She embedded herself in me and though I had resisted for a time there'd be no more of that. The damage was done.

She had my heart in her hand.

Pressing her thighs down to my bed, I arched up, the woman a goddess in my sheets. They already smelled of her and our lovemaking, her soft feminine scent filling the room and making it hers.

Drawing my tongue up her inner thigh, I tasted her juices, which had escaped, her thighs twitching and coming to wrap around my head. She wanted me inside her, her sweet heat, but I held her at bay, tasting her. I needed to remember this, how it felt.

My hand smoothed down the fullness of her deep-ebony toned legs, my body arching up so I could suck her tit, the dark areola peaked and ready to be laved with my tongue.

I went there, grabbing her other breast before I dipped my

head, but she stopped me, her gaze on me in a way that could rip me apart. It was ripping me apart.

Cupping her cheek, I wanted to tell her to choose me, that I'd be there for her.

I really would make it everything for her.

"Gray?"

There were questions in her eyes, questions that caused me to close mine.

Peeling her fingers from my cheek, I spread her legs, filling her like I had that first time, nothing between us. It hadn't been a deliberate thought.

It just felt right.

Her eyes rolled back as she took me in deep, her head rolling on my sheets and truly making them hers. They could be and I wanted her to take them.

I brought her arms back behind her head, extending myself and using my knees to rock into her. My thighs slapped the inside of hers, a burn with every hit to her soft flesh.

Her breasts shook, her eyes closed and I took that moment to kiss her, tell her everything I wanted.

"Stay," seeped from my lips, the ache in my voice a fervent want. "Stay and say you're mine."

I wanted her to feel it, to know how it could be. We could do this. We could be our own forever.

She held me tight with every word, every kiss and thrust between her trembling legs. Her sweat, her passion, I could taste in my mouth and I almost missed the words so quickly. They'd been passion-filled, raw like mine had been.

She'd said, "Yes," and then, "You're my home."

Twenty-Seven

ALICIA

THE NOTES FILLED the wide hall of the church in the most exuberant way, the ones following mine not as loud but just as strong. Laura played with confidence beside me, our duet together not our first but the debut of her playing for a crowd. She'd been an excellent student in the past few weeks, expressing interest in learning to play piano well early on. She'd been patient. She'd been hungry, and today, the world got to see her in this morning's service. Laura had been nervous about playing, naturally some of that old shyness creeping back within her. She had grown in bounds, a lifetime in a few months and that bravery continued on as she pressed those keys with a life that we'd all seen form within her.

One would be hard-pressed to see that eight-year-old of before now, a little girl in her Sunday best while literally a congregation held onto her every sound. She wanted to play at the service, which preceded the church bazaar, all who desired to display a talent invited to play today. This church had been highlighted with the music and feeling of a small town, many voices and instruments performed in only a few hours. It'd been a time of magic and blessings I'd been fortunate to be a part of, a little girl wanting me beside her as she played amongst the lot. Laura had dedicated this performance to her daddy, the man sitting in the front row with his shirt ironed and his hair moussed after a fresh haircut. Gray usually sat in the back during services we'd attended in the past.

He sat up front today.

He'd held Laura's hand just before she came up here, mine in her other, and together, we pushed those nerves full out. She *had* this. The world had always been hers.

I heard nothing of voices, chatter, or even breathing during her playing. It was just Laura with the accompaniment of myself and how the world rang after we were done.

She sat there with the final note, her hands on the keys while applause boomed around her, and leaning, I touched my head on top of hers.

"Look," I told her, smiling wide across her crown. She always smelled of sunshine, heaven's little angel. "They adore you."

She looked up after my words, seeing that adoration, but her vision didn't leave the front row. Gray's booming applause I was sure could be heard well beyond the front row, but he wasn't allowed to do it long.

Laura jumped up from the piano bench but she hadn't made it to him before he made it to her. Down on one knee, he brought his arm around her, a rose he had on the pew in his hand. Upon giving it to her, he spoke words I couldn't hear over the sound in the room, but I didn't need to read lips to know he was proud of her.

Some days I truly didn't believe my life and the decisions I'd made following up to the very point of it. They'd been decisions I hadn't made lightly and would require time to work themselves out completely. I had a life before this place, obligations and commitments well before the town of Mayfield, Kansas. They'd need my care to make sure they panned out, but the toughest hurdle had already been overcome.

I let myself be happy.

The church was a wash of activity following the performance of Laura and several others who dared to put themselves out there for their community. It'd been a day of happiness and smiles and the energy due to it was easy to become addicted to. There was beauty in such simplicity and I myself had been fortunate enough to be at the forefront of a lot of the gleeful chatter. By now, the entire community had pretty much heard of my intent to stay, more than a few hugs of welcome casted my way. The church bazaar followed the performances and I was basically hugged out by the time the event started. So much love was sent my way, the people of this town a true oddity to me. I'd never been cared about as much as I had by so many new people in my life. It was nice.

Ava, Jolene, and myself were placed in charge of the bake sale portion of the bazaar and we started right away in getting the foundation set up and the tasty treats donated, plated, and labeled with signage. Gray had been good for the set up, a strong back and a huge pair of arms to make sure everything was structured in the way it should be structured. He and a few other congregation members contributed to that, and I had to say, put on a nice little show for even some of the married women of the church. The women seemed to have found their way over to Ava, Jolene, and me, talking to us while we set up, yes, but watching the men just the same with subtle smiles. By the time Gray and the other men finished, I'd pretty much heard the voices of the entire female population of the town, everyone at service today and the bazaar.

Gray came over to me after, a hammer in his hand after he set up a makeshift display table to go on top of one of the folding platforms. The man seemed to always have a hammer in his hand these days despite concluding the project for me. I may have been busy recovering from the fallout of deciding to stay here, putting in resumes for local law offices both here and in neighboring towns and cementing my life here, but he was taking on jobs several towns over, his day to day extremely busy.

But I knew it made him so, so happy.

The man's smile couldn't be kept off his face these days and he shined it on me, welcoming me by a touch of the hip. His hand ventured to go higher, until averted eyes by Jolene, Ava, and the other women who lingered in a circus fashion around him let him know now wasn't the time for that, unfortunately. Instead, he offered to brush a kiss on my cheek.

"Are you okay here?" he asked, pulling away. "I have to take Laura back to the house."

"Oh?" I asked, knowing he meant *his house* despite what we'd talked about. We hadn't spoken to Laura yet about the changes that were arising, but not out of fear. We actually planned to take her on a mini vacation outside of the city, make a real thing of it and let her know she and Gray would be moving into my aunt's house with me.

Make a family thing out of it.

Gray had been in an absolute tizzy trying to plan it, and because of that fact, I decided to take the reins, the trip in our near future.

He nodded, a flash of grin to his full lips. He had the kind perfect for sucking and I did often.

He rubbed the smile away a little. "Yeah, she left a plate of cookies for today on the counter. I told her you all look like you got it handled," he paused, gaze sliding over the buffet of goodies that *still* seemed to be coming in. He chuckled. "But she's insistent. She feels bad and stayed up most of the night making them. Well, basically I made them but she helped."

I could only think, *"Could this man be more sweet?"* I was hard-pressed, it took me so long to realize it. He'd been so sharp with me at first, a blade, which cut at the easiest instance. Eventually, that razor edge dulled and I was glad it had.

I told him of course it was fine he left me, more than. I got a soft kiss on my forehead and the ladies behind me a wave, which caused half of them to blush before going away, Ava included. Jolene had the decency to avert her eyes, but Ava came right over, gratefully the appearance ended up being her asking if I was ready to work.

I tapped her shoulder. "Always."

She handed me pies and we went on, setting up the rest of the displays. The bazaar didn't officially start for another twenty minutes or so and we still had several boxes of cakes and things that needed to be broken down. Even the town's local bakery donated items and I had a feeling many would end up on my kitchen table. They all looked so delectable.

I must have been smiling while placing because both Ava *and* Jolene stared at me by the time I got done setting up my last box. My return stare inquisitive, Ava simply brushed my shoulder.

She shrugged. "It's just nice to see you happy," she said, shaking her head a little before using a box cutter to the back of a box. "That everything worked out."

"Worked out?"

Her gaze went up slightly, a smile in her eyes. "Everything with Gray. You guys seem happy."

"We all see it." Jolene cut in with that last part, arranging some pies.

The fact everyone knew what was going on in my personal life though unsaid used to alarm me, but as this was such a small town, it no longer did. It was wonderfully small.

I couldn't stop the smile on my face, agreeing with them. I stepped with a box and was nearly sideswiped by a little girl, Laura's friend Jasmine. It seemed without her cohort, Laura back at the house getting cookies, that the young girl was wild and free and Jolene slid an arm around her niece, the girl looking so much like her with her flourish of red hair.

"We pay attention now, don't we?" she told the young girl, but she tugged on her braid with a smile after she said the words.

"It's fine," I told them both. "And I am happy. It did work out."

It worked out so well it scared me sometimes. There were still some things about Gray that lingered in the wanderings of my brain, but these were things I knew over time I'd gain answers to. It'd just take the time of knowing him and getting to know him beyond those things that no longer needed knowing. I knew the man's heart already though, his soul.

I knew his love.

He was an incredibly good person and maybe the best I'd ever found myself around and that, well, that was enough.

Jolene went on with her tasks, letting Jasmine play near us with a beanbag she kicked around and Ava shook my arm.

"That's so wonderful," she said to me. "And even more that you're *staying* from what I hear."

I was surprised she *hadn't* brought that up sooner, the first to give her two cents most days.

What could I say, I loved the girl.

"Yes," I said and she grinned.

"So Jo's property... you're staying on it and everything?" she asked with a hair flip up, almost an afterthought as she moved onto another box filled with cupcakes.

I nodded. "That's the plan. I still have a lot of things to figure out."

Up until literally a few weeks ago I had been intending to sell, the developer picked out and everything. I had people giving offers well over market value following the write-ups in the many publications my aunt's house had been a part of. It'd actually been helpful for me to find buyers. I had people falling out of my aunt's windows wanting to turn the place into everything from a campground to a resort, the house itself untouched, but the land around it and even part of the town included in the restructuring of the project. They wanted to launch something huge, something that would change this town on its head and though progressive it really wouldn't be the same town. It would change it.

"I can imagine," Ava said, eyes on me. "But everything will be okay. I know it."

"Oh, it will." I smiled at her, leaning on a box. "I'll figure it all out. Well, Gray and I. He's been really helpful with all the decisions and everything. He's going to make sure my aunt's land is treated right."

He'd probably keep up with it until his dying day if I let him.

Would we get that far?

I hoped so and the very thought had me smiling.

Ava gave me a knowing smile and she went silent while we finished setting up. A beanbag hit one of our tables at one point, which got Jasmine chastised by Jolene. I retrieved it for the girl, saying it wasn't a big deal before giving it back to her.

"What do you say?" Jolene questioned, eyeing her.

Dark-green eyes and a huge smile went shy on Jasmine's face.

"Thanks, Ms. Alicia," she said, chewing her lip a little.

I smiled. "No problem and it really isn't a big deal."

That one had been for Jolene, the woman patting Jasmine's shoulder. She guided her off to play, but her niece lingered a second. She followed us around from table to table, playing with the little decorative streamers we placed around the baked items. I figured with her new intrigue Jolene would send her off and I think she would have.

If not for what she said.

"Now that Ms. Alicia is staying everything will be good," she said, smiling wide. "Now that she's not selling everything will be good."

I didn't understand what she'd said and her saying something of that nature was quite odd to me, causing me to look up at her.

I ended up panning *over to* her and I had some eyes before me, ones that'd definitely heard what she said.

Jolene's hands came together and Ava's eyes... well, escaped entirely. It seemed the inside of her arms became her fascination when she crossed them and Jolene put her hand softly on Jasmine's tiny shoulder.

"Run along," she told her. *"Run along"* like she didn't say something weird.

Like she didn't say something weird that involved me.

The young girl skipped off and that left a vacancy in the air, one in which I wanted answers to and no one was giving them, both ladies' eyes on everything but me.

My arms folded, I approached Jolene, her niece the one that said the words.

"What's going on?" I asked. "Why did she say that?"

A breeze of her bright, auburn bangs flipped when she lifted her head. The school teacher opened her mouth perhaps to say something, but Ava seemed to have finally found her voice.

"It's okay, Jolene," she said, her jaw moving a little. "I'll talk to her."

The teacher left us to our peace and more of that silence occurred, which at this point, was really testing my patience. Ava had moved over to one of the pie tables at this point, tapping her fingers on it and I joined her.

"Ava?" I questioned. "What's going on?"

She had no words for me at first, kicking her boot behind her and then...

"What do you want me to say, Alicia?"

My eyes flashed, not understanding.

"Say...?"

She nodded, her eyes sad all of a sudden. I wasn't used to this on her, not at all. She may have been shy sometimes but was never sad.

Nor ashamed.

Her arms moved over the other, her gaze panning over the little world of busy townsfolk, which worked around us.

"We just figured," she started, eyes moving, sight circulating. "We just figured if you saw all this, saw *Mayfield* and everything... Got to know us and all that you wouldn't..."

She said... *us*.

My gaze travelled now, everyone around us working, but in *this* part of the bazaar, this part of my world was crumbling.

"You didn't want me to sell?" I concluded, the reality coming in a chilling wave. "You didn't want me to sell so you were what...? *Nice* to me—"

She had always been nice. She'd always been *there* and well before recently with inviting Gray and me along to functions with her friends. She was always there.

She was always good.

"That's not why I—"

She came closer, but I veered away, my arms tight around me.

Ava's hand closed like she was attempting to reach out, touch me when she truly knew she shouldn't.

Her mouth moved. "That's not what it was like."

"Then what was it like?"

"It was..." Her voice stopped on the end like she was trying to choose her words, her lashes lifted when she seemed to have found them.

"That's what it started as," she admitted, the dagger sharp, the slit inside deep. "But then we got to know each other."

They'd gotten to know me, this town. It'd become less trying to get Josephine's niece not to sell and more about actually liking her at some point, knowledge in which most likely the whole town was in on.

Everyone except me.

The reality had me turn from her, a tremor in my arms. It filled me up, angered me, and even more when I remembered one other person. He'd been *the* person, the one that mattered most with his daughter.

My phone in my hand, I started dialing, but then I heard his voice. My vision panned out the door, the church event room open to the sun. A clear view of the parking lot displayed from here and that's where Gray was, his daughter's hand in his. He let her run out, then tugged her back into a hug.

"Alicia?"

Ava's hand pushed over my shoulder, the hand of whom I thought had been my friend.

"Alicia... it all changed."

Meaning she was actually my friend now. It all was no longer a ruse, but the thing was, it took two people to make a friendship.

And maybe I didn't want to be her friend anymore.

Leaving her hand, I heard her call my name, which I ignored. I needed to ask someone something, his eyes lighting up the minute he watched me cross the threshold of the church.

But then he saw it, saw something in my eyes. The realization caused him to let go of both his smile and Laura's hand, his own guiding behind her shoulder.

"Did you know?" I asked before I even got to him, Laura between us. "Did you know about the town? People pretending to be nice? People pretending to be my—"

He'd gotten to me at this point because I stopped unable to go any further.

My lashes lifted. "Did you know about the town trying to get me not to sell my aunt's estate?"

His gaze travelled over my face in a way that didn't necessarily tell of guilt, but not unknowing either. The very existence of the latter drove the wind clear out of me and he squeezed Laura's arm.

"Laura, go play."

"Laura, stay."

Her attention ventured between us both, not knowing what to do. This man was her father.

But I was her friend.

We'd gained more than that, this girl and me, and because we had, she wasn't moving, Gray pulling her back into a hug since she wasn't.

His face straightened, serious, but he wasn't talking quick enough.

"Did you know?" I asked, truly not a hard question. "Did you know and were you in on it too?"

"Of course I didn't want you to sell, Alicia," he said, shocking the hell out of me in the purest form. He'd been so honest. He shook his head. "I didn't want developers coming in here, slashing up Jo's property."

"So you knew? So you—"

I started to walk away but he used a hand, grabbing me. He made me stay with that hand and he made me listen despite what he'd already done to my heart. He'd done a number on it. He really had.

Breathing, he pushed his hand down my arm.

"I may have heard word about it," he said. "This is a small town, and yes, I may have heard something."

I closed my eyes and he guided me closer, his voice near my ear.

"But listen to me when I say I had *nothing* to do with this," he went on. "I may have not wanted you to sell, but I respected your decision. Damn—" He reconsidered his words when he noticed Laura below. He squeezed me. "Alicia, I helped you for God's sake."

He may have helped me and even respected me, but that didn't leave him victimless. He had knowledge of something he could have shared with me at anytime.

He just chose not to.

Leaving his hands, I couldn't hear anymore.

"Alicia!"

My name called wasn't deep but light, the sound of a little girl.

Her voice truly almost had me turning around, but I couldn't stop my steps, moving forward. Somewhere in the distance I heard a, "Let her go," then a quieter version of the same. "Let her go."

Twenty-Eight

ALICIA

The home of Josephine Bradley rattled that evening, rocked with anger and a storm amongst other things. The wild of winds and rain slammed upon the house after such a perfect day and kept me up, kept me in my head more than I liked. Eventually, I fell back asleep, but came out of it with a dream that had me circulating the house.

As well as ripping up boxes.

I went in search of something I saw as clear as day, needing something, anything of truth. I'd had so many people lie to me, Ava, Jolene...

Even Gray.

He had in a way by omission no matter how unintended. I couldn't trust people like I thought I'd been able to. I questioned everything. If I had rushed into the decision of staying here and if I had should I move forward with the plans to stay. Everything in my head was a screwed-up mess of doubt and confusion, but one thing made sense, the dream I had.

Where is it? I know it's here.

The fifth box I found in my aunt's basement left me empty, the visions in my head I knew had to be true. I hadn't just dreamt them. They *happened* and I had to find the evidence of it, a photograph.

On the sixth box, I found my proof. It'd actually been right underneath a photo my aunt had of herself and her sister, my mom, when they'd been in their youth. I had no idea the time period of the photograph, but my mom's face resembled that of my own young memories.

She looked just like me in her twenties, the same wide eyes and soft features. My mom was beautiful and I was glad I had so many photos such as this at my own home.

Home...

I had no idea where that was for me at the present, but I hoped finding this evidence was the key. Placing the photo of my mom and aunt to the side, I picked up the one underneath.

It was the two of us, my aunt Josephine and myself. I sat back in my nightgown, my bottom touching down in the hallway I'd been ripping boxes I drug up from the basement in. Crossing my legs, I waved my hand over the photograph I remembered being in when it was taken, the memories so fuzzy.

My mom had taken this. I remembered that.

I remembered my mom telling me to smile into the camera, but I hadn't had to. I had my aunt Jo's arms around me, her warm loving embrace. I remembered never wanting to leave it.

She always gave the best hugs.

My head hurting, I pulled for more memories of the woman in the photo, a woman who looked so much like my mom, me. Even a decade over my mom they could have been twins and very similar to myself today in her features, her natural set of wild curls around her head the only difference between us.

I smoothed my hand over the older photograph. This was

when people actually took and developed pictures instead of snapping a photo with their camera phones. It was a different time, a great time.

My eyes itching, I realized I had tears in them when they slid a heated trail down my cheek. I rubbed them away with my sleeve, the soft material I'd found in her closet. My aunt's old nightgowns smelled like amber and honeysuckle. They smelled like her and I loved them.

I smiled at her in the photo.

What should I do?

I called out to her with my mind like she could answer back and the thrashing of the winds on my door almost kept me from hearing the lightest knock ever imaginable. Sitting in the hallway, I had been able to hear it but definitely didn't understand it. It was late, too late for visitors.

In the back of my mind as I got up, I figured it might be Gray for some reason, wanting to fix whatever happened today with a few words and his presence. I wasn't sure it'd be that easy though.

I just didn't know who to trust anymore.

No large frame silhouetted outside the opaque glass so I knew it wasn't him and the figure had been much shorter at my door.

Laura jumped into my arms the moment the door opened.

Alarmed, the little thing pressed her face into my stomach, nearly shivering and covered in rain and the storm's elements.

"Alicia..."

Her trembled cry into my waist had me holding her, my hands folded behind her. She basically shook like a leaf on my stoop and my thoughts immediately traveled toward the depths.

And the fact that her father *wasn't* with her today.

Squatting, I got to her level, pressing my hand to her face. The questions would have ensued if not for her frantic cries.

"Please don't leave. Please don't be mad at my dad."

Her arms pushed around my neck, the strength of this little girl almost made me fall back. Gripping the porch with one hand and her with the other, I cupped the back of her head.

"Laura, what's going on? What are you—"

She peeled away with tears in her eyes, her face flushed and strands of her dark hair sticking to her round cheeks. She was covered in rain, her hair messed about and the fact she'd truly had somehow made her way over here rang clear before me.

"Dad said I had to let you go, but please don't go. Please don't be mad at him."

"Laura—"

"Please, Alicia. Whatever he did I'm sure he's sorry."

"Honey, your daddy didn't do anything." I shook my head, confused. She was speaking a mile a minute and I didn't understand.

The storm gaining behind her, I rose, taking her by the shoulder and guiding her into the house. A child, she went on about her dad and me being mad and I caught up with her as I took her saturated raincoat, then laid her damp boots out to dry. Her clothing had miraculously managed to remain unscathed in all this, but I still got a towel to dry her hair.

"But, but, but why did you leave church then?" she breathed, finally taking a moment to while I squeezed out her pigtails on the couch. None of the curls I put in them remained from earlier that day. After getting them as dry as I could I looked at her.

"I left because I had some things to figure out," I told her, telling her the truth. I put my hands on my lap. "Did you walk all the way over here?"

Her furious nod followed a rub of her eyes. She was still crying and coming down from whatever this was. I decided to take her into the kitchen and get her a cup of cocoa to warm her up. We got her a blanket along the way and I grabbed my cellphone as well, thinking I needed to call her dad.

"Your dad must be in a frenzy," I said, knowing that was putting things lightly. He lived on the other side of town and for her to walk all the way here without him and in a storm at that?

I dialed, her resistance moving toward me when she grabbed my arm.

"Please don't call him. He'll be mad."

Damn right he would, but he needed to know.

I put my hand on her head. "He needs to know you came over here and you shouldn't have, not by yourself anyway."

"He doesn't know I left," she said, peeking up at me with the blanket over her shoulders. "He was sleeping when I left. Please, Alicia. It took him all night to finally go to sleep."

The reality of that had my eyes closing and, eventually, I did hang up the phone.

"He gets a call in a little bit then. You're off the hook."

After acknowledging what I said with a nod, she stood back, a sniffle in her red-tipped nose. I got her cocoa heated up quickly and we took it into the living room, both of us coming down from the excitement of both the evening and the day.

Laura took her cocoa on the couch, the blanket around her shoulders while she lay under my arm.

"You shouldn't have come over here, honey," I told her, shaking my head. "Your dad's going to have a fit."

She said nothing to my words, simply sipped her cocoa and sniffed again.

"Why did you leave?" she edged out, her lashes flickering as she stared at my lap and I sighed, crossing my legs in her direction.

Pushing my hand down her hair, I guided her to look up at me, those cheeks still rosy and sweet.

I smiled at them. "Sometimes grownups need time to work things out."

Her brown eyes traveled around the room.

"That's what Daddy said," she concluded, taking another sip of her chocolate and the words had me laughing a little.

Her daddy was a very intelligent man, and even though I knew that, this all was so much more complicated.

The soft rumble of the storm whooshed around us and Laura sipped her cocoa, no other words about her father said. Nestling herself up on me, she stared at my lap and suddenly tiny fingers slid into the pocket of my bathrobe.

My aunt's photo peeked out the top and I grabbed it for her, smiling when I took her cup and exchanged it for the photograph. Weathered, the two people inside were a little hard to make out, but clearly she knew the older woman was my aunt.

I'd never seen her around my aunt Jo obviously, but she knew her, her small fingers running over the photograph.

"That's me," I told her, watching her. "My aunt Jo and me when I was a kid."

I couldn't have been much older than her. In fact, I knew I couldn't have been, only a few summers spent at this place.

Laura's small fingers travelled down the photograph and when her hand stopped on my aunt, curling on the worn paper, I questioned whether or not I should continue to let her study the photo. Laura had a lot of pain, only a snapshot of which I'd gathered from her dad. He said she'd taken my aunt's death very hard, closed off into herself worse than she'd been.

"Laura?"

She didn't look up at me and the silence sent a tremor into my heart.

My hand smoothing down her shoulder, she leaned into me, her face buried into my side.

"Why did she leave?" came suddenly, her eyes closing and I cupped her cheek, a few tears falling down my fingertips. I didn't know what to say to her, not good at these things.

I'd never been... good with children. I hadn't been until her.

"She really didn't," I told her, hoping, *praying* for the right words. Her tear-stained eyes looked up at me and I smiled at her, that salty trail underneath the pad of my fingers.

"She's with you, Laura. In your heart. She never left."

She'd heard about the afterlife in church and I knew she was aware of the concepts, but still, she was so very young.

Her tiny throat jumped before her words.

"But I miss her," she cried a little, blinking down tears. "I miss her so much."

"And she misses you, but she sees you. I know she sees you every day."

She hugged me after that. She hugged me so hard and I didn't want to let go of her either. My aunt was with her.

She was with both of us.

I told her as such and she nodded, her tears eventually falling away. Her arms moving around my waist, she breathed into me, closing her eyes.

"She sent me you," she said before she fell asleep, and this time, it was my turn to cry. I knew she meant what she said, and in my heart, I think I knew she was right.

I let her sleep as long as I felt she should before daring to move. I needed to call her dad. She'd been there too long with me.

Easing from underneath her, I replaced myself with a pillow, covering her with a blanket before heading into the kitchen. After getting my phone my first thought was to call Gray, but the amount of missed calls on my cell struck an alarm through me. They weren't from Gray.

But from Bastian.

Twenty-Nine

ALICIA

"Alicia... This is very important. Is Grayden near you?"

He had no right to ask this question. He had no right to ask me *anything* for that matter, but this particular question was more than off-limits. I'd been very firm where we left things as far as our relationship was concerned. I'd told him *the truth* for the first time since we developed a relationship together surrounding what I wanted. I told him *my wants* and they didn't include him.

Forcing myself to calm down, I gripped the phone. I only answered because he called me so many times.

"I think I need to hang up now," I told him, the certainty of that decision more than clear. "You don't get to ask about Grayden and me."

"Alicia, this isn't some—" His voice severed into whatever room he was in and he forced a breath into the receiver. "This isn't some jealous phone call from your raging ex. I told you when I'd been there I was at peace with your decision."

In fact he'd been chillingly "at peace," which only confirmed I'd made the right one. He'd been ready to leave, move on if there'd been nothing for him with me. I guess I hadn't been surprised after finding out he'd had affairs behind my back as well if you could even call them that. Two people had to be in an actual committed relationship to cheat on one other.

We were just two people going slow.

He didn't wait for me to come back onto the line before he breathed into the phone again.

"Now, I'm going to repeat my question. Is Grayden with you? This isn't some invasive question. I need to know because the information concerns your well-being."

Whatever bullshit he was spinning I wasn't buying, but the fact he'd called me so many times…

And now the seriousness in his voice.

My jaw moved a little, my legs crossing after I took a slow seat at the kitchen table. I could see Laura from here on the couch, still sleeping where I left her.

"What is this?" I asked, panning away and he asked me next if I had my laptop. I did, working on it just that morning before church.

I entertained at least that part of his call, but only for convenience. He didn't ask about Grayden again, but I assumed he believed he wasn't around because I made no maneuvers to silence my voice or shuffle from the room. Maybe in the end, he just didn't care because of whatever urgent thing he needed to tell me.

"I need you to open your email," he said, the tick in his voice gone and now replaced with a semblance of ease. "I've sent you something and I want you to look at it."

I brought up my account, logging in as I let Laura play on my laptop sometimes. I didn't mind her being on it but I often did have important correspondence there an eight-year-old could easily get into.

Pressing the phone to my ear, I crossed my legs.

"Okay, it's open."

"Good. Do you see my email? I sent you two links."

I had already clicked on the message when he said the words, the two links he referred to there in a no-subject email.

"I'm going to start with I don't feel like I owe you anything, Alicia. But we had a good run and... I couldn't in good faith leave things and *you* in a situation in which I feel could be detrimental to you and your well-being. I don't think you know Grayden like you feel you do. You couldn't possibly."

His accusations of whatever this was he felt he knew about Grayden and me had me pushing my hand off the keys again.

"You're tiptoeing a line, Bastian."

"Well, watch me leap over it," he said, being real. "I need you to open the first link I just sent you. Don't argue. Just do it."

The fact he was commanding me didn't sit well with me. He had a lot of power in our relationship, the majority of the time he took advantage of. Those days were no more, but this, him coming at me with all this noise was even odd for him. Bastian wasn't the type of man to raise his voice or even hell to get people to do what he wanted. He simply would just *be* and people understood that and what it meant. I had been one of those people, but I couldn't ignore all this noise he was in fact sending my way.

My finger smoothing over my trackpad, I pushed the cursor in the direction of the first link.

"I knew I saw his face before," was all he said and I clicked the link, a *New York Times* online article coming up.

"Dalton © Founder Liquidates Assets."

My gaze skimmed over the headline, Bastian speaking before I could travel further down.

"You're seeing an article about the manufacturing company *Dalton*. Have you heard of it?"

I had, though I'd had no dealings with them. My firm

often handled clients who constructed major properties, hotels being one of them. That's how I met Bastian in a hotel construction and companies like *Dalton* supplied the raw materials for the construction. The company based in New York City, I had no direct dealings with them, as my firm was based in Chicago.

"Of course," I told him. "Though, I've never worked with them."

"Well, I have," Bastian went on. "They provided supplies for a few of my hotels on the east coast, but after the scandal, we promptly pulled out and went with another vendor."

"Scandal?"

He, "Mmhmm'ed" into the line. "The article I sent you talks about the CEO. He went MIA about three years ago. Liquidated his assets and everything. The fucker even sold off his *shares*, then went off the grid. Sent the stock market into a tailspin for months."

"Okay, where did he go?"

His silence poked raised flesh along my skin and I moved forward, my gaze finding Laura. She still slept peacefully, undisturbed with the pillow under her head.

"The only evidence of him was what he did with his assets. The fucker sold everything off, little by little until there was nothing left. No one knew why until fraud turned up in his company, embezzlement behind his back, and I guess the man got out before things got hot. Smart, but still a surprise. He probably could have stuck around and worked it out with the support he had. Regardless, that's what he ended up doing with the money, but Davenport himself, no one really knew what was going on with him for another year or so."

He said a lot, made me absorb a lot, but one thing stood out in particular to what he said, one name.

"Davenport?" The name left my voice in a whisper and all Bastian told me to do was scroll down. There'd been a photo accompanying the article I never got to read, the piece explained to me, and had I actually read it I would have seen it.

I would have seen Gray.

He donned a suit, a handsome smile on his face while he stared seemly into the light with his hands together. He'd been fashioned to pose this way, a promotional photo of sorts with his hair smoothed back and his face clean-shaven. The photo in color, no gray resided in streaks of his dark, almost raven-colored locks and something else I noticed, no age was under those bright eyes.

I had no idea why a picture of him was tagged to the byline of this article.

It didn't make sense at all.

"That's *Grayden*, Alicia," Bastian said in my ear like he knew the exact moment I saw him, figured it out. "That's Grayden Davenport, former CEO of *Dalton Inc.*"

My head shook involuntarily, my thoughts trying to catch up with his words and the vision in front of my eyes. No, Grayden wasn't a former CEO.

No, Grayden wasn't one of the richest men in America.

Grayden was a handyman, *my* Grayden was just Grayden.

My chest reeled in shock, my stomach pummeled. Speech wasn't possible and breathing even questionable.

"Alicia, it is him," Bastian went on, once again like he knew, *he knew* I couldn't speak. "I actually met him albeit briefly. His people never really let anyone near him and even our business dealings had been through third parties. I only came across him at a party we both attended in the Hamptons. He'd been drunk off his ass then and not really company I tend to keep."

My head was in my hands, my hair falling around my arms. We weren't talking about the same Gray. Gray didn't drink. Gray didn't party. He hated parties, a social pariah.

My vision took the image again, this man really not Grayden. He didn't have the weight of the world in his eyes, his face so much younger in this photo. It was only things here and there I could make out like his distinguished jawline.

And a smile that could easily capture hearts.

Other than those things this was a different person and completely different than the things Bastian said.

"I don't understand," I kept saying over and over. My hand to the monitor, I touched him, the warm heat from the screen under the pads of my fingers.

"What happened to you?"

My words went out to Gray, the man on the screen before me, but Bastian answered, his voice low in the phone.

"Click on the second link," he said, and though shaking, I did. Another online article popped up but on the New York Police Department's website. No picture accompanied this, but documentation was present. There was a warrant there.

It called for the arrest of a one "Grayden Davenport."

My eyes skimmed, looking for the charges, but Bastian, on his game, gave me that one too. He said it right away and, again, gave my brain no time to catch up.

Nor try to hide the smugness in his voice.

"Kidnapping," he said. "Kidnapping of his own kid."

Thirty

GRAY

A TIMID KNOCK hit my door and I calmed only a little.

It has to be her.

But it wasn't my daughter. It was Alicia, the drips of a steady rain around her as the raindrops hit her red umbrella and fell to the near-flooding ground. In the distance, her rental car sat but it wasn't running nor was there a familiar face in the front seat.

My phone fell from my ear, the woman I'd been calling nonstop standing before me. She hadn't answered one of my calls, and my truck keys in hand, I'd been in the process of heading over to her house.

I dipped into the storm. "Alicia."

The sight of her told of my need for her, her mere presence like a way to recapture air.

"She's missing," I told her, blinking around raindrops. "Laura's missing. I can't find her. I…"

The words accompanied a sickness, which chased itself up my throat and I wondered if not for Alicia grabbing my arm if I'd been heading for the ground. Sometime, someway, she'd guided me out of the rain, my mind blank and the simple construction of words I found a heavy challenge.

"Gray?"

She materialized before me, long, dark hair untouched by the rain and full lips I took every advantage to kiss when I could. They deserved to be kissed, made love to every day.

Closing them, she pushed her hair out of her face, dropping the open umbrella to my carpet before closing my open door. She stayed there, at the door when closed, and sometime in that moment, I got my thoughts back.

"We have to go find her," I said. "Something's wrong. I tried to call you. I don't know why she left."

I could have only slept for a couple hours, but even that sleep had been restless. I'd been concerned about Alicia and where we left things.

I said a lot to her, Alicia, but even still she remained by the door. Approaching her, I would have made it to her had she not raised her hand.

She actually raised to me, *for me* to stop, and her gaze averted as her raincoat dripped droplets to my carpet.

"Alicia, did you *hear* me," I said, not understanding. "Laura's out there—"

"She's fine, Grayden."

She'd finally looked up at me with my name, the *Grayden* on her lips more than tense. Her expression had actually changed when she said it, her eyes sad as if something had caused her pain.

My phone dropped to my side, both her words and demeanor not making sense.

"You know where she is?" I asked and with her nod that calm again only lessened a bit. She said she knew where she was.

But I noticed she didn't tell me.

"What's going on?" I asked and with another step, she

stiffened this time, as if me getting closer would actually hurt her. Her gaze had also averted again and her hand gripped her coat-covered arm like a safety net.

I stood stationary, the warnings in my head going off like alarm bells, her reaction to me and lack of information about my kid.

I shook my head. "Where's my daughter, Alicia?"

She said nothing and I chose to repeat my words again.

"Alicia. Where is Laura—?"

"She's safe, Grayden."

There it was again... Grayden.

She hadn't called me Grayden since I met her, the sudden formality not lost on me.

We stood in a room pregnant with silence, our accompaniment that of the anger that brewed outside. Tree branches rasped at my windows like they were tearing their way inside me, and again, no words of elaboration were said by Alicia.

Testing her, I came forward and despite how closed off she was being I didn't stop. It actually took her saying the command to make me.

My steps froze with the sudden words and my swallow was terribly hard.

"Why?" I asked her, my question of many. Why wouldn't she tell me where Laura was other than the fact she was safe?

And why couldn't I go near her?

My mind had travelled to that of the worst-case scenario in my life many times before. I'd had reasons, but over time, the anxiety of the thoughts lessened. It had partially to do with this town, most with a woman name Josephine, but even more with the woman before me. She allowed me to trust again, trust in people and the possibility of having goodness in my life.

My hand closed around my phone, the device I knew I

ruined in the rain. Either way I hadn't cared in the moment, so much more to care about in the present.

"I just need to know the truth," she whispered, eyes lost and when she lifted her hand, she gathered a tear that clumped in her thick eyelashes. She rubbed it away with the shake of her head.

"I need to know the truth about you and why..." Her voice cracked on the end, her face cringing again with another tear she pushed away. "Why there's a warrant out for your arrest."

Her chosen words unleashed my greatest fear but not in the way I imagined. Real truth, if anyone found out my history and why I couldn't stay in a city for longer than a few months, it'd be bad, but this woman in particular finding out cut me right at the core.

"You don't know what you think you do," I told her, a strong current coming from my lips. "This is so much more complicated than you could ever know."

My words were putting it lightly, a history here she knew nothing about. This had been my fault I knew, but that fact didn't make this moment any easier to deal with.

"That's why I need to know the truth," she said and I noticed she did come here alone. She could have come with other people, authorities, or not even have come at all. She *came here*.

She came here to talk to me.

My fingers pushed into my hair and the way the strands moved around, I knew I was shaking. My gaze lowering, I asked her to take a seat on the couch, noticing right away she made no moves to do so.

"Ask your questions," I told her, remaining where I stood. "And after, you tell me where my kid is."

∼

Alicia

I wasn't going to make any deals with him.

I couldn't.

The best of what I had in me allowed me to come over here unattended. I didn't have to do that. My love for him made me.

That was what made this all so hard, a constant stomach toss making it hard to contain the contents of my insides. Still tasting the bile in my throat, I watched him in my periphery across the room. He ended up taking a chair from his kitchen table, sitting in it on the other side of the room across from me.

I'd taken the couch.

"Alicia, I'll tell you... I'll tell you what you need to know, then you need to tell me where Laura is. It's important. Her safety's at risk."

"Really?" I questioned, looking up at eyes that seemed to have aged even more before me. He'd been scared when I came over, knowing his daughter was missing I wasn't surprised, but that had changed now.

Currently, only sadness remained.

It only displayed at me and I found it hard to look at.

"Because it seems you're the one who might be the danger to her."

He said no words after mine, choosing silence. He shifted before me and when I looked up, his gaze had moved to the window.

His hand slid over his beard.

"I spent a lot of time wondering if what I'd done was the right idea," he said, moving his gaze over to me. "But each time I reflected, every time I looked back and mulled things over, I came to the same conclusion every time. What I did had to be done and never not once have I regretted it."

I saw that in his eyes, so many things I saw I didn't understand. It went beyond me, and like he said, things I didn't understand.

"What happened?" was all I could say, as if he was the photograph, that handsome man who had everything, but had suddenly seemed to have thrown it all away.

His hands dropped between his legs, his chin lowering as well.

"Laura's mom I never got to know," he said. "I didn't care to know. She was ass, ass that I wanted at the time and so many had come before her. I partied like the best of them and have the notches in my belt to prove it."

The man he spoke of sounded so foreign to me, a tale out of a dark storybook.

"I was a playboy like you'd never seen, Alicia," he admitted. "I was rich, powerful, and I used it. Laura's mom just happened to be who I wanted that night and come to find out, she found herself pregnant not long after a thoughtless fuck."

His choice of words had me cringing like it did at the lake, but I wouldn't look away, not this time and he didn't either, his gaze affixed on me.

"I really wouldn't believe it at first," he told me. "And I didn't. It took several paternity tests. After that, it became what did she want. How much, you know?"

His story had him laughing with no humor, the tone incredibly dry in his deep voice.

He looked up. "I didn't want a kid, so I was willing to pay her off to get rid of it. She didn't want that. In fact, she only wanted something I couldn't give her."

"What?" my own voice cracked, him cringing now.

"She wanted a goddamn father for her child," he said, something he'd left out in his explanation at the lake. He said he gave her money.

He didn't say she wanted him.

The reality of that played on Gray's face, his omission clear between us.

He moved his lips. "That's all she wanted, my time and basic child support. I couldn't agree to the former, but the latter, as you know, I gave in to."

He really had been different, so much different before me.

"We came to the agreement that every month I would visit when I paid the support, but only if the child didn't have to be acknowledged," he went on. "Laura doesn't even have my last name."

I noticed that. I noticed it on the warrant.

She was Laura Wallace on there, not Laura Davenport.

Grayden blew into his hands, a breath on them that filled the room.

"Everything was pretty good after that for a while," he went on, dropping his hands. "She got her money and her visits and I got to screw around with whatever piece of ass I could find. I could continue being a bachelor with no ties and no kids."

"What changed?"

My own voice sounded foreign to me and he stared at me, his head tilted.

"The drugs," he said, something he had let me in on before. Laura's mom and her connection with drugs.

"It was the woman's habit that changed things," he said. "Coke her drug of choice. We'd done it at the party we met at, which led to the sex. I pretty much got fried at all the parties I went to but it was only socially. Her mom was on a different level and something I only knew as I'd noticed her stash every time I'd visit her and Laura on our agreed-upon times. Sometimes, I wouldn't even see her for hours on visits. She'd just go to her room and leave me with the baby. Eventually, she started to ask for more money, claiming it was for child support, but I didn't believe her."

Because she needed more money for her habit, the evidence there. I closed my eyes.

"She didn't even want visits anymore eventually," he said, that sad laughter back in his voice. "Just more money, money I knew she was spending on drugs and not our kid, a kid... a kid I was finally starting to see."

His voice changed on the end and he squeezed his eyes.

"I wished I could remember more of those times," he said. "How special Laura had been and her voice... Her laughter was infectious. I was starting to get attached to her, but I was also seeing what was happening with her mom. Eventually, I believed she was taking advantage of the situation and I had to cut her off. I stopped paying her entirely and threatened her if she came for me. Not long after, I started to get the paperwork together to obtain full custody of Laura. I didn't want her near her screwed-up mother and ignored her calls until I could hammer out the details with my attorneys. We were almost done when I got a text from her."

"What did it say?"

The fact he'd said nothing when he had been so upfront with everything now scared me.

As well as the haunted look in his eyes.

His gaze became empty, tortured, and I watched as words formed on his lips.

"It said, 'You made me do this.'"

And that's when his eyes filled with the sheen, a thick glow that made him wipe his eyes with one hand. Dropping it, he shook his head and I wasn't sure I wanted to know what happened next. I wasn't sure I should hear.

"She *sold* her, Alicia," he said, his words retched into open air. A tremor hit his lips with movement. "She sold her for drugs and told me when I tracked her down after that text. She couldn't even remember where she left her. Our baby girl..."

The abyss I fell into resembled a dark cave, the world stopping and my brain unable to form thoughts, only the nightmares. The retelling itself sent Gray into a tailspin, his hands frantically moving, his eyes searching, and his voice choked.

"I had no idea how long she'd been with those people, or many of the details that happened after they took—" His rasp escaped with a pinch upon the bridge of his nose. He shook out of it. "Eventually, I found her, made calls, had people. Thank fucking God I had people."

He looked up when he saw me move, where I should have been the whole time. Sitting at the base of his legs, I held onto him, for dear life if I could have. I didn't want to let go, scared of what would happened if I did.

On my knees I remained at his waist, my arms wrapped around him and my face pushed into his chest.

"What happened to her, Gray?" I asked, closing my eyes between tears. "Did they hurt her?"

I really didn't want the knowledge. It was a need for it the only reason I asked.

So much made sense now, that little girl, her pain...

"I know at least they didn't do that," he said, nearly hyperventilating. He had to take a second, calm himself as if he was reliving it all.

Maybe he was.

Using me, he found his voice again, his arms around me now.

"I was told when my people found her, the dealers explained they hadn't touched her. They had plans for her and she was worth more if she was..."

My stomach rolled this time but I stayed.

I'd stay forever.

It seemed Gray couldn't go on with that train of thought either, his eyes closing.

"They ended up locking her in this room," he said, his voice far away. "Alone and by herself with no one else. I was there when my people located her and I just remembered how she looked."

His stare vacant into the room, so far away like his voice.

"She was completely dirtied," he said. "Covered in her own urine, vomit." His lids lowered, the swallow hard in his throat. "And hadn't been interacted with for days. I spent so much time with her, so many hours getting to know her, *love* her and she..."

His sniff cut him off, his eyes flashing at me.

"She didn't even recognize me, Alicia. In fact, she cowered. It took me singing to her, a song I used to sing to help her go to sleep when she was a toddler. With it, she knew it was me, and eventually, she did let me take her away, away from that place with windows shot out and people passed out on the floor in a heap. We went and that was the last we saw of the place. Her voice completely gone. For over three years it was gone."

My eyes closing, I rubbed his leg. So much pain they'd both been through and it all hit me at his conclusion.

"You took her then, didn't you?" I asked, staring up at him.

He nodded. "I did."

"But why, Grayden? You didn't have to just take her and run."

"But I did," he said, his lashes flashing away. "I couldn't risk her mom coming to her senses and realizing what she'd done. The woman, as fucked up as she was, is Laura's biological mother. She could have a case for a claim over her one day and even if I did get full custody she could have rights to see her. I didn't want her to *see* her. I didn't want her having anything to do with her and mess up her life even more than she had."

And so they escaped, disappeared into the abyss of anonymity. I had no idea where the two had been, but if they'd been places like Mayfield they'd be easy to hide in, disappear in.

"We've been running for three years," he said, his arms finally holding me tight. It'd taken that long, took him that long to notice I was really there...

And he wasn't alone anymore.

He sat in silence like that for so long, me on my knees at his lap and his arms around me. Eventually, that storm stopped and it was just us, us together and holding on for dear life that this all would work out, that we could take back everything we had before he'd admitted the truth and I found out. But I think we both knew with his admission things would change.

How could they not?

"She's at Jasmine's house," I said, pulling away. "She's there, but, Gray, you have to fight. I'm assuming she's the one who put the warrant out for your arrest. Laura's mom?"

He said he'd been scared one day she'd come back to her senses.

His arms falling away, he pushed his hand into his hair.

"Yes."

"Well, what if she's better? It probably took a lot for her to put that warrant out, challenge you and everything you said you were. What if she's gotten herself together?"

"And what if she hasn't?" he challenged himself. "What if that warrant is a way for her to smoke us out? Get us in a place where she can fight for her?"

"So we do like I said, we fight."

"I have nothing, Alicia. We have nothing. There was fraud in my company before I left and I worked out just enough to give Laura and me a chance before putting it all behind us. We literally have little more than the shirts on our backs now."

Bastian mentioned that, how he'd been smart and got out.

I closed my eyes, looking up at him. "You have me."

One resource he hadn't had before and his hands caged my face after the words, his forehead touching mine. His throat jumped, and even this close, the sadness in his eyes pierced my soul.

"We do have you, Alicia," he said, his voice tightening. "But it's not enough. I don't think it will be. I can't take the risk. I can't lose my baby."

The tears flooded my eyes in a river, his voice so final, gut-wrenchingly so.

My hands gripping his shirt, I closed my eyes.

"You can't keep running," I said, my voice shaking. "Someone will find you eventually. You're trying to outrun time."

"It's a risk I have to take," he told me, his thumbs smoothing down my cheeks. "I have to take it for her."

"Well, I won't let you. I can't. You deserve the right to be her dad, for her to have your name and no longer live in fear."

"What will you do if I can't let you do that?" he asked and my silence told him I think all he needed to know.

I wasn't lying. I couldn't let him keep running. I'd fight for him, *her* until I had no more fight in me. That was who I was and the world *I* came from. I had a means and colleagues that could fix this situation for him and I would do it whether he let me or not.

I believed he saw that in my eyes, that fight, and suddenly, I witnessed something I wasn't sure I'd ever see again, his smile so handsome before his lips crashed down on mine.

It'd been a soft kiss, the softest of kisses and it felt so final it broke my heart. He was saying goodbye and I knew right away...

He was letting go.

Thirty-One

ALICIA

Gray made me give him forty-eight hours, forty-eight hours in which he could literally uproot his and Laura's life.

Forty-eight hours in which he could run again.

I hadn't been through what he had. I hadn't seen what he'd seen nor experienced the things that placed so much pain in two people's lives for so long. I was outside of all this, a bystander who achingly wanted to help but didn't have the audacity, *the place* in this to do so. Because of that, I had nothing. I couldn't make the man fight for what was rightfully his, the right to a safe haven with his daughter.

The right to be free.

He wouldn't take that right and I couldn't make him have it, and therefore, he let me go. He had to. He knew I'd fight for him.

I'd do so always.

Many weeks went by after that. In fact, so many I lost count. I started to lose reality of what my life had become versus what it could have been. I was living in post-Grayden Davenport mode, a sickness that couldn't be alleviated with any type of medicine in existence. I was addicted to him, him and his feeling and his love for a child in the beginning he never thought he wanted, but in the end, gave his entire life for. I was addicted to her, his little Laura. I was addicted to the laugh I'd fortunately gotten to hear when she found it within herself again and the life we both could have had to influence each other. I may have been the adult and could teach her things like piano and life lessons, but she taught me so many things too. I learned I had a patience within myself and purpose that went beyond the walls of the office building and conference rooms I found myself in my day to day.

I eventually went back to that life, that world that felt so hollow now in comparison to what I'd literally lived for the better part of a year in a town called Mayfield. It'd been a world of simplicity, purpose I hadn't easily untied myself from upon Grayden's absence. His mobile home had gone vacant within hours and my heart just as emptied. I was bitter for a long time after he left, how he could cut ties and leave things so open between us, but as the days turned into weeks and the weeks turned into months since I'd seen him and his Laura I stopped letting it be about him and me. It became about him, a man who was desperately trying to do the right thing when it came to himself and his young child, and in the end, I found myself hard-pressed to hold anger towards him anymore. In fact, when it all came down to it, the only one I had anger toward was one person.

Myself.

The papers had showed up at my office well after the holidays and into the start of spring, the ones I'd been avoiding since I decided to pack up and leave Mayfield. I actually sat with the developers who wanted to build on my aunt's land with my dad, him looking over everything beside me. I trusted myself and my decisions not a year ago, but now, I'd been resorted to help when asked. I relied upon my attorney father in ways that had me ashamed in regards to handling my business in Mayfield. He took the reins and found me what he considered a perfect monetary deal, absence of any other thought outside of that. Once the meetings concluded, the papers were sent over—to me now.

I signed them.

The action was almost like a symbol of the past, where I was going versus where I'd been. There was nothing there in that town for me now that had changed my life for well past a summer. When I went initially, I believed I'd be there for no more than a week and came back with a lifetime of experiences and lessons I'd take well into the rest of my life. I was sorting through it all and believed it'd literally take me the rest of my life to do so...

But then her letter showed up in the mail.

Thirty-Two

April 16th

Alicia,

Please see the enclosed photos from your aunt's home. With the house becoming a recognized landmark, the town has acquired the home and fashioned it for tours and other things as established in your contract. All personal items have been sold as instructed by you, but I hope you don't mind that I saved these photos and sent them your way. I've been a part of the team that's been going through the house to set up for the tours, but when I found these photos, it didn't feel right to throw them away. They're ones of you, your aunt, and various people around town, and even some of the pair of us in there as kids and I swear to God it's me. I guess we both really have changed.

I hope these photos brighten your day a little, the smiles in them and the beauty in this town. Like I said, it didn't feel right throwing them away and I hope they find a home with you.

There's a lot of history there, a lot of love and it was nice to see it before sending them to you. There's also a sealed envelope addressed to Gray with the photos. I'm assuming your aunt left it for him at some point. As you know, he left Mayfield before you did, so I'm sending it to you in hopes you could forward it to him. I'm not sure of its contents. I didn't open the envelope, but I guess it's not for me anyway. Please try to get it to him if you could. I'm sure it's important if Jo left it for him. We found it in the basement amongst her personal things.

Lastly, I hope you're doing well. I've been thinking a lot about how we left things and what you must think of me after what happened. I've tried apologizing many times to you both in texts and phone calls and I respect the fact that you're not ready to talk to me. I get that as I probably wouldn't be ready to talk to me either. Just know that what I said to you on that last day was true. We may have not wanted you to sell Josephine's land, but just know that this town, I, care about you as if you were one of us. You are one of us, always. I truly and deeply care about you and know forever you will always be my friend even if that feeling is not reciprocated on your end.

Your friend forever and always,
Avaleen Johnson

Thirty-Three

May 25th

My Sweet Grayden,

Today is your birthday, but I know even if I hadn't invited you over today to celebrate it I'd be seeing you. You come by nearly every day to take care of this old woman when you probably shouldn't. You're a young man who should be experiencing life and the world yet you care for me. I'm only too selfish for the attention, which is why I haven't refused your visits. I love them and don't know what I would do without you and your Laura.

You've changed my life since you've both come into it and I hope in our brief time of knowing each other you've both gotten something from me as well. This letter is just an acknowledgement of you, a man who doesn't see the greatness inside himself as he should. I see a lot of pain in your eyes, a lot of hurt I really don't understand, but I hope that one day you'll allow yourself to let it go. I hope you allow yourself to live and experience all the great things life has to offer you and your Laura. You've done such a good job with her and she is only better because of you.

One day you will see who you are. One day you will see what you mean, and on that day, you will heal. You will love and it will be the greatest it could ever be. I know because you will deserve it. You can only love and cherish the best it could be because that's your right due to the beautiful person you are. I'm only regretful that it cannot be this old woman who will steal your heart. I am too old and have had my share of loves. It's your turn. It's your turn to love and you will, and when it happens, it will be amazing.

Live free and love free, my sweet Grayden, and happy 35th birthday to you. You will only have the best cake baked for you with this card. I promise you.

Love,
Josephine, your family always.

Thirty-Four

GRAY

She barely talked to me these days, if at all. The time between exchanges with my daughter was becoming greater and greater, like individual grains of sand pushing through an hourglass. The tower of granules kept building, my chances to connect with her fading with each grain lost. I wasn't sure I had a lot of time with her left and that had nothing to do with us being on the run again. The odds of the authorities catching up with us were the same as they'd always been, a possibility but nothing more than that. I feared I was losing my kid, but in a different way this time.

Her head lowered, Laura sat on the edge of the lake's dock, the great mountains of Colorado around us. Our travels brought us here, nothing more than a map and gas, but we'd stayed for a couple of weeks now, the beauty of the land more than exemplary. I hoped in a way it'd help her, remind her of a similar lake and better times.

Ripples formed when she tossed a rock into the lake before her, her shoes off and her toes skimming the water. She never swam, just looked at the water like she wanted it to take her away. Perhaps, in a way, she did, no matter how farfetched that wish could be of coming to fruition. She understood we weren't going back, that life had taken us here and onward was the only way we were going. We'd been in more motels than I could count, this cabin at the lake a better alternative. I couldn't afford us much and it was only a campground we stayed on, *temporary,* but like I said, I hoped it'd help.

I watched her, unable to even see her eyes beyond her dark hair framing around her face as she studied the water. I had a feeling catching a glance of those big brown eyes would only gut me as, like the sand, they became more and more vacant every day. Her happy kept showing less and less and her laughter had all but gone now.

I found myself in a place where I was questioning everything again, questioning what I told Alicia and everything. I said if I went back to the moment in which I had to decide to fight or stay for a life for my kid I'd make my same decision all over again. I'd run in hopes for a chance at a safe life for her, a life free of her mom and the world I came from. I still felt my decision was best, but now I wondered at what cost.

Closing my eyes, I lifted them to the sky, the sun shining around and so beautiful. This place was stunning and had everything, everything but something stable. Like all things in my daughter's and my life they were short-lived, a temporary paradise before another escape.

My fingers squeezed on the rocking chair I sat in, and lifting my head, I called to Laura. She ignored me at first, not uncommon until I emphasized my voice. I told her of my seriousness and, eventually, she stood, dragging her feet over to me. She got there and I nudged her.

"You finish your homework?" I asked her, back to homeschooling her for now. I was rusty at it but we were making do. I refused to have her get behind in school amongst other things. I was disrupting her life so much already.

Shaking her head, she barely looked at me, my stomach

raw and tossing at the glimpse of sadness I caught in her faded brown eyes. Dropping my hand, I told her to go along and do that, the door of the cabin slamming shut behind her. I waited after that, made myself until that door closed and I knew she was far enough away.

The croak in my throat I kept silent, pushing my hands into my hair. I hadn't slept in what felt like weeks, unable to, always on, always thinking.

Always missing her and regretting.

But there was no going back now and Laura couldn't be the only one who had to accept that. Our fate had been determined, myself the one dropping the ax.

My face in my hands, I listened to nature and the birds call around me for a while, knowing I needed to get it together, but not able to at the moment. I was at rock bottom, the inside of the barrel empty with no escape.

"Why did you have to die?" my mind called out, my hands scrubbing down my face. *"Why did you have to go? You always knew what to do."*

She always believed in me, Josephine. She showed me I was capable of things I never even believed nor thought possible. She allowed me to believe in a world and the possibility of happiness, then let me have it when she dropped her niece into my life. She gave her to me and I truly believed that.

I let it all go like I had everything else, but this wasn't like the last time, money, things, and prestige only that—things. I could easily give up my old life for a potential one of safety for Laura, but the justifications of letting Mayfield and Alicia go were few and far between. I felt I let go of my kid's safety in Mayfield.

And I let go of *my* safe haven in Alicia.

I thought about calling her so many times, just letting her know that Laura and I were safe, just wanting to hear her voice.

I could hear it even now, her voice in the wind like an apparition. She called me, "Gray," then placed her hands in my hair, her touch glorious as she buried her lips there next. I could spend eternity like that, her in my arms as I pushed them around her. She was so warm.

She was home.

"Gray?"

My eyes closed at the sound until I knew it was just too close.

It was *too* familiar.

I looked up and I found her, a soft pink dress moving around the width of her hips and cinching to her tiny waist. Tying behind her neck, the dress left the top of her shoulders exposed, her hair wrapped up and bunched on top of her head in a messy way that displayed the hypnotic tint of her brown eyes, dark and just slightly lighter than the warmth of her ebony skin.

My blinks consisted of many, unsure if I was really seeing her, but the creaks in the floorboards as she came near...

And then her wonderful voice again.

"Grayden," she said, stopping in a perfect ray of the sun. It was like heaven itself had highlighted her, Josephine herself casting that glow.

I sat up, but unable to move more than that.

"Why... Why..."

Speech was that of a challenge, Alicia coming over and out of the light. Stopping, she looked inside the cabin, through the screen door and inside and her smile told me she'd spotted Laura. She always sat at the table to do her homework.

Alicia placed her finger to her lips then, tiptoeing around me so Laura couldn't hear us. She took the other rocking chair reserved for Laura after that, one she never used. My daughter just rarely came outside these days. She could never just *be* like she used to.

Rocking in the chair, Alicia took my hand and I'd forgotten until that very instant what it felt like, how it felt to truly feel something, someone.

I watched her, unable to formulate words, as she clasped my hand then reached into her purse that hung on her shoulder. From inside, she retrieved an envelope and I noticed my name when she placed it front side up on the small wooden table between us.

"Grayden."

My eyes squinted at the cursive, knowing the handwriting right away.

Nodding, she instructed for me to take it, but I couldn't make myself.

I squeezed Alicia's hand instead, bringing it close.

"Why are you here?" I asked her, then closed my eyes when she touched my face.

She was that warm I remembered, that feeling of her skin upon mine.

"My sweet Grayden," she said, reminding me so much of someone else. Only one other had called me that and only one other could. Alicia touched her forehead to mine, then picked up the envelope between us, managing to do so with one hand as I couldn't let hers go.

Leaning back, she read to me then, read to me the final words of a dear friend and I wasn't sure how I was able to sit through it, the woman so right in her words. I had been able to love.

I had been able to heal.

After Alicia was finished, she continued to keep her voice low, no doubt because Laura was inside like I believed before.

"She called me," she admitted, brushing her thumb down my cheek. "Laura called a few days ago. She said she was at a gas station."

I'd taken Laura into town to get supplies, something we'd

done every week. She had been gone for a long time that day, stating she had to go to the bathroom.

Clasping Alicia's hand between mine, I braced it, knowing what I had to say.

"This can't change anything," I told her, but knew this time...

It'd be so hard to let her go.

It'd nearly broken me the first time, and using my hands, Alicia brought them in between us, her thumb brushing my lips.

"But it does," she told me, trying to do the impossible, trying to tell me things were possible I knew weren't. We couldn't go back, my reasons standing.

Alicia's vision panned then, her smile in the direction of the house.

"You can take her home," she said. "Home to me."

"Alicia..." I hated she was doing this, making this so hard for me. I dampened my mouth. "We can't—"

"The charges have been dropped."

My lashes flickered up, a smile I hadn't noticed before. It was one of telling and lit up her entire beautiful face.

I touched it, my fingers roaming her soft lips. "What are you talking about? The charges dropped?"

Her head nodded with my words, that smile doing nothing to fall away. She pushed her hands on my face, making me look at her.

Making me *listen* to her.

She told me a story of a relentless woman, she herself trying to fix this for me. She did this despite my protests. She fought for me when I couldn't even fight for myself.

And thank God for her.

"We found Laura's mom," she said at one point. "My firm and I, we found her and you were right. Once she came to her senses and realized you took her, she put out the warrant."

I suspected as much, coming upon it when I saw my own face on the back of a gas station wall. It'd been the day I decided to leave the state and put as many miles as I could between myself and Laura's mom.

"But she hasn't changed," Alicia stated, her expression sad. "She's still into the same habits. She put the warrant out hoping she could get something out of you. It had nothing to do with Laura."

I wasn't surprised, the woman out of control.

"That made negotiations with her hard, but we managed. She signed over her parental rights in the end, though. We let her know what could happen to her with the allegations you had about what she'd done to Laura. She signed easily after that. She gave up easily."

Gave up...

"She's *yours*, Gray," Alicia told me, nodding with a smile. "Laura is yours, legal and binding. All you have to do is sign the papers. She gave up all rights."

It'd been the worst time to not understand English, to *not* get what she was saying to me and it took her touching my eyes for me to realize I did understand. I got what she was saying to me, the tears on her fingers the evidence.

"She's mine?" I asked her, noticing *her* tears as well. I clasped her cheek, the drops dripping down on my arm with her nod.

"She is," she said. "She's yours."

She's mine...

I closed my eyes, my mind connecting me to a far-off place and a woman in a small town called Mayfield, a woman who gave me the gift of love and more homes than I could possibly imagine, her niece the most important one.

"Let's take her home," Alicia said, then she might have said something else.

Had my lips not met hers first.

Epilogue

ALICIA

My aunt had something in the words she'd never gotten to say. Passing away on Grayden's birthday, she'd never been able to tell him some of the most important words either of us had ever heard, though, I think in Gray's heart he knew. She spoke of family to him. She was his *family,* and in those words, they not only set him free but myself as well. My aunt's will had only talked about her property going to her last remaining kin, speaking of no one in the specifics. I had been blood related yes, and naturally, her estate planner had come for me, but I was a lawyer, a good one, and came from a practice of many who could back me up in any way I needed. We'd been able to spin the wording of her will, stretch it, and pass it on to all deserving. I owned the right to my aunt's property and estate.

But so did a little girl and her dad.

With those specifics, I couldn't legally act on selling her land without the permission of every party involved, and as it turned out, Gray and his daughter didn't want to sell my aunt's estate.

I'd never let him.

The contracts with the developers shredded basically

overnight, and an old woman's property and land technically owned by three were given use to a whole town. Everyone in Mayfield had rights to what Josephine's property had to offer, her living on in every townsperson or local who just wanted to come and see it. Her house had many visitors, a staple and highlight when one came to visit Mayfield. We even had a billboard on the highway to get people to come—Gray's idea and it worked swimmingly. Well, with all the traffic to the local landmark a family couldn't possibly stay there and we didn't.

Gray built a house for us.

It'd been our place and it felt fitting, Josephine's house was for the town of Mayfield and the house Gray built for Laura and me had been for us. It was our piece of this town, a place of love we could call our own. He'd made it three stories, a full basement, and even a large work shed for himself in which he spent many hours, his hobby making small trinkets and gadgets which sold at the country general store downtown. He built Laura's dollhouse in there, a huge home and safe haven for her dolls. I loved that element of the house, but my favorite place I had to say was the sunroom. I got to play piano out there every morning, Laura eating breakfast while Gray had his coffee.

His arms swung around me this morning, our baby between us while I played for our two children at the piano. I formally adopted Laura after the paperwork for her name change went through. I became a Davenport myself shortly before, our wedding quick but in the spring. We didn't want to wait, our only hesitation to get things with Laura and her dad situated. She'd legally become his one year after my aunt's passing, his birthday.

"You will only have the best cake baked for you..."

Little did she know his ultimate gift would be even better. Our baby was expected in the summer, a little boy we decided to name Joseph after my aunt who brought us together. Eventually, my belly wouldn't allow me to play anymore in my sunroom, but that'd be okay.

Like Laura knew I needed a break, she hopped up from her seat at the lounger, her cereal bowl from breakfast this morning empty. Taking a seat beside me on the piano bench, the nine-year-old leaned over, kissing my skirt-clad belly. The quickening flutters of her brother alerted me he knew his sister was there, my smile making her grin.

"What does Joseph want to hear today?" she asked, stretching out her fingers above the keys. She asked that every morning, but she knew the answer every time.

Coming around me, Gray took the seat he placed strategically on my other side, the chair brought in from the kitchen one day, but never returned. He wanted his place too at the piano, his arm sweeping around my waist.

I'd never get over how happy he looked all the time, the weight of the world completely evaporated from his light-colored eyes. He'd let it go. He let it all go. He *healed* and even his beard was gone, his jaw clean-shaven and his hair never longer than the shell of his ears. He had me to help him keep up with it, allowing me the honor of taking on some of those obligations for him. He didn't have to do everything by himself and it wasn't just that he knew that now.

But welcomed the assistance and love.

His lips on my cheek, he closed his eyes, touching his forehead to me before swinging fingers over and brushing Laura's shoulder.

"Play Josephine's Song," he said, the tune Laura herself had actually composed. It'd been with my help, composition classes I'd taken in school a lifetime ago. It'd been an honor to bring the knowledge out and the song had become a staple at church every Sunday, the lead-in to the service. Laura played every week and the town loved her for it.

Curling up under Gray's arm, I rested my head on his

chest, watching his daughter, *our daughter* lead us into what I knew to be another perfect morning. We had so many perfect ones, my highlight before I started my day in town, my own practice right in the heart of it all. People called me crazy for doing that, giving up my potential six-figure salary by working somewhere close to Mayfield but bigger, my own family amongst them. But sometimes it wouldn't hurt people to allow a little crazy into their lives. It allowed for the best life and chances we never would have taken. I took a chance on this town and made friends, *created family*, my friend Ava amongst them all. She'd been the dearest friend I ever had and probably ever would have, something I found out once I allowed myself to forgive her. It took a little while, but we came back to each other. Just like we had when we were kids, two people who hadn't seen each other for almost two decades but were able to reconnect and find a friendship that would take us long into the rest of our lives.

And if not for this town and a woman named Josephine I wouldn't have any of it. Gray and Laura told me on separate occasions she sent me to them, but only I knew the truth. I wasn't sent to them.

They were sent to me.

Click the link below to download book one of Victoria's bestselling series, Found by You!

Download on Amazon

Made in the USA
Las Vegas, NV
24 November 2023